MY FRIEND COUSIN EMMIE

Jane Duncan goes to sea in the new "*Friend*" as Janet and Twice Alexander embark on a lotus-eating voyage back to the West Indian island of St. Jago and the sugar plantation. The perfect ending to their leave, they thought, but, once afloat, trouble in the shape of the perverse and sullen Delia Andrews makes them regret their decision. The two other passengers become enmeshed with the Alexander entourage; Roddy Maclean, young and "mixed up" and, of course, Cousin Emmie herself, dominating the scene in her shapeless and bizarre dresses with her voracious appetite and her uncanny ability to get at the heart of a problem.

Books by Jane Duncan in the
Ulverscroft Large Print Series:

MY FRIENDS FROM CAIRNTON
MY FRIEND MY FATHER
MY FRIEND FLORA
MY FRIEND COUSIN EMMIE

———◆———

This Large Print Edition
is published by kind permission of
MACMILLAN LONDON LTD.
London
and
ST. MARTIN'S PRESS, INC.
New York

JANE DUNCAN

MY FRIEND COUSIN EMMIE

Complete and Unabridged

ULVERSCROFT
Leicester

First Printed in 1964

First Large Print Edition
published May 1978
SBN 0 7089 0136 0

Published by
F. A. Thorpe (Publishing) Ltd.
Anstey, Leicestershire
Printed in England

THIS BOOK IS FOR
MRS. E. JAMES ROGERS

1

A DENT IN THE SILVER

IT was December of 1951 and a dull, sullen south-west-of-England morning when I stood by the ship's rail while all the last-minute bustle of sailing went on about me and discovered in my mind the thought — the thought as complete, concrete, clearly delineated and unexpected as a newly minted silver sixpence found lying on the ground at one's feet — that I was about to sail back to St. Jago and that this was something that I did not want to do.

I do not suppose that there is in anybody's life the right moment for making the wrong discovery, but it seemed to me singularly contrary, even for my ineptitude at this activity called "living", that my moment for discovering that I did not want to go back to St. Jago should have come so inopportunely as to fall within the last half-hour before the ship sailed. But there it was. The moment had come and the discovery had been made.

I have read of people who, on making a discovery like this, simply get off the ship and rearrange their lives without further ado, but my life was not, it seems, like theirs. My life is not like any life of which I have ever read. Mine seems to contain much more of what the authors of books seem to regard as unimportant trivia, and I seem to be much more at the mercy of such trivia than the people in books. Some of this trivia which now stopped me getting off the ship was that our livelihood depended on my husband's engineering job which was based on St. Jago; in the course of our leave we had sold our house in Scotland, and our china, linen, books and other valued possessions were in the hold of the ship; our mastiff dog, Dram, full of inoculations against canine tropical diseases, was on his leash at my side, and our car had already been shipped west by an earlier boat. And, down below me, watching the final bustle along with my husband, was something that surely even the author of a book could not treat as trivial: a young woman of twenty-four called Delia Andrews, who was coming out to St. Jago to spend a holiday with us. The heroine of a novel, no doubt, having made the discovery that I had just made, would leave the ship forthwith and thus avoid all risk of frustration or the repression of her ego, but I, thinking of all the things which I have just noted and many more besides, merely sighed and did nothing. I have not enough character to bend life, the world, people and events to my will. Indeed, for most of the time, I think, I have no character at all. I am merely the prey of every influence, pressure and thrust that life has at its command; I am the straw that is the prey of every wind that blows.

That Delia Andrews was coming to St. Jago with us is fully illustrative of me as a straw in the wind. Sixteen years before, when she was only eight, I had become her governess for a year or so, more or less by accident, in the unwitting way that women of straw like me are persuaded to change overnight from being secretary to Delia's father into being governess to Delia. Then, during this leave, my husband and I had come across her again at a moment when she was at odds with her family and very unhappy, and in a careless moment my husband had suggested that she make this trip with us. That was the moment when I should have made a stand, but the moment happened in the middle of the night, with Delia in floods of tears, so I left the making of my stand until the morning and I can only shrug my shoulders and say that here we were, on board the boat. Delia was aboard the *Pandora* with us, and her car was even now being lowered in its net through the hatch into the hold. With misgiving I looked down to where she stood on the deck below and wished with all my heart that she were safely back in London in the bosom of her wealthy stuffy family, where she would no longer be my responsibility.

The longer one lives, the more habitual it becomes to compromise with life. It becomes so habitual that one, for most of the time, makes the compromise unconsciously, and I now began to seek terms of agreement with life as it was as expertly as any team of diplomats drawing up a treaty of non-aggression between any two irreconcilable enemies.

We could not have had more depressing

weather for our departure, I told myself, than this grey drizzly murk which made the little white ship look like some summer-dressed holidaymaker who, through some displacement in time, had arrived on a deserted storm-swept promenade in the middle of winter. Once back at Guinea Corner, our house in St. Jago, I assured myself, and into the routine of the sugar plantation again, I would feel quite different. And, without any specious self-assurance, I could tell myself with truth that it always depressed me unreasonably to cast off from the shores of Britain, even for a short holiday, and no matter how much I might like the shore of my destination, for I seem to be very deeply rooted in my native soil — or native rock, rather — in the Highlands of Scotland. In a sense, I never really cast off from the shores of Britain at all. The moment of sailing is merely a painful wrenching of the roots that bind me to home, but, after that initial wrench, these roots seem to uncoil and stretch to a limitless length and become a channel of communication from me back to the hilltop in Ross-shire, called Reach-far, where I was born.

5

And so, compromising, making the best of things, as it is called, I turned away from the rail above the fore-deck and began to walk towards the little smoke-room that looked out over the stern of the ship. Dram walking beside me, very stiff-legged, his tail making a round "O" over the end of his broad back, his eyes and ears very alert as he looked with suspicion around this steel and wooden contraption of a vessel that was full of strange noises and smells. When I sat down in the smoke-room, he sat down beside me, raised a large paw on to my knee and looked at me in a questioning way. If often seemed to me that Dram could catch my own mood, and I argued with him much as I had been arguing with myself.

"It's all right," I told him. "You'll come to like it. Ships are great fun, and you'll love Guinea Corner."

He sighed, wrinkled his brows and then turned his large head as the door slid open.

An elderly woman came in from the deck, made her way to one of the little tables on the far side of the room and sat down in a green leather armchair. She was small, thin, dressed from head to foot in an

6

indeterminate drab brown colour, and in this breezy sea-going atmosphere she had, somehow, the effect of a withered autumn leaf that had been picked up in a careless frolic mood by the wind and blown here to be trapped in the crevice that was the green leather armchair. Having settled herself in one corner of the chair which could have held three people of her bulk, and having deposited on the floor at her feet a large, brownish canvas bag and a brown cotton umbrella, she stared across at Dram and me.

"Good-morning," I said.

Her face, which was curiously expressionless, did not indicate that she had heard me, and there was a short interval of silence before her eyes moved from me to the dog who sat beside me.

"It is a very nasty morning indeed," she said then.

Her voice was as expressionless as her face and I had a moment of feeling utterly disconcerted. During this moment she was sitting there looking at me out of her queer, flat, light-brown eyes, and I felt resentfully that she was studying me, considering me, but her face expressed nothing of what she was thinking, neither interest nor lack of interest, approval nor disapproval. Suddenly, after perhaps two minutes of silent staring, she bent from the chair, picked up the canvas bag in one hand, the cotton umbrella in the other, and drifted out on to the deck and, turning a corner, disappeared from sight.

I stared at the sliding door through which she had gone, finding difficulty in believing, now, that she had ever come in, spoken or gone out at all. Looking across at the chair she had occupied, it was difficult to believe that she had ever sat there. The chair looked back at me, more anonymous and more empty than any chair I had ever seen in any public room, I thought, and in the air there remained no faintest vibration, even, of that drab brown visitant. I began to feel more depressed than ever.

I was just about to return to the deck, for that urgency of near-sailing had begun to pervade the air round the ship, when my husband came into the smoke-room.

"Are we off?" I asked.

"Where is Dee?" he asked in the same instant and then repeated:

8

"Where's Dee? I thought she was with you."

As we stood looking at one another, the ship's siren blew and there was no doubt now that we were in motion. The warehouses beyond the windows began to slide past.

"Don't panic," I said. "I don't suppose she has jumped overboard."

He drew a sharp breath, about to make some angry retort, but at that moment a rolling screen rose, disclosing a bar in the corner of the room, and a very freshly scrubbed young steward said: "Good-morning. Mr. and Mrs. Alexander, isn't it? Would you care for a drink before lunch?"

"I'd like a glass of medium sherry, please," I said and went to sit down in a corner of the room.

My husband brought the sherry and a glass of beer for himself and put them on the table, but he did not sit down. "I'll just go and see where Dee is," he said.

"Is that really necessary?" I asked.

He stood looking down at me, frowning. "Janet, what is the matter?"

"I think it is time you stopped behaving

9

like a hen with one chicken. Dee is twenty-four and in no sense a chicken, anyway. Do you realise that for the last week our life has been completely dominated by her?"

"You are talking absolute rubbish." I stared at the wall ahead of me without speaking, and he now sat down across the table from me and went on: "This is a pretty time to indicate that Dee is not very welcome. I take it that that is what you are indicating?"

"Not exactly." I could feel distance growing between us as rapidly as distance was growing between the ship and the shore of the estuary. "What I am indicating is that she has come on this trip with us ostensibly because her family in London interfered in her life too much — clucked round her every minute, as she puts it — and it seems to me that your behaviour makes her coming to us a jumping out of the frying-pan into the fire."

"I'm not clucking round her! I just want to be sure that she is all right and not homesick or anything. A lot of people feel depressed at the start of a journey and — "

"You are telling *me*?" I said and my

voice shook. "Look, you had better get out of here before I throw this glass of sherry! Go on! I mean it. Go away, for God's sake, and leave me to pull myself together before anybody comes in here!"

"Janet — "

"Go and find Dee!" I said, aware that my voice was rising, and he left me and went out on to the deck.

I was sitting with my back to the bar so that the steward could not see my face, and I stared hard at the panelled wall as the tears of mingled confusion and shame began to rise in my eyes. Dram put a paw on my knee and I put my hand on his head.

I was both miserable and ashamed, miserable with a misery that had been growing during this past week, a misery that had reached its culmination this very morning in the discovery that I did not want to go back to St. Jago, and I was ashamed of this outburst of feeling about Dee, but that too was something that had been growing during this past week and had now come to a culmination. I supposed that I was jealous of the girl, and this made me very ashamed, for I have always regarded jealousy as a mean, unworthy emotion which should not be harboured, and it was an emotion which I had never felt before, even when, a few years before, I had thought that my husband was in love with my friend Monica. At that time I had felt that if he wanted to leave me and go to Monica, that was what he must do; he must have what he wanted. That he seemed to want to go to Monica made me sad, but I did not feel jealous of her as I was now feeling of Dee because of his interest in her. Maybe, I thought as I struggled against the tears, it is because I myself love and admire Monica while I neither love nor admire Dee — while I do not really even like Dee? My train of thought stopped as if in front of a blank wall, for this was another new discovery. I had not, until this very moment, been aware that I did not like Dee Andrews. When she was a child I had been fond of her, and until now I had thought that I was fond of her still, but I now knew that if, as my husband had done, I had met her for the first time as a young woman of twenty-four, she would have had no appeal for me. She was too restless, too discontented, too sullen, too old for her years and at the same time too young; she had none of the attributes that draw me to people and none of the attributes that I hope to find in youth. That my husband had been drawn to her seemed to argue some deep basic difference between him and me, a difference of which, until now, I had been utterly unsuspecting.

Behind me, I heard the voice of the steward: "Mrs. Alexander — "

"Yes?"

"If anyone comes in wanting a drink, will you ask them to push this button here?" He indicated a bell-push in the panelling beside the bar. "We are always in a bit of a muddle after sailing and I have to go down and give them a hand in the dining-saloon."

I said that I would do what he asked, and he dropped the screen over the bar and went away.

I was still staring at the wall, but the urge to cry had abated now, when the door from the deck slid open to admit a young man who went towards the bar, then turned away from the closed screen and stood looking at me. He was not less than twenty, I thought, and no more than thirty, but it was impossible to estimate his age more closely than that. He had very strong-growing, slightly curly dark hair, dark eyes and a ruddy skin, and he seemed to exude health and vitality. He moved well, with a control that seemed to be overlaid on a swashbuckling sort of recklessness, and there was a similar air of insouciance in his smile.

"If you want a drink," I said, "the steward said that if you pushed that button there he would come a-runnin' from the dining-saloon."

"I don't want a drink all that much," he said, came over and sat down opposite me. "Mrs. Alexander, I owe you an apology. If I had obeyed my mother I'd have got in touch with you about three weeks ago."

I looked into the gay reckless face. "Oh? And who is your mother?"

"Marion Maclean."

"Marion!"

Marion Maclean was the wife of Rob Maclean, the manager of the Paradise plantation where my husband and I lived in St. Jago. The Macleans had seven sons, but so far I had met only the youngest one,

Sandy, who had not as yet gone home to school in Scotland like his brothers.

"Now which one of the seven are you?" I asked the young man across the table.

"I'm Number Three — Roderick. Mother wrote to me about three weeks ago and said that you and your husband were sailing on the *Pandora* too, and that I was to get in touch with you; but I am dilatory about letters and things and — well, there it is. I didn't write to you, and I'm sorry."

He smiled contritely, and I said: "I don't see that it matters. Here you are now. Are you coming out on holiday?"

"Sort of. I just got through my finals at the university last month and we're now going to hold a family parliament about my future."

He assumed a parody of a heavy pontifical air for a second, and then the youthful gaiety, which betokened all the confidence in the world as to the joyousness of his future, broke through again, and it struck me that he was the very opposite of Dee Andrews. Roddy Maclean was youth incarnate.

"Are you another Maclean engineer?" I asked.

"Oh, lord, yes! There seems to be some natural law that most Macleans are engineers. . . . Listen, would you tell me something? Why is your husband called Twice?"

The sudden change of subject took me by surprise and then I smiled. "I am afraid that I'm responsible for that. His parents christened him Alexander Alexander and I shortened it to Twice. Why?"

"Mother is a very diligent but rather irritating letter-writer. She has kept mentioning Janet and Twice in her letters for the last two years, and if I have asked her once to tell me the origin of the Twice I have asked her a dozen times. She always forgets to answer. It's been haunting me. Do you ever get haunted by things like that?"

"Often. In fact, names and words in general can haunt me more than anything. I still haven't got used to the place-names in St. Jago, for instance — New Hope, Canaan, Content, Paradise — they turn St. Jago into a fantasy world for me."

"St. Jago *is* a fantasy world," he said. "At least Paradise is. It isn't part of things as they are at all," he said with a gravity

16

that sat strangely upon his handsome young face.

He kept on taking me by surprise, this young man. "Things as they are?" I repeated his words.

"That is a bit of private idiom like your Twice," he told me, smiling again. "I divide things into things-as-they-are, things-as-they-seem and things-as-you-wish-they-were."

Looking at him, I repeated his three categories to myself silently and then I asked: "If Paradise isn't things-as-they-are, which is it?"

"A mixture of the other two. It is things as Madame and Sir Ian and my father wish they were, and they do everything in their power to make it seem what they wish it were."

"And what is that — what they wish it were?"

"A feudal plantation, a tropic paradise indeed, where everybody lives in perfect peace and harmony."

"And isn't Paradise nearly that?"

"That's how it seems. But Paradise Estate is part of St. Jago. St. Jago is a West Indian island, and West Indian islands have colour problems and all sorts of other problems and they wriggle like maggots under the surface of Paradise. Of course, people don't like looking at maggots."

"I don't know that I blame them."

His smile broadened to a grin. "But maggots are indubitably part of things-as-they-are," he said.

"But do we have to examine them?" I asked. "I think I belong to the school that is content to let them wriggle away below the surface as long as I don't have to see them."

"It's all right, I suppose," he said, "until they actually pop out, but I am afraid that if I spent much time at Paradise I would begin to turn stones over and actively look for them." He had been patting Dram's head, and now the dog raised a large paw to his knee. "You handsome large lump," he said, scratching the dog's ears and shaking the big head from side to side while I thought: "I haven't deliberately turned a stone over to see what was underneath since I was a child at Reachfar. You have to be young and full of confidence to turn stones over, just to see what is underneath."

In my mind, while the young man played with the dog, a maggot wriggled, the maggot of the knowledge that only a few moments ago I had quarrelled with Twice more grievously than I had ever done in all the time I had known him. We had had many more prolonged, many more violent and noisy quarrels, but never one as grievous as this, never one that arose out of such a depth as this. I sat looking at the young man, admiring him and envying him, envying him his youth that had no responsibilities except to himself, envying him because he could say openly that he disliked St. Jago and its maggots, envying him because he had no restraining ties with other people.

"What is his name?" he asked, still holding the dog by the sides of the head with both hands.

"Dram. It is a short version of his over-fancy kennel-name Drambuie of Kilcarron."

"Dram," he said, giving the dog's head another shake from side to side. "Like Roddy being short for Roderick," and with an upward glance he invited me to call him by this name.

"And I think we had better go down to the kennel," I said. "It must be nearly time for lunch."

Roddy came down with me to the kennel, which was really Dram's own basket in a corner of the luggage room where there was a ring in the wall to which his lead could be tied; and after taking a drink from his own water dish, Dram got into the basket and lay down contentedly.

"He is a very reasonable sort of bloke, that dog," Roddy said.

I patted Dram's head. "He is reasonable about everything except C-A-T-S," I said; but even although I spelled the word, Dram looked at me suspiciously and gave a small and menacing growl.

"But you spelled it!" Roddy protested.

We came out of the room and I shut the door.

"Dram works a great deal by some sort of intuition," I said as we came along the passage and up the steps. "I suppose that even if I spell the word 'cats' I give off some sort of feeling that I am thinking about cats and he picks up the feeling out of the air."

"I suppose people would be a bit like

that too before all this civilisation killed it out of them," Roddy surprised me by saying.

I paused at the top of the companionway at the end of the passage that led to our cabin. "It's not dead in all of us," I said. "I live a lot by intuition. I get feelings about things and about people. Sometimes I wish I didn't. It can be depressing. . . . Well, I must go and wash for lunch."

The ship was primarily a cargo vessel and had accommodation for only twelve passengers, consisting of eight single cabins and two double ones, but this accommodation was very comfortable and every cabin was equipped with its own bathroom. When Roddy left me, he went across to the starboard side of the ship and I turned into our rooms at the end of the passage on the port side, going through the little sitting-room with its two easy chairs and writing-table to the bedroom, off which the bath-room opened. I felt a little uprush of annoyance to find Dee sitting at the dressing-table, combing her hair while she talked to Twice, who was in the bathroom.

"So that means there are only five of us altogether?" she was saying. "That's marvellous! And that old woman won't bother anybody much."

Twice came out of the bathroom, drying his hands, saw me and said: "Oh, there you are! Where have you been? We looked for you in the smoke-room."

"I was putting Dram in his kennel," I said, and looked at Dee, who had turned round on the dressing-table stool.

"There are only five passengers altogether, Twice says," she told me. "There was to be a family of six, but they had to cancel at the last moment. Isn't it marvellous!"

"I don't know if it is," I said. "Five of us may get fairly sick of one another at the end of twelve days."

"We'll wait for you in the little place outside the dining-saloon, Janet," Twice said. "Coming, Dee?"

They went away and I washed and tidied my hair, fighting all the time against a childish desire to cry.

Only four of the five passengers appeared for lunch at the big table in the middle of the dining-saloon. The old lady I had seen in the smoke-room was not there, and Dee and Twice sat on one side of the first officer, and Roddy and I sat on the other at his end of the table, while the captain's chair at the other end stood empty. Captain Davey was still on the bridge with the pilot. "I hope the other passenger is not feeling ill," I said to Mr. Radzow towards the end of the meal. This was no empty conventional remark, for this little ship did not carry a stewardess and it was understood that the sick women passengers would be tended by the unsick ones and I had no wish to spend twelve days below decks with a seasick old woman.

"I think not," the first officer said. He was Polish by birth and he spoke a slightly accented, almost too-perfect English. "She requested that lunch be sent to her cabin."

I had, of course, introduced Roddy to Dee and Twice, and Twice, naturally enough, was interested in this son of his colleague at Paradise and talked to him most of the way through lunch about his engineering studies at Glasgow and his future plans. I was pleased to see a mulish look possess Dee's face at this interference of another personality between Twice and herself. She was quite excessively plain in appearance, with a mere plainness, as opposed to any suggestion of the *jolie laide*, so assertive that it was almost aggressive. Her hair was mousy and badly tended; her eyes were small, round and light hazel; her skin slightly sallow. Her height was less than medium, and her figure unremarkable, but slight rather than full. Physically, her only feature of any appeal for me was what I can only describe as a neatness — neat hands, neat feet and a general neatness of movement, a neatness that, in the way even that her lips moved when she spoke, came near to primness. She was widely travelled for her age and highly intelligent in many ways, but this, along with everything else about her, was, in my eyes, overlaid and dominated by her terrible, edgy self-consciousness, so that, by her very shrinking away from people, she contrived to thrust herself and her self-consciousness on the notice of every-one, just as now I felt that Mr. Radzow and all the junior officers who were lunch-ing at little tables round the wall must be aware that Dee was sulking because Twice was giving some of his attention to Roddy.

When lunch was over, Mr. Radzow asked in a general way if we would like to go round the ship with him on his afternoon inspection, but I said that I would prefer to retire to my cabin with a book, which I did. I hoped that Twice would soon join me in the cabin so that we might talk and close this rift which had opened so suddenly and ominously between us; and although I took from the box of new books which had been delivered from London to the ship for us a novel called *But not for Love* which had been very well reviewed and which I had been longing to read, I did not read it but sat against the pillows of my bed, the book lying unopened on the eiderdown, hoping that Twice would come, and listening for the click of the door that led into the little sitting-room. At last it came, and I sat up straight in the bed, tears in my eyes, my apology for my anger of the forenoon already on my lips.

"Miss Jan, may I come in? It's Dee," the voice said, and: "As if I didn't know it was you!" I thought as I lay back and thrust my hands, that were shaking with disappointment and anger, under the eiderdown.

"Yes, come in, Dee," I said as calmly

as I could. "But I thought you had gone round the ship with the others?"

"I was with them, but they don't really want me."

She stood at the end of my bed and began to pick with her neat little fingers at a thread on the corner of the eiderdown. "They are down in the engine-room talking about nothing but engines."

I wanted to laugh, and I think I was smiling when I said: "But, Dee, Twice and Roddy are both engineers, and engineers always prefer talking about engines to talking about anything else."

"Who is this Roddy Maclean, anyway?" she asked next, her face sullen.

"His father, Rob Maclean, is the manager of Paradise, where we are going, and his mother, Marion Maclean, is my best friend in St. Jago."

"Did you know he was to be on this boat?"

"No, I didn't."

"It seems funny to me that out of all the boats going to St. Jago we should be travelling on one that has a friend of yours in it."

Her voice was suspicious, as if I had

made an assignation with Roddy to travel on this boat; but even although I knew with certainty that she did not mean to imply this, I felt myself growing angry, and I tried to conceal the anger as I said: "I think you have got the wrong end of the stick, Dee. What would be funny is if any white person whose home was in St. Jago was travelling on this or any other boat to the island and I *didn't* know him. The St. Jagoan white community is very small, you know." She stared at me sullenly. "What have you against Roddy Maclean?" I asked.

"Nothing, I suppose" — she picked at the eiderdown — "except that he is just in the way. I wanted it to be just Twice and me — and you, of course."

I felt that I had been added to her chosen group rather ineptly as an afterthought, for the sweet sake of politeness, and longed to slap her sullen little face.

"Pity," I said. "We should have chartered the ship instead of merely buying passages."

"You are not being very nice," she told me.

"Perhaps not. Perhaps it is because I

think you are being extremely silly, Dee. You can't expect to have the whole ship to yourself and generally have everything just as you want it."

"You are angry with me!"

"No, I am not angry with you, Dee," I said, and it was true to the degree that I was more irritated than angry. "I simply think you are being silly, as I said. Now — "

"I don't want the whole ship to myself!" she said sullenly.

"What do you want then ?"

"It's — oh, I can't explain."

"Look, there is a box of books over there. Have a look through it and find something to read, Dee."

"I don't want to read."

"Well, I do!"

She dropped the corner of the eiderdown and stared at me. "You don't want me in here ?"

"Frankly, no."

"Oh, I wish I'd never come on this ship! You're horrid! You're all horrid!" she said and fled out and along the passage, leaving the outer door swinging open behind her. I got out of bed, banged the door shut and threw myself back into the bed in such a fit of rage and shame that I was trembling all over.

I did not see Twice again until dinner-time, for he and Roddy had, in the end, spent the whole afternoon below with the chief engineer and had then gone to have a drink with the first officer in his cabin, so that Captain Davey and I were already at table when Twice, Roddy and the two officers came into the saloon. The chair opposite to me, on the captain's left, was empty, for the old lady had again elected to dine in her cabin, but I was more aware of another empty chair, which was Dee's, and sat waiting with foreboding until, about halfway through dinner, Twice said: "Where is Dee?"

I finished the remark I was making to Roddy beside me before I looked across at him and said: "Down below, I suppose."

His blue eyes looked hardly back at me. "Is she feeling ill?"

"I shouldn't think so, but I haven't seen her since just after lunch," and I turned back to Roddy.

"If you'll excuse me," Twice said,

getting up, "I'll go down below for a moment."

As he went out, I was as fully aware as if he had spoken it to me in words that Roddy Maclean knew that Dee and I had been quarrelling that afternoon and that Twice and I were quarrelling now. I could feel the knowledge emanating from him just as enmity had emanated from Dram when I had spelled the word "cats" that forenoon; and even as this analogy came into my mind, he said: "There is something going on down below that will surprise you, I think."

For a horrid moment I thought that by "down below" he meant Dee's cabin where Twice now was, and I repeated: "Down below?"

"In Dram's kennel. He has had the ship's kittens in there all the afternoon, playing with them."

"Kittens? Playing with them?" For a moment I forgot about Twice, Dee and everything. "Oh, Mr. Radzow, he'll kill them! He is terrible about cats!"

"No. They have been with him since lunch," Mr. Radzow assured me. "He seems to like them very much."

"He loves them," Roddy assured me. "Probably it is because they are so young. They are only six weeks old."

"We had to have the mother cat put down at Bristol," the chief engineer told us. "She had a tumour, the vet said, but two of the hands wanted to keep the kittens, so we have three of them on board."

"As long as Dram doesn't harm them," I said as Twice returned to the table. I looked across at him. "What is this I hear about Dram playing in a kindly way with cats ?" I asked.

"True enough," he said shortly.

"Is Dee not coming to dinner ?"

"No. She is feeling a bit off," he said to the table at large.

"She'll probably be all right by to-morrow," Captain Davey said.

"Probably," said Twice, looking sternly across at me, and I felt the word to constitute a threat.

"Would anyone like to play Scrabble after dinner ?" Mr. Radzow asked.

"You and your Scrabble!" the chief told him. "It's sheer victimisation of the passengers, that's all it is !"

"What is Scrabble ?" I asked.

"It's a sort of spelling game," Roddy told me. "Quite good fun."

"I'm not a games player, but I can spell an odd word here and there. I'll play, Mr. Radzow, if a beginner won't be a bore."

"Me too," Roddy said.

"I suppose I'll have to," the chief said, and Mr. Radzow smiled. "Splendid!" he said. "Let us go up."

I played Scrabble in the smoke-room until nearly midnight, while Twice, at another table, played cards with some of the junior officers and glanced at me now and again in an angry way, but at long last even Mr. Radzow tired of this means of extending his English vocabulary and there was nothing for it but to go below to our cabin.

"What the hell did you do to Dee this afternoon?" Twice blazed at me the moment we were inside.

"Me? *I* didn't do anything!"

People who love one another know in an instinctive way a great deal about one another, but this does not mean that they always use that knowledge in a beneficent way. I loved Twice very much; I knew a great deal about him, and one of the things I knew best was how to make him even angrier with me than he was already.

"Stop clowning!" he said, coming towards me in a menacing way. "What did you do to her?"

"Nothing, I tell you! It was *you* who did it" — I began to whine lugubriously in imitation of Dee — "going away looking at those horrid nasty engines and paying no attention to poor little Dee. And talking to that horrid Roddy Maclean and those nasty engineering officers and leaving little Dee all lonely and droopy and miserable!"

"Stop that! Stop it at once!"

But I did not stop. My face as sullen as I could make it, I picked at a corner of the window curtain with my fingers and whined on: "I wanted it to be just Twice and me on this boat — and you, of course. I wanted it to be just ourselves — "

I raised my eyelids to observe the effect of my performance, to find Twice coming slowly across the small floor towards me, moving like one of the larger members of the cat tribe, his fingers already curved to take a grip of me and shake me. Twice and I have got the better of many a crisis by physical violence for the reason, I think, that we can never find the words, especially when we are angry, for the feelings that lie between us, and now, as I saw the menace in his approach, I snatched my hair-brush from the dressing-table and threw it at him with all my force. Even at my calmest, I have no aim, and, angry as I was now, the brush went wide by a good yard; but Twice, unlike me, is quick of eye and hand, so he caught the brush in full flight, hurled it back, aimed in such a way that it whistled past my ear, making me shut my eyes and duck so that I lost my balance while the brush flew on through the open doorway to the bathroom, bounced off the far wall and clattered with a splash into the lavatory pan. I had fallen on to one of the beds, and Twice seized me by the shoulders and shook me till my teeth rattled.

It was at this stage, as a rule, that I began to cry with shame at behaving so badly, with sorrow at quarrelling with Twice, and for a complex of other reasons, so that, suddenly, we were no longer angry but ready to dissolve into love-making or laughter, but on this night I was neither ashamed nor sorry and I did not begin to cry. Instead, as soon as he released his grip on me, I sat up and panted venomously: "How that destructive little brat would love to see this! You'd better go and fetch her!"

Sitting on the other bed now, panting with rage as I was, Twice said: "What the hell's got into you?"

"It seems to me that whatever it is is in *you*!"

"What do you mean?"

I rose, went to the dressing-table and sat down with my back to him while, my hands shaking, I began to take the pins out of my hair.

"I suppose it flatters your forty-one-year-old vanity to be gazed at starry-eyed!" I said viciously.

"Great God Almighty — "

"Stop shouting! You might have picked something with eyes that could *look* starry and a bit less like the eyes of a dead cod!"

"Look here — "

"No, I won't. I've looked at the two of you enough today, not to mention this last week, and it gives me what my old Air Force chums called The Sick!"

"Now, Janet, listen — "

"I will *not* listen! If you need an audience, it's two doors down on your left," I said, went into the bathroom and banged and bolted the door.

I had rescued my hair-brush from the lavatory pan and had begun to wash it, when I heard the door of the bedroom slam shut; and as I wrenched open the door of the bathroom the outer door of the sitting-room slammed and I heard Twice's angry steps die away along the passage until there was no sound but the wash of the water against the hull of the ship. For a second I had a panic-stricken urge to run after him, but then I saw the dent in the silver back of the brush between my hands, and, my anger rising again, I went back to the bathroom and rubbed more soap into the bristles before scrubbing them furiously with the nailbrush.

It was a long time before Twice came back. I do not know by the clock how long it was, for I turned the lights out when I got into bed by way of showing, when he chose to return, that I had gone uncaring to sleep, but between the time when the doors slammed shut and then softly opened again, it seemed to me that I had lived through at least a century of even grimmer historic weather than that which prevails in this twentieth century of ours. During that century I had promised myself that if ever Twice came back to me I would apologise to him kneeling, offer to find a second Dee for him and never quarrel with him again, but as soon as the door opened and he was moving quietly about the room, all my promises to myself shattered to fragments and it was as much as I could do not to sit up in bed and scream at him like a virago accusations of his having spent this last century in Dee's cabin even although I knew that such accusations were utterly false.

I did not sleep a great deal that night, and probably Twice did not sleep much either; but when morning came and I knew he was awake, I was afraid to open my eyes because I did not want to quarrel any more and yet knew that the quarrel must continue, although I had no very clear idea of what, precisely, we were quarrelling about.

The cabin steward came in with a tray of tea, and it was useless for either of us to pretend any longer to be asleep, but when we sat up in our beds we did not look at one another and we did not speak until we were both holding cups of tea and Twice said in a cold, even voice: "What did you mean last night when you said Dee was destructive?"

"I don't suppose it matters what I meant."

"What you mean is that you don't know what you meant."

I turned my head and looked at him, and his blue eyes looked sternly back at me.

"I know very well what I meant," I told him.

"Then what did you mean?"

"I meant what I said — that she is destructive."

He looked momentarily exasperated, took a grip on himself and managed to ask calmly: "Destructive in what way?"

"In many ways, I suppose, but the obvious one is that she has already destroyed the peace between you and me."

He drew a sharp breath and said: "You can't blame Dee because *you* started throwing things!"

"Oh yes I can and I do. That hair-brush of mine is badly dented with you throwing it into the bathroom — more destruction — but I don't blame you for that. I blame Dee," I said, staring at the wall ahead of me.

"That is simply bloody-minded and unreasonable!"

"These are two characteristics of mine that you have been aware of for years, but bloody-minded and unreasonable or not, I maintain that Dee Andrews is by nature destructive and I don't want to discuss her any further."

"But, Janet, don't you see how impossible all this is? I mean, we have invited her to come with us — "

"You invited her."

"But, damn it, you concurred!"

"I didn't get a chance to do anything else."

There was a prolonged silence while we both drank tea, until Twice laid aside his cup, got out of his bed, came to sit on the edge of mine and said: "Janet, you must try to explain to me what has happened."

"Nothing has happened except that you have convinced yourself that I have been so horrid to your poor little Dee that she is afraid to come out of her cabin."

"And haven't you been? When she came in here yesterday to talk to you, you told her to clear out, she says."

"Yes, so I did. But she didn't come in here to talk to me. She came in to belly-ache because you were talking to the engineers and not to her. That is different from coming in here to talk to me."

"You don't feel you are splitting hairs?"

"Perhaps I am, but this is one of the times when the thickness of the parts of a split hair is important — important to me, anyway. But we won't bother about that at the moment. The point is that you are in a tizzy because here we are with Dee in our ménage and you think that she and I are not going to get along. You are mistaken. She and I will get along all right when she gets hungry enough to come out of her huff and her cabin. *She* will get along with me — or else!"

"For God's sake! Why didn't you say before we left London that you disliked her so much?"

"I couldn't. I didn't know about it then."

"My God, but you can be maddening!"

"There's no point in blowing your top," I told him. "It is your fault that she is here, and your fault that I dislike her even more now than I disliked her yesterday afternoon."

"My fault? For Pete's sake, why?"

"Because you charged in here last night and attacked me because of her. Do you expect me to love her for that?"

"But, Janet, if you had seen her last night when I came down during dinner! You don't seem to realise how you can pulverise people, especially a little creature like Dee, with this primitive thunder of yours!"

"It seems to me that a little primitive thunder and thinking is very much in order. As for getting pulverised, doesn't it occur to you that it can happen to me too although I am nearly five feet nine?"

"You? Pulverised? One might as well attack Ben Wyvis with a toffee-hammer!"

"Have it your own way," I told him. "But the situation between you, Dee and me will be all right if you cut out the drama and the heroics, Twice. Let's have no more of your rushing at me asking what I have done to her. Take it from here that I will do to her what I bloody well think fit, that's all, and you are at liberty to do the same. You can even spend your whole life with her if you like, until such time as I get around to murdering her."

"I simply don't know what's got into you."

"Dee Andrews has got into me and I have already told you she is destructive. And if you don't like it, that's too bad, because you started it. But for you, she wouldn't be here."

"Janet," he appealed to me, "you realise that you are worrying me quite badly?"

"I didn't sleep much last night either."

"But why do you dislike her so?"

"I dislike anybody who can do this to you and me."

"But she isn't doing anything!"

I stared at the hair-brush on the dressing-table, at the dent in its silver back.

"She doesn't have to do anything. I dislike her for what she is."

"For what she is? And what do you think she is?"

"I can't tell you in words. She is simply something that I dislike."

"You are talking absolute rubbish!" he told me angrily. "And there is something disgusting about this — about you being jealous because I take an interest in a youngster who is unhappy. I thought you had more stature than that!"

I drew breath to make some angry retort, but was struck again by the idea that had come to me the night before, the idea that this rupture between Twice and me would please Dee, and I swallowed the words while I stared at the wall and decided that I was going to stop this quarrel, not, primarily, to achieve peace with Twice, but because, by achieving peace, I felt that I would be in some obscure way making a stand against the malign influence of Dee.

"I honestly don't think I am jealous of her, Twice," I said, "and I apologise for all the filthy things I have said to you. I don't mind, honestly, how much time you spend with her, but equally I expect you not to mind how I choose to deal with her. In other words, if she comes in here bellyaching that you are neglecting her, there is liable to be a repetition of what happened yesterday. After all, it is pretty absurd for a girl to come complaining to *me* that she is being neglected by *my* husband, don't you think?"

Twice smiled a little. "She didn't think of it like that, Janet."

"Then I think she should have done. This is part of what I dislike in her. She is so damned inept!"

"That is because she is so uncertain of herself."

"Maybe. Anyway, she is your pigeon. I'll do my best to cope, Twice, but it would help if you drew her a few diagrams about not coming to *me* with her complaints about you. Dammit, I think that is what made me so angry yesterday — it is all so complicated — but I'd get mad at anybody who criticised you, and for *her* to do it was too much altogether."

Twice leaned towards me and kissed me on the cheek, then took my hand in his and sat looking down at it. "I feel that I am being circumgyrated by subtlety," he said, "but, anyway, I apologise for last night."

"So do I. And, Twice, I really will do my best with this thing."

"I know you will," he assured me,

"but I wish you liked her. It would be so much easier, you being you."

"Everything can't be easy in this vale of tears, and right now you had better get dressed and go along to her cabin and make sure that she hasn't jumped overboard or something."

While Twice bathed and shaved, I sat staring at my hair-brush and thinking of the situation. Delia was twenty-four and Twice and I were forty-one — we could have had a daughter of her age, I told myself, but I had no parental feeling towards this girl now although my liking for her as a child had been of a near-maternal kind. She did not even arouse in me the liking that I felt for most young people, the liking that I had felt at once the day before for young Roddy Maclean or for the young seaman who looked after Dram and the kittens.

As a rule, Twice and I reacted in a similar way to people, and I could think of no other instance of his being drawn towards someone whom I found inimical, and this worried me in a deep-down gnawing way, influencing my every thought about Dee. Twice and I have no children.

We married late, I had a miscarriage at my first pregnancy and could not have another child; but by an earlier marriage Twice had a son whom he had not seen since infancy but who must now be only a little younger than Dee. It struck me now that I had always thought that Twice had accepted our childless state just as I had done but that this might not be so. After a bitter struggle, I had arrived at the acceptance, an acceptance reputed to be more difficult for the female than for the male, but it was possible, I now thought, that Twice had not achieved acceptance as I had, after all. Staring at the dented hair-brush, I found myself thinking: "If only it had been anyone other than Dee Andrews!"

2

QUEER THINGS HAPPEN AT SEA

BY the time I went up to the dining-saloon Twice and Dee had already breakfasted and were out on deck somewhere, but I had a pleasant meal with Roddy Maclean and went with him to take Dram for a walk afterwards. When he opened the door of the luggage-room, two seamen, Dram and the three kittens were in there, the seamen sitting on a bench and Dram lying on the floor, with the kittens jumping and gambolling all over him, playing with his ears and tail, and he did not look in the least enthusiastic when I suggested that he should come up on deck for a walk.

"You'll 'ave to take 'is kittens as well. Mrs. Alexander," one of the seamen advised me, and that is what we did, going up on deck in a procession, I leading Dram, and Roddy and the sailors carrying a kitten each while Dram kept a wary eye on them.

We went up to the upper after-deck outside the smoke-room, which was no more than a gallery screened on three sides to a height of some four feet with steel mesh, and there the men put the kittens down and I unhooked Dram's lead; and although normally he was full of energy and ran miles in the course of a day, he at once lay down again and began to play with the kittens.

"It's all very disconcerting," I said to Roddy. "His whole character seems to have changed."

"It must be love," Roddy said, "or maybe it's the sea. They always say that queer things happen at sea."

I found Roddy an amusing and agreeable companion, very relaxed and easy, the exact opposite of the tense and self-consciously self-centred Dee; and while she and Twice went about the ship, Roddy and I sat contentedly on the little gallery. Dee and Twice spent most of the forenoon on the bridge, for the *Pandora* was an informal little ship, and Dee, I gathered, was allowed to take over the wheel from the steersman on duty and keep the ship on her tied course between two points of the compass

while Twice and Captain Davey or whatever officer was on duty sat about yarning.

In this way the forenoon passed, and at
lunch Dee looked happy, but she spoke to
hardly anyone at the table except Twice,
which made me feel slightly irritable. Her
monopolisation of him was so complete
that she seemed to me to resent his address-
ing a word to anybody else, and it amazed
me that Twice seemed to be unaware of
this fixation of hers. Or was he aware of it
and flattered by it? But this thought I
dismissed as being derogatory of him, and
I concluded that he was unaware of the
degree of her fixation, while I, probably,
was exaggerating Dee's wish to monopolise
him. When lunch was over, the three of
us sat on at table for a little after Roddy
and the officers had gone — the old lady
was again having lunch in her cabin —
and Dee said: "Captain Davey is a friend
of yours, isn't he, Miss Jan?"

It was the first direct remark she had
made to me since our exchange in the cabin
the day before, and even as she spoke the
words I was aware that she was being
consciously magnanimous in thus addres-
sing me, displaying to Twice her generous

forgiveness of my "nastiness" to her of the day before.

"Yes," I said. "His daughter Dorothy came out to spend a holiday with Twice and me just like you now, and she married the estate schoolmaster at Paradise and — "

"Just quite *unlike* me!" Dee broke in. "You needn't think you are going to marry *me* off to the first man who comes along, because you're not!" Whereupon she rose from the table and marched out of the saloon.

"The little brat!" said Twice, frowning at the glass-doors that swung shut behind her.

"The inept little fool to do that in front of Twice!" I thought, but aloud I said: "Wait a minute, Twice. Maybe that was partly my fault. I should have remembered how sensitive she is about this marriage thing when she has just broken her engagement to Alan Stewart and everything."

"But if she is going to fly off like that all the time, life is just not going to be possible! Damn it, I wouldn't have believed it if I hadn't seen it!"

"Oh, darling, she'll settle down," I said,

and then I laughed. "Dash it, everything is getting wrong end up on this ship. Last week nobody would have convinced me that Dram would fall in love with a bunch of kittens, and last night nobody would have convinced me that I would ever take Dee's side against you, but here I am doing it. Look here, you'd better not sit here talking to *me*. That will only make things worse."

"Don't be ridiculous! I'll sit and talk to you any time I like!"

"Twice, you have got to humour her during the voyage, at least. Never mind me. I'm all right. I'm going down to the cabin to have a flop with my book. All I ask is that you keep her out of *there*!"

"I am not going to spend my days humouring her, as you call it," Twice said, his chin sticking out in its aggressive way. "I've got some work to do, and I am coming down to the cabin to do it, and that is that."

I shrugged my shoulders. "Please yourself."

Down below, I got on to my bed with my book, and Twice took his brief-case out to the writing-table in our sitting-room and set to work, but it was not very long before I heard the tap at the door and Dee was in there.

"Twice, aren't you coming up to the bridge?"

"Not this afternoon, Dee. I want to go through these specifications."

"It isn't that. You are angry because I was rude after lunch."

With exasperation I thought that she was less adult than she was when I knew her at eight years old.

"Yes, you were rude. But I'm not angry about it. It isn't that important."

I did not at all like the sound of Twice's voice and put the eiderdown back in preparation for sudden intervention.

"I am sorry I was rude, Twice."

"Then that's all right."

"I didn't mean to be."

Twice did not speak, but I heard an impatient rustling of the papers he had been studying.

"Aren't you coming up on deck?" she persisted as if she felt that he must come in return for her apology.

"No. I have work to do, Dee."

"Then I'd better go." Her voice was dreary and I heard her feet go away along the passage dragging in a discouraged way.

There was a short interval of silence from the next room and then Twice came to stand at the foot of my bed.

"Dammit, that girl needs psycho-analysis or something! If you suspected this, as you implied last night, why the blazes didn't you say something before we got aboard this bloody ship?"

"Darling, I didn't know how she was until yesterday, don't you see? You know how slowly my mind works about things. It was only yesterday that the feeling came over me that — "

"Oh, you and your feelings!"

"They are a sight more informative than all your logic and reason!" I snapped at at him. "*You* can't see anything unless it's in a geometric design on paper or somebody drives it through your skull with a mallet!"

"There is no point in our having another shouting match," he said. "Get on with your book and I'll go back out there, but I'll bolt that damned door!"

The afternoon, however, was not a success. I could not concentrate on my book and, judging from the suppressed oaths and impatient shiftings of the chair in the adjoining room, Twice was not very happy either. After about half an hour I rose, put on my coat, fetched Dram, with his kittens cavorting behind him, and went up on deck, where I found Roddy Maclean all alone on the gallery outside the smoke-room.

"Have you seen Dee, Roddy?" I asked.

"Yes. She's in the little lounge outside the saloon writing letters."

Relieved that Dee had not plunged into the grey waters of the Atlantic, I sat down beside him, but before very long Captain Davey, accompanied by an officer called Mr. Carter, who was in charge of the dining-saloon, came along and asked me to join them in the smoke-room. They looked so grave that I at once made up my mind that Dee had indeed tried to jump overboard, had been restrained by main force and that I was now being summoned to a drumhead court-martial as her legal guardian.

"It's this old woman in Cabin Five, Missis Janet," the captain said, using the St. Jagoan version of my name that he had picked up from his daughter, and I was so relieved that I looked much more interested than I felt in his fifth passenger. "She is down there in that cabin doing nothing but eat all day, Carter here tells me. It won't do, you know. It isn't healthy," he told me accusingly.

My first impulse was to laugh, for Captain Davey was a big, ruddy-faced traditional-looking sea-dog and his heavy pink jowls positively joggled with disapproval of the old lady's unseamanlike behaviour. "She'll get a liver a fathom long," he continued with an air of dire threat. "She's got to be got up out of there!"

"I don't see why," I said. "If that is the way she likes to travel, let her get on with it. Maybe she will come up when we get to warmer water."

"If she hasn't died of jaundice by then." Captain Davey was lugubrious. "Look here, Missis Janet, I wish you'd go down and see her. Nobody's seen her since she came on board except old Dooley, the cabin steward. She must be some sort of crank and next thing you know she'll be trying to jump overboard or preach religion to the crew."

I did my best to argue my way out of this duty, but Captain Davey was not to be laughed out of or argued out of or in any other way coaxed out of his sense of responsibility for his unseamanlike passenger, and I was borne to the door of her cabin in my straw-in-the-wind way at four o'clock tea-time by Mr. Carter and the steward Dooley. Dooley knocked at the door.

"Tea, madam!"

There was no sound from inside except that of the catch on the door being slipped back. I found myself shivering, apostrophised myself roundly but silently, and Dooley opened the door and went it.

" 'Afternoon, madam," he said. "Very nice up on deck today. By the way, Mr. Carter, the dinin'-saloon officer, and Mrs. Alexander, one of the passengers, is here to see you."

"What for?" came the flat voice. It had not even the upward lilt of the interrogative. But for the presence of Mr. Carter I would have bolted like a rabbit for the upper-deck, but as is well known, the men of the British Merchant Service are famed for their intrepidity and also have a great

56

respect for the wishes of their captains, so he seized me by the upper arm and, more or less thrusting me before him, precipitated us both into the small cabin.

"Good-afternoon, Miss Morrison," he said. "Just came down to see that everything was to your satisfaction, you know."

She looked up at him levelly from the armchair under the window. "I would have informed you if it wasn't," she said, not emphatically or rudely or anything but as a bald statement of fact.

Again I wanted to run. There was a slight clatter as Dooley released too soon his grip on one end of the metal tea-tray so that it fell sharply to the table-top, and then Dooley did run, out into the passage, closing the door behind him.

"Not thinking of coming up on deck for a bit?" Mr. Carter asked her with what I thought was enviable aplomb. "It's getting quite warm already, you know."

"No," she said flatly, staring at him out of her dull eyes for a moment before turning her gaze to me.

"You — you are feeling quite well, Miss Morrison?" I said nervously, feeling that she was forcing me into speech.

"Yes."

I felt that my hands and feet were growing larger by the second and that soon the the cabin would not hold them.

"Then that's splendid," I said stupidly, knowing that my attempt to smile was utterly sickly and unsuccessful. "I hope you enjoy your tea," and I turned towards the door.

"You'd better stay and have some tea now you're here," she said, and I felt rather than heard the words hit me like little pebbles between the shoulder-blades. "Tell that man," she added to Mr. Carter, "to bring Mrs. Alexander's tea down here."

I turned back from the doorway. Mr. Carter turned his back to Miss Morrison, raised his eyebrows at me and then winked. I sat down on the little stool by the dressing-table and said: "That will be very nice. Would you do that, Mr. Carter, please? And will you tell my husband where I am?"

"Certainly, Mrs. Alexander," he said and went out. The door closed and there we were.

Twice knows quite well where I am, I

58

thought, but when Mr. Carter tells him he will know that I am not liking this, and maybe he will come and stand in the passage outside or something, for I am really not liking this one bit and she is a quite horrible old woman and I wish I were miles away and . . .

"Is that big man with the white teeth your husband?" Miss Morrison asked, and, although her tone was as expressionless as ever, she contrived to make Twice sound like an orang-outang.

"Yes," I said.

"That makes a difference," she commented.

This floored me. I longed to ask her the nature of the difference that was made by the relationship between Twice and me, but I could not think of the words to frame the question.

"I saw him with that girl with the brown hair," she said; and this is a difficult thing to describe, for, although there was no expression of any kind in her voice, no implication of any sort, the fact that she made the comment at all gave it an undercurrent of sinister meaning, as if Twice were a tycoon in the white slave traffic.

"That is Delia Andrews, a young friend of mine who is travelling with us," I told her, laying a definite emphasis on the word "mine".

She had poured herself out some tea, although Dooley had not, as yet, arrived with mine, and she now began to chew at a sandwich in a ruminative way, staring blankly at the wall ahead of her.

"And there's a young man up there," she said, "a good-looking young man," and I had the immediate conviction that she disapproved of good looks, and of good looks in young men in particular.

At that moment Dooley arrived with my tea-tray, and when he had gone out and I was pouring out a cup I thought that there were about ten days of this voyage to go and it would be a pity to quarrel outright with this old woman thus early if it could possibly be avoided.

"It is kind of you to let me have tea with you, Miss Morrison," I said, "for maybe you would prefer to be left alone?"

I was quite prepared for her to tell me flatly that she did so prefer; I visualised myself telling Captain Davey forthright that this was her preference and thus

60

clinching the matter for good and all, so I was pulled up short when she said: "I don't like being alone. I don't like travelling alone either. I've never done it before and I don't like it."

It seems absurd to say that I felt that everything had changed, for, outwardly, nothing had changed at all. The old woman still sat there, her face and voice as flat and expressionless as ever, as she munched at her sandwich; she was as unfriendly and distant as she had ever been; she had merely made one more of her bald statements of fact, but, for me, everything had changed. I think this was because I had found out something about her, something that humanised her — she was travelling alone and she did not like it. In her own words, to know this about her "made a difference".

"I am sorry," I said. "But you have friends in St. Jago?"

"Not friends," she said. "Cousins."

The precision of this, the differentiation between friends and cousins, had the effect of repressing me again, as if once more I had come up with a bump against a stone wall. Talk, I thought. Get this tea over. Get it behind.

"St. Jago is a lovely island. Have you been there before?" I asked.

"No."

"I think you will find it very beautiful. My husband and I are on a sugar estate out there — it is called Paradise and it almost *is*. We have grown very fond of it."

"I don't suppose I'll like it. I don't like foreign places and foreigners," she said after a moment and took another sandwich. "It is difficult enough to know where you are if you stay at home in your own country."

"Miss Morrison, why did you come on this trip then?"

"I wanted to get away from London for a bit," she said, but she did not amplify her statement and we sat facing one another in the small intimate room in silence until I said: "Do you mind if I smoke in your cabin, Miss Morrison?"

"Aren't you going to eat any more?"

"I've had two sandwiches and a piece of cake — that is more than I usually eat at tea-time."

"Then I'll have the rest from your tray." She reached across and tipped the two remaining sandwiches and some cake on to her own plate. "You should keep your strength up at sea, and it is silly to waste the food. Smoke if you want to. I don't smoke myself, but I like the smell of cigarettes. My friend Miss Murgatroyd used to smoke like a chimney."

"Has she stopped then?"

"Yes."

"I've never even tried to stop. It is a bad habit, I suppose, but there it is."

"It's no worse than a lot of habits people have, as Fanny — that's Miss Murgatroyd — says. And if it's harmful, it harms only yourself. People have a lot of habits that harm other people too, like people that talk too much."

I made no comment, virtuously determined not to be accused of having the harmful habit of talking too much.

"Does anybody on this ship play chess?" she asked next. "Or bridge?"

"Well, nobody has played so far, but I am sure some of them do. My husband plays chess and bridge; and the captain plays bridge, I know. Do you play?"

"Yes."

"Then I am sure you can get a game after dinner if you come up. Will you?"

"I might," she said, as if turning the matter over in her mind.

"We were playing Scrabble after dinner last night," I said.

"What's that?"

"It's a spelling game. Quite good fun and not too difficult for non-games people like me. It was the first officer who produced it. He is Polish and I think it widens his English vocabulary."

"Polish? I don't like foreigners."

"He is very nice," I said, feeling irritable with her again.

"I didn't think much of that Captain Davey either," she added. "He is far too sure of himself."

"I think I prefer the captains of the ships I sail in to be fairly sure of themselves," I said nastily.

She looked at me out of her pale, expressionless eyes. "He is sure of himself about everything, not only ships," she said to me firmly. "His brain runs along lines like an old tram-car. I don't like people like that."

Captain Davey was by way of being a friend of mine and I could have hit her for being critical of him, but the annoying thing was that what she had said was singularly acute and exactly correct. Captain Davey was a completely conventional example of his race, his age, his class and the service in which he was employed, and his mind would neither embrace nor consider anything or anyone that departed from its accepted norm, such as, for instance, misogynistic old women who preferred meals in their cabins to meals at his captain's table in the dining-saloon. It was over two years since I had first met Captain Davey, but I had never appreciated this fact about him until now when I sat opposite this old woman in this little cabin, and the fact that she had caused me to re-appraise him did not in the least make me like her any better. That is how I am. I will go further and say that I think that that is how humanity is. We do not, in general, care to have the less attractive, more mundane facts which we have contrived to ignore pushed under our noses, and so I sat staring in front of me, silenced again, wishing that I could say: "And Captain Davey doesn't think much of you either — he thinks you are an old crank!"

"I suppose I had better come up for

dinner tonight," she said next. "If I don't, that captain will make up his mind that I am a crank. That's the word he would use — crank."

I was so stunned by this that I do not think I spoke another word to her, and when Dooley came in to take away the tea-things I took my opportunity and ran like a stag for my own cabin.

I was still there when Twice came down to wash before dinner. I had already changed and sat looking at him while he came in without speaking, took off his shirt and frowned at his own face in the mirror, took off a shoe and frowned at the sea beyond the window.

"I don't like that youth Maclean," he said suddenly. "There is something queer about him."

I emitted a long howl, flapping my fingers in front of my mouth to make a noise like a Red Indian war-cry.

"Are you off your nut?" he asked.

"Probably. There is an old woman in Cabin Five. There is something queer about her too. In fact, this ship is a floating loony bin. What, specifically, is queer about Roddy Maclean?"

"He knows no more about engineering than a hole in the wall."

"Aha! The ultimate in the diagnosis of insanity. All those who know nothing about engineering are ipso facto dotty. *That's* what's wrong with me! I know nothing about eng— "

Twice threw a shoe with a bang on to the floor. "Can you possibly stop being unfunny?" he asked.

"Look, Twice," I said gravely, "can't you recognise an escape mechanism when you see one? I spent the afternoon in Cabin Five with a queer old woman to oblige Captain Davey. Then I came in here and sat thinking about Dee, and now you come in and say Roddy Maclean is queer. My hours and my days are being devoured by queer people and I'm sick of it, and I don't give a damn for any of them, and I don't want to talk about them, and that's all there's to it!"

Twice went into the bathroom and slammed the door, and I wanted to burst into tears, but, instead, I went off up to the smoke-room, where I sat talking to Roddy Maclean, watching for queerness to break out of him like ectoplasm until the others gathered for dinner, trying to evade the haunted feeling I had that some intangible wedge was being driven inexorably through the fabric of the relationship between Twice and myself.

Miss Morrison, to Captain Davey's gratification, at first, appeared in the saloon for dinner, but by the time she had eaten her way through the third course I found that he was looking at me as if to blame me for bringing this hungry death's head to the feast. Miss Morrison sat beside him, in the brown tweed coat and skirt in which she had come on board, eating prodigiously and speaking no word unless asked a direct question, and even then, sometimes, she would make no reply other than a flat stare, which indicated that the question was too basically silly to merit an answer.

Further down the table, Dee sat playing about with her food, her face downcast, a sullen aura all about her, while Twice talked to the chief and Mr. Radzow; but even while he talked I could see that Twice was only too aware of the sulky silence that was Dee alongside of him. The effect of Miss Morrison's prodigious eating and ill manners, Captain Davey's accusing glances, Dee's sulky lumpishness and Twice's discomfort altogether had on me was to make me slightly hysterical, and it seemed that the atmosphere round the table had a similar effect on Roddy Maclean, who sat beside me, with the result that he and I became more and more uproarious. I do not know how it began, but very soon we were playing a game of conversing in nothing but literary quotations and, dazzled with our own brilliance, we screamed with laughter at one another while Roddy said to me: "Mesee, Madam, you have a pretty wit!" and I replied with a coy: "Oh, Mr. Rochester!" It was when we recovered from this fit of laughter that I saw Twice, very unamused, glaring up the table at me, and in the same instant I saw a small mean light of triumph flash into Dee's eyes, betokening her pleasure in Twice's annoyance with me. Although I admitted in my mind that he had every reason to be annoyed with my puerility, this little flash of malice had the effect of making me more strained, hysterical and puerile than ever.

When dinner was over we repaired to the smoke-room, and Captain Davey and Miss

Morrison settled down to play bridge against Twice and the chief while Roddy and I sat down in a far corner of the room, as far from the earnest bridge table as possible, for Miss Morrison, although saying nothing, contrived to convey that this would be no light-hearted game.

"Sit down, Dee," I said.

"Like to play Scrabble?" Roddy asked, looking up at her where she hovered between us.

She looked from him to me and back again.

"No," she said. "I am going down to my cabin."

She turned and went away, but as she went out I saw her glance at the back of Twice's head, a glance that accused him of being foully traitorous to abandon her thus for a game of bridge.

"I wouldn't let it worry you too much, Missis Janet," said Roddy's voice quietly and intimately, and I jerked my head round, realising that I had been staring fixedly at the door where Dee had gone out.

The words sounded to me as if they were the only normal, reasonable words I had heard spoken since I had come on board this ship, the only words that belonged to the plane on which I lived my life, and my first impulse on hearing them was towards tears of relief.

"It is difficult not to worry about her," I said.

"Has she been ill?"

"No. Not exactly."

I looked down at the green leather top of the table between us and thought that this young man was of Dee's generation and that he might be able to understand her better than Twice, and I could if I were to enlist his help, so I looked up at him and told him the circumstances that had led up to her coming on this trip with us. "It was all meant to be helpful," I ended, "but I am beginning to wonder if it wasn't a ghastly mistake. I do wish she were having a better time."

Marion Maclean, Roddy's mother, was a very sympathetic woman to whom I always found it easy to talk, and although I had never talked intimately with her I always felt that she would be sympathetic if one went to her in trouble. Roddy seemed to have inherited some of this sympathy that I felt to be in his mother, and in him it was a trait strangely feminine in one so masculine.

"She is so self-conscious," I said, "and she always seems to feel that nobody is interested in her or wants her."

"It isn't that exactly," he surprised me by saying. "She may say that she feels like that, but I think it is more that she is one of these people who wants to be part of a relationship without giving anything of herself away. She wants Twice to give her his whole attention while she keeps herself undivided and intact. It is like wanting to have your cake and eat it too. It can't be done."

"You are a bright boy for your age, Roddy."

"Not very." He seemed to withdraw into himself a little, looking down at the table. "You don't have to be very bright to see that Dee has got her wires crossed somewhere. Of course, that's awfully easy to do at our age." He looked up at me suddenly with a grin that was half-rueful, half-mischievous. "Youth and all that, you know."

"It is particularly easy for young women to get their wires crossed as you call it.

I was a young woman once and I know. Young men seem to be more fortunate if you are anything to go by."

"I've got no wires to cross," he told me lightly. "Everything is easy and straightforward for a bloke like me. Dee is rich, isn't she? I don't suppose that is any help."

"No. I don't think it is."

"The world is arranged all wrong. Dee is the earnest sort, she craves a mission in life. Now I am the type that should have been born rich. I'd have had a whale of a time!"

"I bet you would," I agreed with him.

While the bridge-game went on across the room, Roddy and I now began to read the books we had brought with us, but for the first few moments, although I had my book open, I did not read. I was covertly studying Roddy Maclean, remembering how Twice, earlier, had said that there was something queer about him. To me, Roddy seemed anything but queer; he seemed to be a more normal, better balanced person at this moment than any of the rest of us as he sat opposite me reading, with a concentration that was almost palpable, a cheap edition of Thackeray's *Vanity Fair*. When, earlier, I had remarked upon his choice of reading matter, he had explained that, now that he had completed his engineering studies, he was trying to catch up with a few of the classics which he had never had time to read before. Twice could say what he liked, but I wished that Dee were sitting there as alive and interested as Roddy was in his book and everything about him, instead of as she was, for even now she was probably sitting in her cabin, brooding, as she picked at the corner of her handkerchief.

I closed my book for a moment and laid it on the table while I took out my cigarettes, and Roddy looked up.

"Cigarette?" I said.

"Thanks." Holding a lighted match across to me, he looked down at the novel on the table. "Is that any good?"

"Very good indeed, I think. Would you like to read it when I've finished?"

"It's a new novel, isn't it? No, thanks."

"Are you pursuing a policy of classics only?"

"I think maybe it's better for an engineering type like me with limited time to concentrate on what's supposed to be the best. *But Not For Love*," he read from the jacket of my book. "It's a wet sort of title, isn't it?"

I felt a touch of irritation and thought that, after all, this young man was not the son of Rob Maclean for nothing, for Rob regarded reading, unless it was a scientific paper on the regeneration of steam or the maceration of sugar cane juice, as a waste of time.

"I wouldn't say that," I replied. "Before you pass judgment on that title, I think you want to read a few more classics. It's a question of knowing enough."

"Knowing enough?"

"These four words come from one of Shakespeare's comedies. 'Men have died from time to time and worms have eaten them but not for love.' "

"Oh, I see. Yes. That does make it sound a bit less wet. And you think it is a good book?"

"Yes, I do. S. T. Bennett, whoever he or she may be, knows a lot about people and can put into good English what he or she knows."

We talked for a little longer about

books, then read again until there was a stir of movement across the room as the bridge game ended and I looked round as I heard the expressionless voice of Miss Morrison.

"It is a long time," she said, "since I saw three people play such a poor game," whereupon she picked up the canvas bag that lay on the floor by her feet, went out of the room and disappeared down the companionway. Flabbergasted, the three men stared at one another for a moment before they began to laugh, and then Captain Davey said: *"There's* a crank for you, *if* you like!" and I had a mischievous urge to tell him that Miss Morrison knew that that was precisely the word he would use to describe her.

"Where is Dee?" Twice asked, joining Roddy and me.

"She went down to her cabin right after dinner," I told him, picking up my book and cigarettes, "and I am going down now. Good-night, Roddy."

Without waiting for Twice, I set off, but he followed me at once, and as soon as he was inside our cabin, with his back against the closed door, battle was joined.

"The least you could have done tonight was to pay a little attention to that kid along there," he said, "instead of giggling with that youth Maclean like the parish flirt at the Sunday School Picnic!"

"Oh, well, I haven't done the least I could have done," I said.

"Janet, what the hell is the matter with you?"

"Maybe I am in need of psycho-analysis, or was it for Dee that you recommended that? You listen to me, Twice Alexander. I am not going to get into a shipboard routine of having a nightly row about Dee Andrews and a morningly making-up of our differences in preparation for the next nightly row. As far as Dee is concerned, you continue to go your way and I'll go mine."

"Your way being into a shipboard flirtation with a youth half your age? My God, woman, you are forty-two!"

"Not till next March. And can you draw me a scientific diagram to show the difference between my giggling with Roddy Maclean and you giggling with Dee? Except that you don't giggle. I wish to God you did!"

"Now, Janet, you know perfectly well that the thing of Dee and me is quite different from you and that youth Maclean. He's attracted to you — anyone with half an eye can see it."

"And isn't Dee attracted to you? A blind man could see her glowering at anyone who says a word to you."

"Don't talk rubbish! I am talking about sex — there is no sex in Dee, but it leaks out of every one of Maclean's pores!"

"Well, I hadn't noticed it."

"We have been through all this before with Don Candlesham. You didn't notice that either until the whole island was talking and then you said I should have told you. Well, I am telling you about this lot right now at the start!" he half shouted.

"Stop bawling, Twice. The point is, you are quite wrong about Roddy Maclean. He only talks to me because there is nobody else."

"So I'm quite wrong, am I? And there is nobody else? There are all the ship's officers, there's me, there's Dee. Wouldn't it be more natural for him to spend his time with *her*?"

"If *she* were anywhere near natural, it

might be, but as she is since we came aboard this ship I wouldn't blame a louse for avoiding her much less a good-looking young man."

"So he is good-looking?"

"Yes, good-looking. If you are even half honest you have to admit that."

"I wouldn't trust him a bloody inch!"

"That doesn't affect his looks." I had taken the pins out of my hair and I turned round on the stool with my hairbrush in my hand, looking down at the dent in the silver. "Twice," I said, "we shouldn't be quarrelling like this about Roddy Maclean, you know. I know we giggled at dinner, but it was sort of strain and hysteria, what with that old woman eating like a horse and Dee glowering, and then you starting to glower too. Then up in the smoke-room we did ask her to sit with us, and Roddy suggested that we should play scrabble or something but she wouldn't. She just went off to her cabin."

"She probably got the idea you didn't want her and I hardly blame her."

"Twice, I think you're being bloody unfair. I'm not responsible for the ideas she gets!"

"Aren't you? After larking all through dinner with that young fool?"

I turned round towards the looking-glass so that my back was towards him. "I am not going to talk about this any more," I said.

In the glass I saw him make a sudden violent movement behind me as if he were going to shake me as he had done the evening before, but the impulse died and he sank down limply on the bed.

"I just don't understand what is happening," he said. "I just don't understand any of it."

I spoke into the looking-glass, which showed the side of his head as he sat looking down at the floor. "I don't either, but there is one thing that I see and that is that during these years since — since . . ." I hesitated, for this was something that we never spoke about, ". . . since I lost the baby, you and I have been so close together that we have been almost a single person. It was you who did that for us, Twice. It was you who brought me back to life and welded me to yourself that time when I wanted nothing but to die. But two people, no matter how close they are, can never turn into one composite person.

We are still two people and we have discovered that we have separate likes and dislikes. You are fond of Dee although she tries your patience at times, but I dislike her and I am repelled by her and I cannot be patient with her at all. I like Roddy Maclean, but he repels you. To accuse me of flirting with him is nonsense and you know it."

While I spoke Twice had moved down the bed and now had his arm round me where I sat at the dressing-table.

"Sitting here, I know that," he said. "Sitting here like this, everything is all right. But up there — " He rolled his eyes at the ceiling and sighed.

"Up there, this destructive thing I feel in Dee is at work," I said, "and, heaven knows, that old woman Morrison is no help to anybody either. Come, let's get to bed."

It was a long time after we put our lights out before I slept. I lay listening to the wash of the sea against the side of the ship, listening to Twice's breathing in the bed alongside mine, and felt very safe and secure. If only, I wished, it were possible to let people pass heedlessly and unheeded by as the Atlantic water flowed past this ship, closing in over its wake so that its passing left no mark, but the sea of life is of a different water from the Atlantic. The Dees create a strain, the Miss Morrisons make you giggle, the Roddys are willing to giggle with you, and before you know where you are the still waters of your life with Twice take on the treacherous swirl of a whirlpool. I made all sorts of resolutions to try harder with Dee and avoid Roddy as much as I could, and it is little wonder that when I did go to sleep I had a nightmare which I have never forgotten, in which Miss Morrison, dressed in Captain Davey's uniform, ate the steering-wheel of the ship, which was made of ginger-bread; and as the alarm bell for boat stations rang and I was hunting desperately for Twice in the engine-room of the helpless ship, I woke up sweating with terror.

3

"PEOPLE ARE THEMSELVES
FIRST — "

THE next day, it struck me that I was not perhaps the only one of the ship's company to have resolved upon a mending of ways the night before, for Miss Morrison, having broken out of her seclusion by coming to dinner, appeared at breakfast the next morning to the acute embarrassment of one and all, and especially of Captain Davey. She was dressed for the day in her brown tweed coat and skirt, a felt hat of the same brownish non-colour as her faded hair, and came into the saloon carrying the canvas bag in one hand and the brown cotton umbrella in the other, depositing these on the floor on either side of her chair. The captain, and indeed all of us, watched with interest while she ate half a grapefruit, a plate of cereal and a kipper, and some toast; but when she then asked for bacon and eggs, Roddy and Mr.

Radzow abruptly excused themselves and left, closely followed by Twice and Dee. Gradually, as she demolished piece after piece of toast, the captain and everybody else left the table too, so I also got up.

"Where are you going?" she asked then.

"Nowhere," I said stupidly. "At least, I — "

"Then sit down," she said and took a roll from a basket, buttered it and popped it into the canvas bag at her feet.

I sat down obediently while she finished her meal, but I did not know why she had asked me to stay, for she did not speak to me any more until she said: "I am ready now," and picked up the bag and the umbrella. "Where is the best place to sit?"

I conducted her to the little gallery deck outside the smoke-room, which looked out over the stern of the ship. "I think this is nice and sheltered, don't you?" I asked.

"It's all right," she said without enthusiasm.

She sat hunched in her chair, her tweed collar rising round her ears to meet the brim of her brown felt hat so that very little of her sallow face showed between, and she did not move or speak for a long time. The roundish hat looked rather like a carapace and it was something like being in the company of a hibernating tortoise and not very cheerful; so I rose and went along past the smoke-room windows to the main deck in the centre of the ship, whereupon I noticed what looked like a second and third good resolution being put into practice. Roddy and Dee were standing by the rail, talking as if Roddy had decided to help Dee over her troubles, and Dee was actually laughing, as if after her solitary cogitations in her cabin the night before she had resolved to be more approachable and sociable. Further along the deck, near the bridge, I saw Twice talking to Captain Davey, who was planing wood for the model ship he was building. I turned back to the gallery and Miss Morrison with a virtuous feeling of not being one to disturb or distract the attention of anybody, especially of Dee.

I had just sat down quietly and was opening my book when Miss Morrison poked her head out like a tortoise hearing the first rustle of spring and said in a voice like the croak of a raven in mid-November: "That is a very silly little girl you have travelling with you."

"Silly? In what way?"

"No particular way. Just silly," she said and retired into hibernation again, while I sat staring at her helplessly.

This was the third day out and the days began to settle into a routine, as days at sea, especially in small ships, tend to do, and my part in this routine seemed to be to occupy the little gallery with Miss Morrison for most of the day while, now that we were in warmer waters, the others played deck games and splashed about in the canvas swimming-pool which had been set up on the after-deck below our gallery. Dee was still subject to fits of sulks, and I continued to be wary in her presence, but she was a great deal more reasonable in her attitude to Twice, and I discovered that I had Roddy Maclean to thank for this.

One morning at breakfast Miss Morrison announced that she intended to wash her hair that forenoon and that I would thus be deprived of her company, but I do not think I let her know how delighted I was at this deprivation, how relieved I was to be free of the hibernating tortoise that croaked like a raven about twice between breakfast and lunch and perhaps twice again between lunch and tea. Miss Morrison never made any remark that was cheerful, and three doomful phrases recurred and recurred in her conversation: "I don't like . . ." and "That makes a difference . . ." and "You never know what might happen . . .", this last being the deepest, most sinister raven's croak of all that confidently expected the very worst.

I had just settled on the gallery in solitary luxury with my book when Roddy arrived, looking like a dashing pirate in nothing but blue bathing trunks, leading Dram with his bevy of kittens. Roddy sat down on the deck and began to tease the kittens with a washer tied to the end of a length of string.

"Where is Dee?" I asked him.

"Up on the bridge steering the ship. It bores me blue. They won't let you wiggle her about or turn her round or anything — you have to keep her between two points of the compass the whole time."

I laughed. "Maybe the owners wouldn't care for it if they found out their ships were going in circles in mid-Atlantic."

"I don't think she *can* go in circles. I think you could leave her alone and she'd make for St. Jago Bay from sheer force of habit. But steering doesn't bore Dee. She'd do it all day."

By this stage in the voyage Roddy had told me that he was twenty-three, while Dee was twenty-four, but I could not rid myself of the impression that Roddy was the older. I think this was because he seemed to me to be so much better balanced than Dee was.

"You are very good for Dee, Roddy," I said now. "She is much less moody than when we left England."

He looked up at me slantwise from under his dark eyebrows, a brilliant mischievous glance.

"She only puts up with me when Twice isn't available."

"I know she has a sort of fixation about Twice. I think it is because he is so different from her own father — maybe Twice is the sort of father she would have liked to have."

"Maybe. Pity we can't choose our parents." He swept the washer on its string in a wide circle over the deck, the kittens dancing after it. "But Dee is one of those people who wants to crawl inside somebody and lie down. That's what she does with Twice. She does it with anybody who will let her do it, and if they don't let her she crawls inside herself."

"You are quite a sage, Roddy."

"No. It's just that I like people, especially the complex ones like Dee. When she was talking about Twice yesterday, I was trying to tell her that nobody gets all of anybody and that anybody is lucky who can get some of somebody, especially somebody like Twice. I was trying to tell her that he would be a different man if he weren't married to you" — he glanced up and swept the string round again — "and that she might not like him so much as he would be with you not affecting him." He paused for a moment, watching the kittens, and I said nothing. "She couldn't see that. That people can be changed by their relationships. It is interesting to talk to somebody like that who hasn't a clue about people or human relationships."

"She hasn't had much chance, with her mother dying when she was a baby, being at school away in Canada all through the war, and her father being such a stick."

"I know. She told me," he said.

It astonished me that anyone so young as Roddy could have grasped so quickly and acutely the situation between Twice, Dee and me, and this grasp must have been largely intuitive, for the situation had not been obvious enough to be noticed by any of the other people on the ship, I think. This quality in him drew me towards him, and I was still more attracted by his seemingly altruistic desire to help to ease the situation, for he did not talk of Dee as if he were attracted to her as a young man is attracted to a young woman. He talked of her more as if she were a clinical study or as if she were a problem in human relations who could be handled successfully only by a skilled technique which he was interested to devise and deploy.

On the day that we crossed the Tropic of Cancer, sailing in water of that saxe blue colour that illustrates the high seas in school atlases and headed for the Mona Passage that would take us through between the islands of Hispaniola into the Caribbean, where the water is of a deeper, clearer blue than the cartographers have yet invented, Roddy achieved a triumph by persuading Dee to unpack her swimsuit, put it on and gambol in the canvas pool as gaily as the young officers and himself. I sat beside Miss Morrison on the gallery above the pool, watching the nonsense in which Twice came to join before lunch, and thanked Roddy from the bottom of my heart.

"There's that silly little girl," said Miss Morrison's flat voice suddenly, and when I looked at her the face had poked out from under the brown felt carapace. "I wouldn't let her go swimming half naked with that young man and all these young officers. You never know what might happen."

"Oh, nonsense, Miss Morrison!" I said, but the face had disappeared between the brownish tweed coat and the felt hat as if, having sent its little dart through the new-found cushioning round the core of my discomfort about Dee, it had withdrawn contentedly into its wintry hibernation. Her hand reached down into the canvas bag and drew out a bar of chocolate, to which she gave her whole attention until just before lunch, when the pool emptied and the swimmers ran away to change. Miss Morrison now took her umbrella in one hand, the bag in the other, rose from her chair and said: "They'll all get their death of cold jumping in and out of that pool." She then went down to her cabin to get ready for lunch.

About three the following morning I awoke and heard the swish of the water past the side of the ship, but I also heard something else, the sinister sound of husky breathing which I had heard for the first time about three months ago when, shortly after we arrived in Scotland from St. Jago, Twice had come down with a severe attack of bronchitis. I switched on my light and sat up. Across the cabin, Twice also was sitting up in bed, his face flushed, his breathing labouring.

"Sorry, darling," he said. "Seem to have got a cold."

My first thought was that there was no doctor on this little ship, and my second thought was: "There is *nobody* on this ship but Miss Morrison!" Recognising this to be the thin end of the wedge of hysteria, I swung my feet out of bed, and before I could stop myself I had said: "Oh, damn and blast that old woman!"

"What old woman?" Twice croaked.

"Miss Morrison. She *said* you'd all

get chills wallowing about in that pool."

I have a morbid terror of illness, for I always tend to be afraid of things that I cannot understand; and although I have a normal housewife's knowledge of nursing minor ailments, that does not make me any less inwardly afraid. The attack, as it happened, was not a severe one, and Twice was up and about again at the end of two days, although he now eschewed the swimming-pool and became a spectator like Miss Morrison and myself. I mention the attack, however, because of that lurid moment in the early morning when, in the dizzy panic that attacked my mind, the first image to emerge was the sallow expressionless face of the old woman. It invested her with a curious significance for me; it altered her aspect so that I could no longer laugh at her as the "Performing Eater", as Roddy called her, and I found in myself, and at the same time despised in myself, a tendency to surround her with a mental taboo as if she were not merely a sour disgruntled old woman but some sort of oracle.

When I said that Twice had become a spectator at the water sports in the swimming-pool like Miss Morrison and myself, I do not mean to imply that he sat with us on the smoke-room gallery, for he could not bear to be in the company of the old woman.

"I don't see why you loathe her so," I said to him at bedtime one night. "She has a lot in common with you."

"Meaning what?"

"She says that Dee is a silly little thing that needs looking after, which is more or less what you think, and she says that she doesn't trust Roddy Maclean, which is another thing like you. I differ from her on both counts, but I still don't loathe her as you do. Why do you?"

"I don't really know. It is some of your intuition stuff, I suppose. There is something unnatural about her that makes me itch between my scalp and my brain. Why doesn't she trust Roddy Maclean?"

"Miss Morrison never explains her whys. She just says 'I don't like that young man. I don't trust him', and leaves it at that."

"Stop that croaking! You give me the creeps."

"Why don't *you* trust Roddy, Twice?"

I felt very grateful to Roddy for the

trouble he was taking over Dee, and I would have liked Twice to be grateful to him too.

"There is something queer about him," Twice said now, "but I can't put a finger on it. He is the queerest engineering type I have ever met and I've met a few. Oh, you can laugh if you like, but he is the first engineer I have ever seen who just isn't interested in engineering. And there's another thing — he spends a lot of time with Dee, but I don't think he really likes her."

"Then it's all the more decent of him to bother with her, surely," I said. "And he seems to be very good for her. She is a lot more reasonable and normal and like her age."

"I grant you that, but to bother with her when he's not attracted to her is *not* reasonable or normal or like *his* age. There is nothing more selfish than a virile young man where uninteresting young women are concerned. I was such a bloke once and I know. Say what you like, Roddy Maclean is fonder of *you* than he is of Dee."

"Twice, don't start that nonsense again!"

"I'm not starting it again. I've never left off thinking it. I don't mean any more that there is a thing starting between you as I thought at first, but you have some definite appeal for that youth and he likes you and he can't help showing it."

"And he admires *you*. Aren't we so lucky to be so liked and admired? No, but seriously, Twice, he told me a very good thing he had said to Dee. He told her that nobody gets all of anybody and that anybody is lucky who can get some of somebody, especially of somebody like you. It seems that she had been moaning to him that you were neglecting her."

Twice smiled. "I'll probably come round to the bloke in the end. We all love ourselves so much that we almost *have* to love anyone who admires us. But he is still a bloody queer engineer."

"Oh, people are themselves first and engineers and things afterwards!" I said impatiently.

Quite suddenly one forenoon just before lunch, when Dee had changed out of her swimsuit into a thin cotton dress and appeared on the little gallery, I noticed that, so gradually that it had been imperceptible, she had changed in the course of the voyage from an ugly little duckling into a pretty little elf. While she stood in the breeze by the gallery rail, drinking orange squash and talking to Mr. Radzow, I realised that physically she was of a type diametrically opposed to myself. I am a tall, fairish-skinned woman better suited to the climate of Britain than to the tropics. British clothes suit me — severe clothes made of heavy materials — and my skin and hair thrive and look better in the cold and wind than they do in the heat and humidity of the tropics. Delia, it was now apparent, was exactly the opposite. In London, her skin had looked muddy and sallow and her hair dull, but now the skin had an apricot glow and the hair had sun-bleached streaks in its light brown that were very pleasing above the darker brows and hazel eyes. And the thin cotton dress became her, showing the neatness of the arms and hands and the fineness of the waist, while the small apricot-coloured feet in the flat white linen sandals displayed all their neat elegance that had, in London, been concealed under heavy British winter leather.

"Your Dee is a fetching little baggage," I told Twice under cover of the general conversation, for in the pre-lunch half-hour all the ship's officers who were not on night duty and now asleep joined us on the smoke-room gallery.

"You are not the only one to notice that," Twice said, and I followed his glance to Roddy, who was standing alone at the other end of the gallery, his eyes fixed thoughtfully on Dee. "That young man has a more natural look in his eye."

At that moment Miss Morrison poked out from under the carapace of the felt hat, took a grip with each hand on bag and umbrella, and gave a little cough. She did this every day when she considered that it was high time that we went down to lunch, but the cough coming at the moment when it did, when I was full of a new relief about Dee, made me hear again the flat voice saying: "That's a silly little girl. I don't like that man Maclean," and at its sound in my mind the whole world seemed to change. The sky seemed to darken, the sea to become dull. The music of the waves past the ship's side became a horrid thrust of ocean against puny steel, and the pleasant shipboard company standing around fragmented into a mere group of people who were all alone and separate in their trials and sorrows. And Dee, the pretty smiling elf, was once more Delia Andrews, the difficult child of a stuffy disapproving family.

"Well, lunch," said Captain Davey.

I got up and joined the group and we all trooped below, but the wind that swept along the deck seemed to mourn in the wake of the bright moment that had fled.

That afternoon I lay on my bed in my cabin and read, for I felt that I could not bear another afternoon of Miss Morrison on the gallery, but when I went above at tea-time it was only to be informed that Twice, Dee and Roddy were having tea in the chief's cabin after making yet another inspection of the engine-room, so there were Miss Morrison and I, tête-à-tête. Having nodded without words to acknowledge my arrival, she ate a considerable amount of bread and butter, tucked what remained away in the bag and said: "That girl of yours has been down around the engines all the afternoon."

To reply to her felt like scaling the wall of disapproval that she contrived to set up, but I said: "Delia is interested in all aspects of ships. She comes of a shipping family."

"I suppose your husband can look after her," she said, as if she grudged the supposition and even the words to express it.

I felt irritation spark up in me. "Why should she need looking after? What in the world can happen to her?"

"You never know what might happen."

I cursed myself for giving her this opening for her favourite croak, puffed out an exasperated breath and lit a cigarette while she set about a plate of cake. After some munching without words, she took a sip of tea and then fixed her expressionless eyes on me. "But I suppose your husband being there makes a difference." She took another piece of cake. "I wouldn't bring a young girl like that abroad like this — not that sort of young girl."

"What sort of young girl?" I snapped.

"A young girl like that among all these men. Men don't understand a young girl like that."

"A young girl like what?"

"Like her."

I could have screamed with frustration and exasperation, for she seemed to crystallise all my vague fears and nebulous sense of responsibility for Dee, turning them into sharp needle-points that stabbed at my mind, and it seemed unjust that she should be able to do this and yet withhold from me any guidance that might help me.

"Rubbish!" I said angrily. "Dee is a much-travelled sensible young woman."

This is what I wished were true, and I said it vehemently as if I could thus make it to be true, but Miss Morrison had contrived to make me more aware than ever that it was far from true, and for this I could cheerfully have killed her, but being too inhibited to kill my fellow-passengers on transatlantic ships, I changed the subject, albeit abruptly.

"Two more days and we'll be landing in St. Jago Bay," I said.

Miss Morrison took another piece of cake, took a bite out of it and looked without enthusiasm out to sea.

"Are you coming out to spend a holiday?" I asked, for, although the voyage was nearly over, neither I nor anyone else aboard the ship knew any more about her than her name and the fact that she had cousins in St. Jago. Ships are proverbially as conducive as barbers' chairs to the exchange of life histories and hospital experiences, but Miss Morrison seemed to have neither life history, nor hospital experience. I have a strong dislike of prying openly into people's reserves, although I spend much of my time studying chance acquaintances and trying to deduce facts about them, so that hitherto I had asked Miss Morrison no direct questions; but today she had annoyed me so much that I thought I would try to pay her out by making enquiries about her, a thing that I felt she would dislike intensely.

"No," she said. "I never go for holidays. I don't like them." The going was hard and heavy, I thought, but I had the energy of real annoyance to bring to my task.

"Oh, of course. You said earlier that you were going to visit your cousins."

"I may not visit them. I'll see when I get there."

Obstinate old beast, I thought, but I'll break you down yet into open rudeness if nothing else.

"I know most of the English people in St. Jago," I pursued doggedly. "Who are your cousins?"

"They're Scots — not English."

"Then I am bound to know them, being a Scot myself. Who are they?"

I felt that I shouted the last three words: "WHO ARE THEY?" while hitting Miss Morrison three dull thuds upon the head with a rubber truncheon, but I could not have done, for she merely stared at me over her piece of cake with her face as void of expression as ever and said: "Charlotte Dulac. She married a foreigner. And her son Ian."

In truth and in fact, it was Miss Morrison who hit me, and it might as well have been over the head with a rubber truncheon. Ringing from left to right through my bemused brain was the voice of Madame Dulac, the owner of Paradise Estate where Twice and I lived, saying: "Emmie Morrison, my cousin in London — a quite impossible person, my dear," and ringing from right to left was the barking voice of her son, Sir Ian, saying: "Old Cousin Emmie — mad as a perishin' hatter, Missis Janet."

"Why," I heard myself say in a voice that mingled all the irritation, annoyance and exasperation of these shipboard days with relief that Miss Morrison had human, flesh-and-blood relations and was not some supernatural monster out of the ocean, "*you* are Cousin Emmie!"

I stared at her in wide-eyed amazement. I would not have been any more disconcerted in that moment if the ship's siren had blown and Neptune himself had risen from the deep surrounded by a court of mermaids and tritons with wreathed horns; but Cousin Emmie merely helped herself to the last piece of cake and looked at me as expressionlessly as ever.

"I had a letter from Madame just before we sailed," I said. "How odd that she didn't mention that you were sailing too. She must have forgotten."

Cousin Emmie swallowed a mouthful of cake and said: "I didn't bother to write saying I was coming. I don't like writing letters," and she took another bite of cake. "She married a foreigner but he's dead now. Just as well. I don't like foreigners."

"But you must have heard Twice and Roddy Maclean and me mention Paradise!" I expostulated, following my own train of thought.

"That doesn't make any difference."

"But it is a point of contact, a common factor between us all!"

"No it isn't."

"But — but — " I felt that there was something that I wanted to say but I could not find the words.

"Like people saying the world is a small place," she said, picking a raisin out of her cake, examining it closely and then eating it, "but it isn't. Compared to the size of the people in it, it is very big, and to say it isn't is just idle talk. I don't like idle talk."

I sat staring at her, stunned into silence, and this seemed to suit her admirably, for she said nothing further either. She did not ask for news of her cousins or make any enquiries about Paradise. She simply ate her way through her piece of cake, and then it was time to go below to our cabins to change for the evening.

I could hardly wait to get below, to see Twice and apprise him of my discovery and generally to blow off in a steam of words my irritation at Cousin Emmie, which seemed, now, to be generating in greater volume than ever.

". . . and she didn't bother to write telling them she was coming!" I ended.

"Madame will hit the roof when she arrives. You know how Madame hates anything unexpected or disorganised that isn't her own personal unexpectedness or disorganisation."

"Just you take yourself along to Sparks' office after dinner, my pet, and radio your friend Sir Ian," Twice told me. "The old dame didn't swear you to secrecy, after all, and you can be a gossipy woman for once. Just say 'Miss Emmie Morrison on board coming visit Paradise'. I think it will be your good deed for the day."

"You think so? Madame doesn't hold with her at all, you know. She is the one who plays chess by telephone from Kensington with a friend in St. John's Wood or somewhere — Cousin Emmie, I mean."

"All the more reason for giving Madame fair warning of her. It will be easier for the rest of us if the major storm is over before we get to Paradise."

Immediately after dinner I sent the cable as dictated by Twice, and before breakfast the next morning Dooley brought Sir Ian's reply to our cabin: "Grateful for news is she travelling alone query reply urgent meeting you customs Ian Dulac."

"What does he mean, 'is she travelling alone'?" I asked.

Twice stared at the cable form. "What he says, presumably. Is she travelling alone query."

"Well, is she? Us four passengers and the ship's company are here."

"He knows about the ship's company." Twice went on frowning at the form. "Reply urgent. Is she travelling alone?"

"I say, I wonder if she has a demon lover and Sir Ian's afraid she is bringing him to Paradise?"

"Don't be such a fool! I tell you what — let's do this." He found a piece of paper and wrote: "Greetings from all — repeat all — passengers, namely Morrison, Andrews, Maclean, Alexanders."

"Brilliant! But what if the demon lover's name is Andrews?"

"You would think of the millionth chance. Let's risk it."

We sent the cable; there was a day and a half of radio silence and the little white ship sailed proudly into the harbour of St. Jago Bay to tie up at the newly constructed passenger and cargo wharf.

"Well," said Dee, coming down from the

bridge with Captain Davey, the pilot and Roddy, "did I make a nice job of bringing her in?"

"Splendid thing, this new wharf," Captain Davey said. "Those old lighters were a menace. Yes, there's his Old Nibs down there."

Down below, on the wharf, his "Old Nibs" Sir Ian Dulac, in his immaculate white drill suit and pith helmet, looked like a figure cut from a picture of St. Jago of fifty years ago and stuck on to this glossy highly coloured modern picture of the new pier and the St. Jago of today. In 1951 the white men of the island no longer wore white drill and pith helmets. The modern uniform was light-weight gaberdine in pale grey or fawn and light-weight straw hats, the uniform that Rob Maclean, standing with his wife Marion and youngest son Sandy, beside Sir Ian, was wearing. All about the firm white figure the bustle of tying up the ship went on with much gesticulation and shouting by negro wharf-hands dressed in khaki drill trousers and violently coloured "tourist" shirts, and behind him stretched the length of the pier, through the Customs sheds to the iron gates beyond which was all the garish colour of the pier market, a blatantly artificial affair set up by the more opportunist negroes for the fleecing of tourists from cruise ships. They sold "native arts and crafts" in the form of necklaces made from brightly coloured seeds, ashtrays and knick-knacks made from wood or polished ox-horn, and hats and baskets made from sisal and decorated with raffia embroidery. It seemed to me symbolic of this moment in the history of the island that in this second Sir Ian seemed to be superimposed on the scene without being an integral part of it, and yet that, in this same second, he should still dominate it, as a picture, by virtue of the sparkling white suit standing among all the raging colour and sun-baked squalor of the new but already dirty and garbage-laden pier. In 1951 men like Sir Ian were anachronistic figures in St. Jago, and yet they still dominated the picture of island life by their long island lineage which gave them an air of feudal command, by their wealth which was the only god that the new St. Jago could as yet recognise and, not least, by their grim integrity which the new St. Jago could not understand but, by long tradition, could not do other than respect.

"There's Sir Ian," I said to Cousin Emmie, who was standing beside me dressed to go ashore in the same clothes that she had worn when she left England and during every day of the voyage — the brown tweed coat and skirt, the felt hat, the brown umbrella and the brown canvas bag — but in honour of the arrival she had added the skins of two small brown animals whose heads kissed each other in death at the back of her neck and whose limp tails hung over each of her shoulders, connected in front, across her scrawny throat, by a frayed brown silk cord. "Beside Mr. and Mrs. Maclean and the little boy," I amplified as she made no response, "the only white people on the pier."

She still made no response but continued to stare down at the crowd and the bustle with a flat, disinterested detachment.

How anyone who had never landed in St. Jago before could be detached from and disinterested in this scene was something that I could not comprehend. I who had been in the port many times, although I had never before landed here from England, having hitherto come out by air, felt a wild thrill of excitement. Four crowded months in Scotland and England had been enough to overlie my mind with a patina less exotic than this. My eyes had forgotten the riotous colour; my ears had forgotten the mixture of raucous clamour and melodious song, which is the sound of the negro at work; and my nose had forgotten the smell of the island, which is compounded of spices and fermented fruit, the heavy scent of lilies and the foetid stench of human sweat.

Dee, hopping with excitement, darting from one point of the ship's rail to another, clinging to Twice's arm and pointing first to the clamour of the market and then to the white buildings of the luxury Peak Hotel remote on its promontory above the harbour, was making, I thought, the normal reaction to a landing in St. Jago. Cousin Emmie displayed neither pleasure nor disappointment, excitement nor undue phlegm. She merely waited, brown and expressionless, for what would happen next, which was the lowering of the gangway.

As soon as it was in position, Sir Ian, followed by the Macleans, began to climb on board, and as soon as his highly polished black shoe hit the deck he took the pith helmet from his head, lowered his white eyebrows in his ruddy face, strode towards Cousin Emmie and plunged into speech, and I knew that I now was really and truly back in St. Jago.

"Now then, Emmie, what's the meanin' o' this? Why didn't ye write to Mother? Wouldn't have known ye were comin', dammit, if I hadn't accidentally got a look at the passenger list. What the devil ye doin' here? Tell me that!"

I think that during the two days since I had known of Cousin Emmie's status as Cousin Emmie of Paradise, as it were, I had been unconsciously anticipating with pleasure this moment with a spiteful feeling of: "Just wait till Sir Ian sees her! That will shake her confounded calm!" And probably that was why the great moment of the meeting fell flat. My conviction that Sir Ian would "shake" Cousin Emmie could not have been more erroneous. Slowly and without smile or frown, she looked up into his face with her flat brown eyes and said: "So here you are, Ian," as if to imply that this was exactly the unfortunate luck that she expected life to hold in store for her. Round about us there was a babel of greeting as the Macleans brought Captain Davey messages from his daughter and welcomed their son, and I was conscious that Twice was doing what should have been my own job of introducing Dee to Roddy's parents, but all this by-passed me, so fascinated was I at the family reunion between Sir Ian and Cousin Emmie.

"Now then, Emmie," he said threateningly in response to her greeting, "don't go standin' there like a wooden image. What you *doin'* here? Tell me that!"

"I just thought I'd come and I came," she said, quite unmoved by his fierce aspect; and then, as if she were already tired of the sight of him, she stared away shorewards beyond wharf, market and town to the distant scrub-covered mountains.

"That woman Murgatroyd ain't with you?" Sir Ian asked, staring round the deck in a suspicious way.

"No," said Cousin Emmie, her eyes still on the distance.

"That's one God's blessin', anyway,"

said Sir Ian and mopped his forehead with a large white handkerchief.

I passed from disappointment in my expectations regarding this meeting between cousins to something that was strangely like triumph that, after all, the citadel of the calm of Cousin Emmie had not fallen to the onslaught. It pleased me to discover that Sir Ian, who could bully all of us on Paradise Estate, from Rob Maclean, his manager, down to old Ezekiel, his negro groom, could make no more impression on Cousin Emmie than I could.

At this moment my attention was distracted by a strange procession that was coming towards us along the deck and was made up of Twice, two seamen and Dram, who was tenderly carrying a ship's kitten in his large mouth while the other two cavorted round his feet.

"By Jove," said Sir Ian, "what a dog!"

"You don't know the half of it, sir," Twice said. "At home this brute killed every cat at sight, and now look at him."

I sank down on a hatch cover, and, with infinite care, Dram deposited the hairy grey-and-white bundle in my lap before sitting down with an expression of besotted pleasure on his face. I am not a cat lover, really, but the kitten was appealing and I stroked it, and at every stroke and every purr Dram gave a satisfied "Uff!" of pleasure.

"That's Charlie, Mrs. Alexander," one of the seamen said. "Charlie's 'is favourite."

" 'E's goin' to miss Charlie, sir," the other seaman assured Twice. "So we just said down below — didn't we, Andy? — that 'e should get Charlie to take ashore with 'im."

"That's right," Andy agreed, and they both looked at Twice and me with happy expectation which seemed to be reflected on the face of Dram.

All I could say was: "Thank you very much. It is very kind of you. We'll love to have Charlie."

All I could think was that the world was turning upside-down. The Alexander family had acquired a cat, a thing that, an hour ago, I should have regarded as beyond all possibility or probability, and I felt somehow that I wanted to blame Cousin Emmie.

4

"LIKING PEOPLE IS VERY DIFFICULT"

ALTHOUGH I cannot record an eye-witness account of Cousin Emmie's reception at the Great House of Paradise by Madame Dulac, who was, if anything, slightly more outspoken than her son Sir Ian, I can record with truth that the reception left her quite unaltered and in no whit abashed. As Dee had done, albeit in a manner quite different, she seemed to undergo an extraordinary physical adaptation to the tropical way of life so that the woman who, on board the *Pandora*, had moved in a narrow orbit between her cabin, the smoke-room gallery and the dining-saloon, now tramped tirelessly in the tropic heat about the paths and roads of the vast plantation while younger women like Marion Maclean and myself never went anywhere except by car. She had now acquired a beige-figured, black silk dress which had once belonged to the stout little Madame Dulac and which hung in loose superfluous folds about the shrunken form of Cousin Emmie. She also carried, as always, the canvas bag, but the brown cotton umbrella had now been replaced by a large dark green parasol with a heavy bone handle which I remembered noticing, once, in the huge storage cellars under the Great House. The bag, as always, contained a few articles of food-stuffs, and now, in the humid heat, it smelled sourly of cheese or in a sickly way of slightly fermented bananas or oranges, for Cousin Emmie could not pass an orange or a banana tree in any garden without furtively nipping off a fruit or two and popping them into the bag anent some future pang of intense hunger.

Although at the age of forty-one I should have been old enough to know better, I had never lost, and still have not lost, my childish faith that tomorrow will be a lovely day and it had been my ill-conceived notion while aboard the ship that, as soon as we landed, Cousin Emmie would disappear into the maw of the Great House and go right out of my life, while

Dee, escorted by Roddy Maclean, would join in the gaiety of the young social life of the island and stop bothering me. My Highland grandmother was reputed to have second sight and to be able to foretell the future, and if I have inherited her gift, as some people have implied from time to time, I can only conclude that I have inherited it in an astigmatic form. The lovely tomorrows that I foresee quite often dawn in sheets of rain which turns to sleet as the day goes on.

All went well enough in the few days before Christmas, although Cousin Emmie visited me most days for coffee in the forenoon or tea in the afternoon and popped any biscuits that were left over into the bag, a habit which I had thought she would discontinue when in private houses as opposed to ships in which she had paid for her passage, but I still had to learn that Cousin Emmie was impervious to change. Dee, however, made up for the static quality of Cousin Emmie by changing from moment to moment, and I seemed to live in a state of permanent mental breathlessness from my efforts to keep pace.

The Paradise year was divided into two

precise halves, January to June being the harvesting period when the sugar cane was reaped, the processing plant and rum distillery put into action and the year's crop of sugar milled and its crop of rum distilled. This was called the In-Crop period, and the months from July to December were the Out-of-Crop period when repairs and maintenance to the plant were carried out and the preparations made for the next year's crop. In December, therefore, we were just at the end of the Out-of-Crop when the final adjustments to the factory were being made, steam trials being run, boilers, turbines and cranes being tested. And this year on Paradise there was more than the usual pre-crop anxiety and excitement, for this was the second year of a three-year plan of expansion, and while Twice had been on leave Rob Maclean and the other engineers had been installing a chain of five new crushing mills which had been supplied by Twice's firm in Britain.

And Paradise, of course, was not Twice's only concern. He was chief engineer for Allied Plant Limited in the Caribbean area at this time, and, although the Paradise expansion was the biggest scheme he had on hand, there were other schemes in other islands as well as the Allied Plant office in St. Jago Bay making calls on his attention. As soon as Paradise went into Crop at the beginning of January, he planned, if all went well, to leave on a tour of the other islands, leaving me at Guinea Corner. I was not looking forward to this, for Twice and I had never been apart since we married, and, besides, I was a little afraid that he might come home from a trip to ask: "Where is Dee?" and I would have to reply: "I buried her under the fig tree in the back garden."

In those last few days before Christmas Twice was too busy at the sugar factory to spend much time in the house, so he saw very little of Dee, which was something he appeared neither to notice nor regret, but Dee made up for this, too, as she made up for Cousin Emmie's static quality, by missing the company of Twice in a way that made her pick at the edges of curtains by the hour, and but for Roddy Maclean either she or I would have gone screaming crazy within the first few days at Guinea Corner, for I could not begin to understand the way she could abandon herself to melancholy boredom. When I had been her age I invariably escaped out of boredom into something, and mischief as frequently as anything, and I think I would have preferred it if Dee had been like this, even if she had caused me some anxiety. I would have found anything, I think, less wearing than her moods of gloomy discontented introspection. However, she spent a fair part of each day with Roddy and he took her to the Estate Club and to the Peak Hotel, where he introduced her to most of the young European set. She seemed to be happy enough on these outings, but she had no talent for making friends, and as the days moved on towards Christmas I became more and more grateful to Roddy for bothering with her at all, for he did not seem to be attracted to her now any more than when we were on the ship, so that his interest in her seemed to be actuated by sheer benevolence.

If, however, I felt that Roddy was benevolent, Twice still distrusted him, and, indeed, the fabric of life was crisscrossed with threads of dislike and distrust. Dee liked Twice and Roddy and was developing a liking for Cousin Emmie, while she disliked both Sir Ian and Madame Dulac and, to some extent I think, myself, while I liked Twice, Roddy and the Dulacs but could raise little enthusiasm for Cousin Emmie or Dee. The small enclosed society being what it was, we all did our best to put a good face on things with the exception of two members. Cousin Emmie tried to put no face on anything and Madame Dulac made no secret of her dislike for her cousin.

Madame and Cousin Emmie could not have been more different or have been iller bed-fellows. Where Cousin Emmie wandered aimlessly about the estate, Madame was the power and the throne, and her abounding energies were always aimed with tremendous force at some object or another. When Madame was not meting out from her office on the Great House veranda feudal justice to the some four thousand negroes who depended on Paradise for their livelihood, she was raising funds for a new ward at the hospital in the Bay. When she was not bossing a gang of labourers who were planting a new shrubbery in the Great House garden, she was ringing up the Colonial Secretary about

Customs dues or the Minister of Works about the disgraceful state of the North Coast highway. The sight of Cousin Emmie drifting about with her parasol and canvas bag infuriated her, but where others would have quailed, Cousin Emmie drifted on unconcerned. And Madame, time and again, said to Cousin Emmie the very words that I always longed to say but for which I had not the courage and which were: "Oh, rubbish, Emmie! Hold your tongue!" But Cousin Emmie did not take offence and neither did she hold her tongue. The next moment she would give vent to another croak beginning: "I don't like — "

"Emmie," said Madame in a firm voice one morning when she, Marion and I had met at the Great House to arrange the Christmas Dance at the Estate Club, "you must have some dresses made for the festive season. You cannot wear those cast-off rags of mine for ever. You look like the maiden aunt of a vicar."

"I am the maiden aunt of a vicar," said Cousin Emmie flatly. "James, Peter's second boy, became Vicar of Foldesley last year."

There was a short charged silence before Madame said: "Tchah! Go away, Emmie! Marion, Janet and I have business to attend to."

Neither hurt at this summary dismissal nor triumphant at her verbal defeat of Madame, showing no expression of any kind, Cousin Emmie drifted away along the veranda like a dried-up autumn leaf in a light wind.

"Marion," said Madame impatiently, "get a message down to Mattie Fitt and tell her to come up here with some patterns. Emmie is really an extremely trying woman. Now, let us get on with this entertainment at the club."

Matilda Fitt was an island institution. Her clientele was made up mainly of the older ladies such as Madame who had worked out a system over the years by which when they took a holiday away from the island they brought back a few dresses from their favourite shops and these were copied by Miss Matilda in various colours and materials until such time as the ladies paid another visit to the home country and returned with some new designs. The ladies dressed by Miss Matilda by this means bore always upon them the indelible stamp of their home towns, so that old Mrs. Buckley represented sartorially her native English cathedral town, Miss Maud Poynter had all the style of New York's less exclusive stores, and Madame Dulac was, in this outpost of empire, the far-flung battle line of the matron's department of the best shop in Princes Street, Edinburgh. To slightly younger people like myself and Marion Maclean, this method of dressing was known as "clothes by Missfitt" and the garments themselves referred to as "missfitts". This, however, is a digression.

During the afternoon following the meeting about the dance I told Dee with some catty enjoyment of Cousin Emmie's setting-down of Madame by her announcement that she was indeed the maiden aunt of a vicar, for a setting-down or even a momentary silencing of Madame Dulac was not an event to go unremarked or unrecorded.

Dee was duly amused at my tale, but after a moment she said thoughtfully: "I think it is unfair, though, that people don't like Cousin Emmie just because she has a knack of hitting on the truth."

I thought of Cousin Emmie's prophecy about chills when the swimming-pool was set up on the ship and of how Twice had gone down with bronchitis.

"That's quite true, Dee. She hits on truths that one wishes weren't there."

"Miss Jan, I know you don't like her, but I do, the more I get to know her. You won't mind, will you?"

"Dee, don't be absurd! You have every right to like anyone you choose."

"Liking people is very difficult. It often puts you wrong with someone else you like."

"It shouldn't if people are reasonable. I think it would be wrong of me to mind your liking Cousin Emmie."

"That's what Roddy says. He says the world needs all the liking we can do. Roddy says some very queer things."

I did not find what Roddy had said "queer", for I thought very much as he did, but this was not the first time I had been astonished by Dee's quotations of things that Roddy had said to her.

"You like Roddy, don't you, Dee?"

"Yes. He is kind and good at explaining things, and he's not all sexy and things."

A faint flush suffused her tanned fore-

126

head as she spoke the last words, and I noted that this was the first time since we had met her in London that I had heard her mention the word "sex" and I wondered if there was some psychological block in her in this connection. It might account for much of her difficult moodiness, I thought.

"There is another great friend of yours I don't like," she went on in almost a masochistic way as if she were making an unnecessary confession just for the sheer misery of it. "Don Candlesham."

This made me wonder how wrong people can be about one another, for if Dee had wished to bring my grey hairs through worry to the grave, the best way she could have done it was to form an attachment for Don Candlesham, the most ruthless lady-killer in what I had seen of the western world. I could barely conceal my delight that she disliked him as I said: "He is not much of a friend of mine, Dee. I had a bigger fish-wife row with him once than I've ever had with anybody in this island."

"He isn't? Everybody seems to think he is. Well, I'm glad, because I think he's horrid. Cousin Emmie doesn't like him either," she added.

"I didn't know she had met him."

"Oh yes. Round at the club one night. He called in when she was there."

"She comes to the club?"

Dee laughed. "She has to have coffee and a sandwich between dinner and bed, Miss Jan! Sashie de Marnay is nice though, isn't he?"

"Very nice, Dee. Now Sashie really is a special friend of mine. I am very glad you like him."

"Roddy says — "

"Yes?"

"Roddy said Sashie — "

"He said Sashie was a homosexual, is that it?" I asked.

"A *queer* was what Roddy said." Her face flushed scarlet. "Miss Jan, I know it means something queer about sex, but I don't know what and I couldn't ask Roddy, but I wouldn't like it if Sashie was what Roddy made it sound like when he said it!" she said in a muddled rush, the phrases tumbling over one another.

For once, I was in full sympathy with Dee, took hold of her hand, which was shaking, and said: "Darling, it isn't true about Sashie, but a homosexual is a person who prefers people of his own sex to those of the other sex, a man who can fall in love with another man." She was gripping my hand between both of her own while I went on: " 'Queer' is the slang expression that people like Roddy use for it, but that's rather cheek, really. Why are the Roddys so sure that they are the normal ones and that the others are so queer?"

She smiled in a tremulous way. "I suppose you think it's qu — " She stumbled over the word, smiled a little and went on: " — queer and terribly ungrown-up of me not to know about this, but — well — I just didn't."

"I was older than you are before I knew about it," I comforted her, but I was amazed that in her day and age, even in the milieu of her stuffy family, Dee could be so innocent, and found myself thinking: "If only she would read a bit more instead of mooning about!"

Later in the evening I told Twice of this part of our conversation and said: "Don't you think it odd that she knows so little about some things? After all, she didn't spend all her time in the schoolroom or in the stuffy bosom of the Andrews family.

She was out on her own in London for a bit and had some pretty raffish friends if what her aunt told me is true, and yet she didn't know about homosexuality. Things are different now from when I grew up. You'd think she would have had some sort of clue."

Twice frowned thoughtfully before he said: "I think people have their own types of knowledge. What I mean is, that facts about things you are interested in stick to you automatically. An engineering fact will stick to me without any effort on my part, and things about literature and language stick to you like leeches where other facts just go over our heads. Dee doesn't seem to have much interest in sexual matters, unlike most people, so I suppose that anything she saw or heard that was of a homosexual nature just went over her head and didn't register."

"Maybe," I said. "She is certainly odd about sex. She seems to have some sort of guilt complex," for I was remembering that after I had explained to her about Roddy's and his friends use of the word "queer" she had asked: "Is it terribly wrong for people to be like that?"

"There you have me, Dee," I told her. "I am no good at drawing lines about right and wrong."

"But Sashie — isn't?"

"Definitely not."

I did not tell her that the reason for Sashie's mincing, dancing walk was that he had lost both legs while serving as a fighter pilot during the war and that he could walk in no other way on his artificial legs, for this was a closely guarded secret of his, a secret which he screened still further by an affected manner of speech and a choice of clothes more brightly coloured and less conservative than those favoured by most men.

"Sashie is a very shy, private sort of person, really," I went on, "and that affected manner is a defence more than anything."

"It works too," she said with evaluating appreciation. "It works far better than that defiant thing I went in for with the family at home. It makes people leave him alone. They're scared of him."

"But you are not?"

"No. I like him. He lets me help him in the wine store."

"You know about wines?"

"I had to learn about them when Uncle Archie left me the London house. He was quite a connoisseur. He wrote a book about the Bordeaux district and another one about Jerez. The cellar was crammed with wine, so I had to find out which to keep and which to sell and what the value of it all was."

Heigh-ho, I thought, Dee's upbringing and education may not have included any handy hints on homosexuality, but trust an Andrews not to lose money on the sale of a cellarful of inherited wine; but this thought was rapidly followed by the idea that it was no wonder that she was subject to moods and irrational fixations. She had been so bandied about and harried by her family and her own nature that she had never had a chance to find herself.

"Miss Jan, do look at Dram carrying Charlie out of the sun!" she said next, so light-heartedly that it was difficult to believe that she was the same girl of those first days on the ship or the one who had spent the whole forenoon of the day before picking at the corner of a venetian blind.

Dram and Charlie spent all their time together. In the cool of the early morning and in the comparative cool of the last daylight hour, they were wildly energetic, hunting mongoose in the sugar cane and playing their own form of "tag" in the garden, but in the heat of the day they lay in the shade of a round clump of hibiscus on the lawn, and as the sun moved round to invade their shade they moved round the clump to a new spot. Charlie was extremely lazy, and Dram was most frequently the first to get up, stretch himself and seek a cooler spot, and now he picked up Charlie by the scruff of the neck and, carrying him round the shrubs, deposited him tenderly in the new place before lying down beside him. There was something irresistibly comical in the large dog with the limp lazy cat hanging from his mouth walking solemnly and with an almost ritual air round the clump of hibiscus, and Dee and I, more at ease with one another than usual, began to giggle.

"That dog looks silly carrying that cat about like that. It is very unnatural," said the voice of Cousin Emmie.

I felt that a raven had croaked in the

bright sunlight as her shadow fell on the veranda floor and the flat voice came to my ears, but Dee said: "Charlie likes it, Miss Morrison. If you make Dram put him down he will spit at you."

"And Charlie is an unnatural name for a cat. I don't like these unnatural goings-on," Cousin Emmie said, sitting down, placing the canvas bag open-mouthed on the floor and arranging the parasol against her chair, while I, feeling that I was being driven against my will by some irresistible force, went through to the kitchen to ask for tea to be brought in.

When tea was over and Cousin Emmie had chosen a piece of cake for the bag, Dee tactfully took her away for a drive in her car, leaving me gratefully alone, and I found myself thinking of Dee's many antagonisms to people. Her dislike of Madame Dulac was straightforward.

"She does nothing but bully people and interfere with them — asking in that silly way why a pretty girl like me wasn't married, just like Aunt Angela and people!" Dee had said angrily after meeting Madame for the first time.

It seemed that she regarded Madame

as an extension of authority as manifested in her own family at home and disliked her for this reason, but some of her antipathies were less easy to understand, as difficult to understand, indeed, as some of her attachments, such as her attachment to Cousin Emmie, for instance.

I had not been alone for very long when the Rolls from the Great House drove in and disgorged Sir Ian on the doorstep and he stamped up the steps with a fierce look on his face and said: " 'Afternoon, me dear. Is Emmie here?"

"She was," I said. "She and Dee went off for a drive about fifteen minutes ago."

"Dammit, there's no need for your guests to be drivin' her about. There are three cars round at the house an' people to drive her."

"It's all right, Sir Ian. She and Dee get along very well together."

"I wish she an' mother got on. House isn't fit to live in. I can't think what brought Emmie out here, anyway. 'Smatter o' fact, I can. Mother'n I are the only ones o' her generation o' the family that's left. She has nobody in England now except a coupla nephews — both parsons an' not the kind to want Emmie around, an' now that she an' this Murgatroyd woman have fallen out she's feelin' the draught. I don't see why they had to fall out at this stage o' the game."

"Who *is* Miss Murgatroyd, Sir Ian?" I asked, for, although I had heard this name mentioned only twice in my life, it had a special place in my mind, for in memory I could hear Cousin Emmie, at our very first encounter in her cabin in the *Pandora*, saying: "My friend Miss Murgatroyd smoked like a chimney." I had paid little heed to this remark at the time, but now that I had seen more of Cousin Emmie — you will notice that I do not say "knew" more of Cousin Emmie — it had a new significance, for Miss Murgatroyd was the only person I had ever heard her refer to as a friend. Miss Murgatroyd loomed in my mind a fabulous unknown, a creature of great power and mystery, the only living creature, it seemed, with whom Cousin Emmie had ever formed a bond.

"She an' Emmie have been sharin' a flat in London for about forty years, ever since they came back from Salonika in 1918, anyway, an' probably before that.

Big woman like a camel that wears woollen stockin's."

"And they have parted now?"

"Yes, an' for good, it seems."

"After getting on together since 1918? What were they doing in Salonika?"

"That was a very fine show in its way. Emmie has a decoration, ye know, an' I believe the Murgatroyd woman got somethin' as well. Ye see, me dear, Emmie is the sort 'o black sheep o' the family — that's how Mother sees her, anyway. Emmie was always a damn' nuisance to her people — wouldn't settle down, ye know, an' in the end they let her go in for nursin' and she did very well at it an' got all her certificates an' everything, but she was always dabblin' about with different things an' got mixed up in the suffragette carry-on an' all that. That was where she met Fanny Murgatroyd. Fanny! Wish you could see her — more like a camel, as I said. Anyway, Fanny Murgatroyd was a doctor — weren't many women doctors at that time — and in 1914, when the war started, she an' Emmie an' one or two others set up an ambulance unit an' finished up in Salonika."

"But I think that's terrific!" I said. "To look at Cousin Emmie, you wouldn't think she'd ever been anywhere or done anything!"

"She's done plenty in her time an' she's still doin' it. Mother ain't fit to live with."

"It's a pity she and Miss Murgatroyd have quarrelled, though. She must find it very odd after such a long time."

As is my hot-headed wont, I was becoming more sympathetic towards Cousin Emmie and admiring her more by the second, but let me point out that the Cousin Emmie I was admiring was a gallant figure with a medal pinned to her white nurse's apron who had braved the mud and malaria of Salonika, a figure I had created for my own delectation and not the old woman who, less than half an hour before, had come croaking on to my veranda, although I did not realise this in that moment. Human relationships are very complex, or, in the words of Dee, "Liking people is very difficult", not for the reason that Dee had given, particularly, but because one is never sure whether one is liking the real person or some glamorised version of that person that one has oneself invented. In this moment Cousin Emmie was wearing, for me, a halo of glory.

"The thing that surprises me," Sir Ian said, "is that Emmie an' the Murgatroyd woman stuck together for so long. Emmie's a damn' queer woman, Missis Janet. She seems to go at everything from the wrong end, if ye see what I mean."

"I don't really," I told him.

"I'm not good at explainin', but say I meet a fellah in a bar or at somebody's dinner-table, I am prepared to like the fellah until I find out somethin' that makes me *not* like him, like meetin' that fellah Somerset in Twice's office at the Bay an' then comin' to think later on that he's a bit of a fool, don't ye know. But Emmie, she don't go about things like that. Emmie just naturally hates the perishin' sight of everybody to start with an' then takes a likin' to the odd one here and there later on. Damned unnatural, I call it."

It seemed to me that life would be much simpler if people were less individual in their opinions about what was natural and what was not, but I supposed it was the way of mankind to take oneself as the norm, as Sir Ian was doing now, and regard any deviation from oneself as unnatural; but it also struck me that this tendency of Cousin Emmie's to dislike at sight and come to liking later, unwillingly if at all, was also descriptive of Dee. When Sir Ian arrived, I had been trying to find reasons for her antipathies, but I now saw that it would be simpler to accept the antipathies as her normal reaction to people and study her few attachments which were the departures from her norm. Looked at in this way, her attitude to myself, which was about ninety per cent hostile, I always felt, was explained. In London she had sought me out because she had had an affection for me when she was a child, but that remembered bond had not held and, seen again in the flesh, I had slipped into the mass of humanity to which she was naturally averse and to which she referred in hostile tones, pouting the word out, as "people". "I think people are awful!" she often said, and: "Why is it that people can't let me alone?"

Just as Sir Ian was leaving, Sashie de Marnay was driven in in one of the Peak Hotel cars and came skipping gaily up the steps.

"What brings you here in the height of the tourist season and with Christmas just upon us?" I greeted him.

"Tes beaux yeux, darling, and news, Sir Ian, news! Guess who dropped into the Peak off an aeroplane today?"

"Martha's aunt after another divorce," I said. "I give up. Tell."

"Isobel Denholm!"

"Den— That big red-haired girl from Mount Melody?" Sir Ian asked.

"That very one, my sweet."

"By Jove! How is she? Is her brother with her?"

"Redder-haired than ever. No," Sashie said, taking the questions in an orderly fashion.

"By Jove! I must get back to the house an' tell Mother. She'll be delighted an' she's in need o' delightin'. You know what Mother is about old island families. We'll have to get Miss Isobel up for Christmas dinner. By Jove, this is splendid!"

When Sir Ian had gone away, Sashie gave me his mischievous smile and said: "Dear me, it is very comfortable to come to the country and meet some nice normal people for a change."

"If normal you can call us," I said. "What really brought you away from the big city today?"

"I was over at the settlement by the river arranging about a few vegetables. Your difficult child is not at home today?"

"What makes you think she is difficult?" I asked, for, although I knew Sashie to be fairly acute, he had surprised me.

He shrugged his slight shoulders. "Ça se voit."

"Actually, Dee isn't easy," I admitted, "but she likes *you*, by the way. You ought to be pleased. She doesn't like many people."

"There is the young Maclean."

"Yes. She likes Roddy."

"She must like very divergent types. There could be no two people less alike than young Maclean and me."

"She likes Twice too."

"Darling, *everybody* likes Twice, but I should have thought that liking him and young Maclean she would have written me off as too utterly effete."

"She asked me only today if you were a homosexual."

"My *dear*! What *did* you say?" he asked.

"I said you were an affected ass but that I didn't think you were queerer than that. As a matter of fact, if I had said that you were a homo I don't think it would have made any difference. She forms her likes and dislikes by some odd standards of her own — like all the rest of us, I suppose."

"Those you have named are all males, I note."

"That's not the standard either. She is fond of that awful old Miss Morrison — Madame's Cousin Emmie. But let's not talk about Dee, Sashie. It's a waste of time with you here to bring the great world into the backwater of Paradise. What goes on at the Peak? I read about the Duke of Grampian in the newspaper. Any other distinguished visitors?"

"The word 'distinguished' is a little inexact — all our guests at the Peak are distinguished for something although the somethings may not be to all tastes. We have that drunken woman who writes the plays about existentialism, and a young gentleman who is euphemistically referred to as her secretary. We have two male film stars and three female ones, none of whom speak to each other. We have three pairs of homosexuals and two of Lesbians, and we have old Lady McIndoe again with her eight Pekingese and her kennelmaid. The place is a sink, darling, but an utter sink."

"Sashie, surely homosexuality is commoner than it used to be?"

"I don't know. It is becoming more open, perhaps. I don't mind it really — it is a more social way of controlling the population than the atom bomb, after all."

"The things you think of! Dee tells me she has been helping you in the wine store. She's not a nuisance to you, I hope?"

"Quite the reverse, my sweet," he assured me. "She knows a great deal about wine and can be a tremendous help."

"Then that's all right. There isn't much for her to do here, and there will be less when Crop starts."

"How does she come to *be* here?" he asked.

I told him how Dee came to be with us and ended: "Twice had something of a rush of blood to the head over her"; and then because Sashie and I shared an intimacy that I had with few people, I added: "I think Twice regrets more than I do that we have no children of our own, Sashie."

"This situation of Dee and Twice is worrying you, darling?"

"No, not really, but I do wish I liked her better."

"She is very difficult to like," Sashie said, and it struck me that this very afternoon Dee had used the same words in a different way when she said: "Liking people is very difficult" and I felt that there was a causal relation between her words and Sashie's.

"You find that?" I asked. "You find her difficult to like?"

"Yes. I am afraid I do, dear."

"Why?"

"That is something I cannot tell you." He looked at me gravely for once, without a trace of his mischievous satirical manner. "There is something in her that I find antagonistic but I don't know what it is." His face took on its normal, lightly satirical expression again. "But, of course, what I feel is not serious. If it amuses her and takes her off your hands to come to us at the Peak, let her come as often as she likes. We are delighted to be of service to our friends in any possible way, as you know."

Shortly before Twice came home, Sashie had to leave, and when Twice came in with his usual greeting of: "What sort of afternoon?" I told him of Sashie's visit, but I did not tell him that we had talked about Dee and this was something that I did not like, although I felt it was better so, because never before had it been part of my life with Twice to have reserves, to have subjects that were not mentioned between us in this way. We did not talk of the loss of our child, it is true, but that was a silence based on a deep tacit agreement between us, while this silence about Dee was based on a deep tacit disagreement between us. Between such silences there is all the difference in the world; and although I had told Sashie that I was not worried, this silence was always present like a little black cloud on the horizon of my mind.

5

"NOBODY WANTS ME!"

NATURALLY enough, it was in the Great House of Paradise that the powerful personality of Madame Dulac flowed at full strength, and Christmas night of 1951 might have been, to all appearances, half a century back in time. The house itself was a lot more than fifty years old, and so was much that it contained, but the whole atmosphere was redolent of the late Victorian period when Madame had arrived from Edinburgh as a bride.

When she first came to Paradise she had made the Great House look as much like her wealthy Edinburgh home as possible and her taste in interior decoration had never changed, so that in the huge drawing-room the grand piano stood decently clad in its Indian shawl and garniture of silver-framed photographs while a little table beside it was a feature that was of great amusement to Twice and myself.

This table was loaded with curios from "foreign parts" — parts, that is, that were foreign to Edinburgh — so that there were several shells that could have been picked up in hundreds on any St. Jagoan beach and a palm leaf fan when Paradise bristled with a wide variety of palm trees. India, however, was also represented on this table by a hollowed-out elephant's foot in which reposed the representative of Africa, which was a blown ostrich egg that shone in the lamplight as smugly as the bald pate of any Victorian paterfamilias.

The party was a large one, for Madame also retained spacious Victorian ideas of entertaining which, with all the servants and appurtenances of the Great House, she was still able to put into effect, and it was not until after the lavish dinner was over and the women had scattered to various bedrooms that I had an opportunity to speak to Isobel Denholm.

"Hello, Janet," she said. "Gosh, it's good to see you again," and turned to look at Dee, who was by my side.

"Isobel, this is Dee Andrews, who's staying with us at Guinea Corner."

The two girls smiled at one another.

"Madame introduced us before dinner," Isobel said, "but I didn't know you were staying with Janet and Twice."

I knew that Isobel was twenty-one and Dee twenty-four, but Isobel looked much the older. Where Dee was a very small creature, Isobel was tall and rangy in a long-legged way that made me think of what I had read of the Amazons. Where Dee's colouring was faint and delicate, indeterminate and easily submerged as a house sparrow's can be by the more brightly plumaged birds, Isobel's brilliant red hair, which stood out round her head in short springy curls, and her vivid blue eyes, flaunted themselves upon the sight with the stridency of a vivid-plumaged cockatoo. But it was not the difference in physical appearance between them that seemed to reverse the order of their ages; it was some emanation from the personality of Isobel. She had changed greatly in the course of a year, I noticed, while she and Dee stood talking together and I powdered my face. The most striking difference was that she was much quieter, stiller. A year ago her manner had been as strident as her appearance, aggressive and brooding by turns, and, largely to annoy her horrid old bully of a grandmother, she had spoken in a slang, interspersed with oaths, that reminded me of early gangster films. A year ago Isobel had been uneasy company, tense, suspicious, alternating between wild gaiety and fits of unbalanced rage, and as I looked at her now and listened to her deep voice, which still had the accent of America but had lost all its stridency, which still had the idiom of America without the slang and coarseness, I found myself thinking: "What a blessing that old Mrs. Denholm is dead!"

"Everything is very different from last year, Janet," she said to me.

"Yes, Isobel. Everything is very much improved, I think, if you want a frank opinion. How is David?"

She smiled. "Improved," she said.

"Who is David?" Dee asked.

"My twin brother. He and I gave Janet and them all here quite a bit of trouble last year." She turned to me again. "Gosh, but you and Twice and Madame and Sir Ian and everybody were good to us!"

"Oh, nonsense," I said. "Let's go along to the drawing-room."

The younger people were dancing, and Don Candlesham and Roddy at once came forward to partner Dee and Isobel, so I went to sit with Madame, Cousin Emmie and one or two of the older women. Miss Matilda Fitt had been faced with something of a problem for her technique of dressmaking when asked to make an evening dress for Cousin Emmie, for the latter, to the best of my knowledge, had brought with her to St. Jago no clothes except some shapeless cardigans and the brown tweed coat and skirt. Miss Fitt, therefore, had had to copy Madame's current evening pattern for Cousin Emmie, and the current pattern was a lowish-necked, sleeveless dress, fairly straight in the skirt, but with flowing panels hanging from the waist in front and from the shoulders at the back. This dress was made in velvet for the winter and chiffon for the summer, and tonight, on Madame, in lilac velvet, it looked very well and very dignified. On Cousin Emmie, in velvet, in the colour undescriptively known as "old gold" — for no textile can have the true colour of metal — it looked like what it was, a misfit in measurement, style, colour and everything else for the woman who was wearing it. To me, it was worse than a misfit, for Cousin Emmie, with the long panels hanging limply about her, made me think of one of those cemetery monuments so common in Scotland, a brown freestone pillar with a brown freestone urn on top that has brown freestone cloths hanging out of it, and all the depression that she tended to induce in me came over me at full strength so that I became so low in spirit that I could have wept.

Old Mrs. Buckley, like Madame, had spent a long married life in the island and had come to love it, and she had been talking with interest about Twice's firm's new branch in St. Jago Bay. "And this is to be the centre for the Caribbean?" she continued now. "What a splendid thing for the island. Of course, my dear, your husband will be away a good deal but you like it here at Paradise, don't you?"

"Very much. And the trips will be short, you know. Just hops by air from one island to another."

"I don't like all this air travel," said Cousin Emmie. "You never know what might happen."

"Oh, nonsense, Miss Morrison," Mrs. Buckley said. "I go home to England by air every second year to see my daughter. It's splendid! They even give you free champagne!"

"I don't like champagne. It's bad for rheumatism," said Cousin Emmie.

"Rheumatism, Emmie?" said Madame, who had been talking to someone else but felt impelled as always to quell her cousin. "Nonsense! You can't get rheumatism here. But when you go back to England eat plenty of parsley. Old Uncle Willie was crippled with rheumatism for years and he almost lived on parsley."

"I don't like parsley, Lottie," said Cousin Emmie, "and I don't like champagne either," she added to Mrs. Buckley, quite unquelled.

This party at the Great House was, of course, but the preliminary canter in the Paradise Christmas marathon which could only be described as an annual endurance test, for every house broke out into a rash of parties so that for about ten days one was, as Twice put it in the old soldier's phrase, "either in bed or out of barracks". The effect of this marathon on myself was one of stupefaction, for, although an occasional social gathering stimulates me, a social whirl literally makes me giddy. I think that this stems from the first ten years of my life spent on the lonely hilltop of Reachfar where visitors were rare treats, and where, for hours at a time, I wandered about with only my dog for company. To be in the company of other people continuously makes me think in my not very scientific way that the atom being bombarded inside the atomic pile must feel as I do when one personality after another makes its impact on me; but instead of breaking and creating a great surge of energy as I understand that the atom does, I merely turn into a be-numbed bemused mass and cease to feel any impact at all.

It was a tradition at Paradise that the Cropping season started on the first Tuesday of the New Year, but New Year's Day of 1952 was itself a Tuesday so that we had a week to recover from the marathon before being plunged into the dull routine of Crop, when the factory and distillery would be running for twenty-four hours a day and none of the menfolk were happy when out of sight and sound of the plant, so that life became centred in the Paradise valley.

On the afternoon of the first Saturday of the New Year, having emerged to some degree from the coma which what Madame called "the festive season" had induced in me, I drove with Twice down to St. Jago Bay, where he dropped me at the Peak Hotel to visit my friend Sashie. Dee and Roddy had left Paradise in Dee's car in the forenoon and I did not know where they had gone; but as Sashie and I sat having tea in his bedroom, for this was the height of the tourist season, and even Sashie's and Don's private sitting-room was let, I saw Dee standing alone under a tree outside on the lawn, her face heavy and sullen as she picked with her neat little fingers at the rough bark, while, away beyond her, down on the beach, I could see Roddy, Isobel and some twenty other young people playing some crude form of water polo.

"Oh, God," I said to Sashie, "look at Dee!"

"I'd just as soon not if you don't mind," he said. "I am beginning to find her uncommonly tiresome. She has been lumping about like that for the last week."

In a self-pitying way I began to feel that life was being very hard and cruel to me. I had thought that Dee, squired by Roddy, had found her social feet and that she was enjoying herself, and in the course of the Christmas marathon I had been too stupefied to pay detailed attention to her.

"But what is the matter with her, Sashie?"

"Quite a number of things, I think. Dee is by nature the opposite of a little ray of sunshine. She comes into one's life like a little cloud of gloom and she has varying degrees of cloud to spread over every situation. Her main trouble at the Peak here, however, is Isobel Denholm."

"Isobel? Why? I thought they got along all right. They spent two afternoons together up at Mount Melody this week."

"Mount Melody is not the Peak, my sweet," Sashie said. "You see, when Dee used to come down here before Isobel came, she was Don's and my pet lamb, but since Isobel joined us and Don and I regard Isobel as something of a lamb, too,

Dee does not like that. Dee doesn't want to share anybody with anybody."

"But, Sashie, it's too silly! This is how she is about Twice — or was, anyway, while we were on the ship and he was free all day. She wanted him to look at nobody but her. The odd thing is that she doesn't mind so much his going to work all day, but as soon as he comes in in the evening she gets touchy and ready to think that I want to exclude her and so on. And maybe I do want to exclude her at that, for she monopolises Twice so. Anyway, it is all very straining."

"How right you are! Far be it from me to complain, but Don simply refuses to be strained and I am left to take the brunt of Dee's black looks. I feel like forbidding her to enter the place. You see, Isobel is here in a business way. She intends to turn Mount Melody into a hotel, and we have given her the run of this place so that she can see exactly how we work. She has already done a year on the financial side of things in a hotel in New York."

"You think it is a good idea, Sashie — Mount Melody as a hotel?"

"My dear, it can't miss! Isobel is going

to need a little capital at the start — a lot of the Denholm money is tied up in various things in the States and she can't get at it — so if Twice and you have a pound or two to invest, don't hesitate. Don and I are going in with our spare fiver."

"You two really got in on the ground floor of the tourist boom in this island," I told him.

"And you and Twice were almost our first guests, my sweet. You brought us luck. But for that, I should probably have wrung your foster-daughter's neck by now."

"You are one of the few people she likes, Sashie, as I told you. Do try to be patient with her. I know it's difficult."

"Very," Sashie agreed and we both looked out of the window again.

Dee had moved to another tree, but she might as well have stayed where she was, for she was again picking at the trunk, her gloomy eyes fixed on the gay crowd splashing about in the shallow water beyond the silver sand.

"Crop starts at Paradise on Tuesday," I told Sashie, "and Roddy is starting work at the factory. If you hear rumours of murder up there you will know that I have probably gone for Dee with a cutlass."

At six in the morning of the following Tuesday the siren at the factory blew a prolonged ululating blast that echoed across the valley basin of Paradise, penetrated to every precipitous valley in the surrounding hills and told the inhabitants of every shack on the highest mountains round about that the 1952 Crop had begun. The swing-over from Out-of-Crop to In-Crop had a peculiar drama of its own, for the field labour, who, in the main, spent the Out-of-Crop months in the high hills tilling their own few acres of land to raise maize and yams, now descended in their hundreds to the valley, their savagely sharp cutlasses balanced on their shoulders, to cut the cane. These cutters were the young and strong men and women — the men would cut, the women would pile the cut cane into heaps and place on each the family tally-mark of a mysteriously tied cane blade — but they were followed by grandmothers, who would cook the family dinner, and by grandfathers, who would still cut a little cane between sleeps in the sun, and by little children, who were too young to be left at home. From all points of the compass they came, converging on the factory at the centre of the valley which was the pulsing heart of their lives and sustenance, and they came with a gaiety, the young and strong with speed in their ugly loping walk, the children with the grandfathers on donkey-back and the grandmothers also perched on donkeys between the big panniers that contained the cooking pots and the enamel plates. And the donkeys went pad-padding by on their neat little hooves, their heads nod-nodding and shaking the gaudy sprays of bougainvillaea that had been put into their bridle bands to celebrate this start of another Crop.

The whole great valley came to noisy pulsing life in the course of a few hours. For the last day or two, we who lived there had been conscious of a stir of power from the factory, a noise akin to that of an orchestra tuning up, as the boilers were fired, steam raised and one piece of machinery after another given a final turn-over, and on the day before the whistle blew we had heard a different note come in, a deeper diapason, when a few tons of cane were put through the crushing mills so that their pressures could be finally adjusted; but after the blast on the siren, the orchestra was in full volume, from the high yet musical shrill of the fiddles as steam at pressure screamed into the evaporating vessels to the deep organ note of the crushing mills themselves, as they gaped for and then groaned as they pulverised and swallowed the tough fibrous tons of cane and sent the juice in a tinkling river along the troughs to the tanks. And against this great orchestral background the men and women sang and shouted in the fields, the grandmothers crooned beside the cooking fires, the children called to one another and laughed as they played, and the tractors, with their long trains of cane carts, each carrying a five-ton bundle tied with chains, kept up a steady percussion beat of diesel engines as they plied to and fro from fields to factory.

I had seen all this before, but it still had for me all the freshness and excitement that belongs to any great act of creation, the freshness and excitement that is permanent in a great work of art, the wonder and joy that used to recur for me with every spring and harvest when I was a child, the wonder and joy that is in every Easter morning for the true believer.

I had taken a chair out to the upper veranda outside my bedroom early in the morning and was sitting there with my sewing in my lap when Dee came out to join me.

"Why are you sitting up here?" she asked.

"Watching Crop start. Isn't it terribly exciting! Do look at that donkey in the hat with pink roses!"

Dee looked out across the broad valley. "I thought they would have a machine for cutting the sugar cane, like they have for wheat at home, only bigger, you know."

I suddenly felt very flat and began to do my embroidery. "I believe they have them in the States and Cuba and places," I said, "but they have never introduced them here yet. They might cause a revolution — like the spinning jenny in the cotton industry at home last century. Mechanical harvesters would put a lot of people out of work."

"It's got to happen some day surely," she said.

"Oh yes, I suppose so. Some day."

An old grandmother, her white frizzy hair tied up in a bright bandana, went past on her donkey, the pots and pans clashing about her, and she called: "Mawnin', Missis!"

"Good-morning!" I called back and said to Dee: "But the mechanical harvesters won't wish me good-morning as they pass."

"Miss Jan, you *are* childish!" she said. "When shall I be able to go round the factory?"

"Certainly not today. Probably not till next week. The first few days are always tricky until the plant settles down."

"Oh, well, I think I'll run down to St. Jago Bay."

"Do that," I said and she went away.

Glad to be rid of her, I dropped the sewing into my lap and looked out over the valley again, but the music and the gaiety had gone out of it. Dee was right, of course. One day — a day not very distant — the mechanical harvesters would come; ther would be no more donkeys with bougainvillaea in their bridles, and it was as well to face it — I did not want to be here in this island when that happened. It was only certain days in the year, such as this start of Crop and Christmas with Madame's dinner-party, that made life in the island bearable for me, and all these things would die away. Most people nowadays celebrated Christmas in the luxury hotels in the Bay; and on most plantations, already, Crop did not begin with bougainvillaea-bedecked donkeys but with an argument about cane-loaders' wages and the like. To go through trouble and misery day by day with anyone, you have to love that person deeply and I recognised the fact that I did not love this island enough to go with it through the troubles and misery of its economic and political future.

Another family party on three donkeys passed by and again I called good-morning and waved to the children, and behind me a voice said: "Exhilarating, isn't it?"

I turned to see Roddy in shorts and open-necked shirt standing in the bedroom doorway behind me.

"I didn't see you arrive," I said. "Good-morning."

"I came up the drive, but you were too

busy looking out over the valley so I just came up. I don't blame you. This is the best Paradise has to offer."

"Haul a chair out of there and sit down."

"This is all right," he said and sat down on the veranda floor.

"I thought you were starting work at the factory today?"

"I've got a day's grace. Dad doesn't want to be bothered with me today, which suits everybody. I'd rather be here today where I can see what goes on than be shut in the power-house. I love the start of Crop. I've loved it ever since I was a kid."

"Has it changed much, Roddy?" I asked. "I think it is immensely thrilling."

"It's less thrilling than it used to be — the tractors, you know. All the haulage used to be by teams of mules and oxen, all decked up with flowers, and some of them would bolt and others wouldn't move at all, and it was all terrific."

"Like going to the coal boat at home when I was a kid. There was a horse called Pearl that sat down on the pier with her cart once and smashed it to matchwood."

We watched another family go past, and

Roddy said: "Has Dee gone down to the Peak?"

"She said the Bay," I told him. "I don't know whether she meant the Peak or not."

"Oh, definitely the Peak. She has a bit of a thing for de Marnay."

"I know she likes Sashie."

"I'd be inclined to use a stronger word. I may be wrong. Dee has odd tastes. Jim Maxwell and Bill Taylor and that lot have it that de Marnay is a queer, but I'm not sure he really is — he gives me the feeling that he is masquerading."

I looked down at Roddy's dark head and tanned face, which was turned away from me as he looked out across the valley, and I had a sudden feeling that a very acute intelligence was at work behind this swash-buckling façade of his. He had come too close for comfort to the truth about Sashie de Marney, anyhow, and I said: "But surely to masquerade in that way argues a form of what you call queerness in itself? Like those men that dress up as women?"

"That's true. Isn't he by way of being a buddy of yours?"

"Yes. I am very fond of Sashie. He is very intelligent and sympathetic."

"A lot of homosexuals are like that," Roddy said, and suddenly he turned to look at me with a flashing smile. "But they don't have the appeal for types like me that they might have for a woman."

"I can understand that," I smiled back at him and I thought how strange it was that Dee had said he was not "sexy and things", for in my eyes the most immediately noticeable thing about Roddy was his masculinity and virility. These things were even more marked in him than they were in Don Candlesham, the island Casanova, for in Don's case the first thing to strike one was the perfection of the physical structure and the emanation of sex came second.

After lunch, for which Dee did not return, I came up to the top veranda again and sat thinking of what Roddy had said and felt that it might explain Sashie's ill-temper about Dee of the Saturday before. Sashie, as a rule, was waspish, mischievous or satirical about humanity in general, but he was seldom sufficiently moved by or involved with anyone for his temper to be affected. If, however, as Roddy had implied, Dee had fallen in love with him, I felt it probable that Sashie would be acutely embarrassed, for I thought that a large part of the reason for his affected masquerade was that it might help him to avoid sex entanglements. If Dee had formed an attachment to him, she was headed, I knew with sure foreboding, for real unhappiness; but Dee being what she was, I did not feel that I could advise her, warn her or help her in any way.

She did not arrive home until nearly dinner-time when Twice was upstairs changing, and as soon as she came into the house I saw that she was sunk in gloom.

"What is the matter, Dee?"

"Nothing." She began to pick at the sash of her dress, her face as ugly and heavy as lead, and then: "I'm not going back to that Peak Hotel! They're horrible! All three of them — that Don and Sashie and Isobel — just horrible!"

"Why? What happened? What did they do?"

"Nothing. People can be horrible without doing anything. They just don't want me — that's all."

"Dee, I really think you imagine things."

"No, I don't! I hate them all!"

"But what happened?"

"Nothing. Nothing happened outside. It was inside me it happened. You wouldn't understand. Nobody wants me!"

"Dee, I can't bear to have you miserable like this. If you don't go to the Peak, where all the young people go, it is going to be so dull for you now that Crop has started and Roddy is working and everything. Dee, are you tired of being here? Would you like to go back to England?"

"Oh — " Her eyes became round, she stared at me for a moment and then went flying out of the room and upstairs, and I heard the door of her room slam shut.

It seems almost unnecessary to record that, no more than thirty seconds later, Twice arrived in the drawing-room, naked except for a pair of drill slacks, his blue eyes blazing.

"What have you done to Dee?" he snapped at me.

"Go and ask her!" I snapped back and marched out of the room and up to my own bedroom.

It was not very long before Twice came barging in there next.

"What's all this about you sending her back to England?"

It would be tedious to record all the explanation and the argument that ensued and which culminated with us all in Dee's bedroom, where she lay on the bed, her face bloated with tears, sobbing while I assured her insincerely that the last thing I wanted was that she should go back to England, that Guinea Corner would be miserable without her, that Twice and I would miss her dreadfully from our lives, and that I, when Twice went away round the islands, would pine with loneliness all by myself. In the end, she became calm, asked Twice if he would carry a tray upstairs for her so that the servants would not know she had been crying, and apologised for making a scene. ". . . but it was just that I felt that nobody wants me."

Feeling that I was being socially blackmailed almost beyond bearing and also feeling exhausted, I left her and came downstairs.

Later, when Twice came down, I said to him: "The awful thing is that it is true that nobody wants her — she makes them so that they don't want her."

Twice sat down, frowning. "I thought she had settled down. Of course, I've been busy since we got back, what with getting ready for Crop and the festive season and all, but she seemed to be all right."

I sighed. "She will come round, I suppose. The longer I live, the more convinced I become that affluence and leisure are the joint curses of humanity. If she had her living to earn she couldn't afford all this nonsense. Did you get out of her what happened at the Peak today?"

"No. Nothing except the they-don't-want-me thing."

"The only person who can handle her is Roddy Maclean and you have to go and take him for your ruddy power-house!" I said.

"*I* have no hand in putting Roddy Maclean in the power-house," Twice said angrily. "I'd rather see that power-house without *him* in it."

"Twice, what have you against Roddy?"

"I don't know. I just don't trust him."

"You sound exactly like Cousin Emmie," I told him snappishly.

The next afternoon, although he could ill spare the time, Twice took Dee on her promised trip round the factory and she came home with him about six in the evening, very gay and bright and with what seemed to me to be an amazing grasp of the workings of the complex plant. It was difficult to believe that the young woman who sat at dinner discussing so intelligently the working of the evaporators was the same person who, the day before, had wailed like a child the words: "Nobody wants me!" When dinner was over, she went off to the club to play badminton, and I said something of this to Twice and he said: "I know. She has more grasp of the real nature of the turbines in that power-house after half an hour in there than Roddy Maclean will ever have."

"It seems to me, though," I said, "that Roddy has a grasp of something more important than turbines. He is one of the happiest people I have ever seen. I wish he could teach Dee something of his own design for living. Not that I am complaining about Dee really, because I thought of a thing today."

"What?"

"I have complained that she caused destruction between you and me with all those rows on the ship and everything, but that isn't true. She has made you and me more aware of one another. I had begun to take you for granted a bit, I think, and I had nearly forgotten what a nice sort of bloke you are until I saw you being so good to Dee."

Twice grinned at me. "Something similar has crossed my own mind," he said. "I was thinking in bed last night that the great thing about you is that one knows exactly where one is, whether it is in heaven or the dog-house, because you make no bones about telling one and it is a great deal to be thankful for. Another thing I was thinking about, or hoping rather, was that you are not going to have too bad a time with Dee while I am away."

"I have been thinking about that too and making all sorts of resolutions, Twice. I will do my very best, but if she has gone off home to England in a huff by the time you come back, will you try to believe that it truly isn't my fault?"

"After last night's how-d'ye-do, I'll believe you every time, but you know, Janet, when she told me you had told her to go back to England I don't think she meant to be destructive between you and me as you call it."

"Darling, I don't think she means to tell lies either, for that is what happened last night. That was a real whopper she told you that first time you went in to see her, but she didn't see it like that. It is that she sees everything from her own dismal point of view — the minute I said the word England she decided I wanted to send her home and I truly believe that is the last place she wants to go. In a way, she makes me think of Cousin Emmie. *She* never sees anything either except from her own dismal point of view."

6

"LOVE AND OBLIQUENESS"

WATCHED day and night by its staff, the factory behaved like a model industrial plant for the first week of Crop. There is a semi-medical term which is "nurse's sleep" to describe the restful doze that a nurse can fall into without ever losing consciousness of her patient and his needs, and there ought also to be a semi-engineering term "engineer's sleep" to describe the sort of rest taken by Twice and Rob Maclean during the first week of a Paradise Crop. Guinea Corner was about three-quarters of a mile as the crow flies to the south-west of the factory, and Olympus, the Macleans' house, about the same distance to the north-west, and the night breeze in the early months of the year at Paradise blows from the east. Every note of the sugar-processing symphony was carried to the two houses and in through the mosquito

175

mesh on the bedroom windows. To such as myself the sound was just a massive hum that was soothing until broken momentarily by the day-shift siren at six in the morning, but for Rob and Twice it analysed itself down into single notes, so that at bed-time Twice would say: "They've got that molasses pump speeded up again, damn them!" and in the middle of the night, more than half asleep, he would turn over and I would hear him mutter: "That brake on Number Three basket is a bit rough."

On the tenth evening of Crop, I was packing Twice's suit-cases for his trip to the southern islands while he sat on the bed arranging the papers in his brief-case.

"I know I am a big grown-up boy now," he said suddenly, "but I don't want to go away from home one bit."

"Darling, I don't want it either, but there it is and a fortnight isn't all that long."

"It won't be a fortnight long if I can help it. You are sure you will be all right?"

"Of course!"

We went on with our separate jobs, both a little ashamed of ourselves and trying to adjust ourselves to this new departure in our lives, for since we had first met in 1945 there had not been a single day that had not largely been spent in the company of one another.

"And you are not to worry about Dee and me while you are away," I told him.

He had finished arranging his papers and had taken one shoe off preparatory to having a bath before dinner. He sat on the edge of the bed with the shoe dangling from his hand by its lace.

"I wish to God we had never brought her out here!" he said suddenly.

Since the evening when we quarrelled on board the ship we had tacitly avoided serious discussion of Dee, and had gone on from day to day, coping with her moods as they came, but for the most part avoiding mention of her when we were alone. On my part, the reason for this was that I was afraid that discussion of her might lead to another quarrel between us, for I could now understand Twice's liking for her even less than I had understood it that first evening at sea. Since the "nobody-wants-me" scene of about a week before, I was less in sympathy with Dee than ever because my attitude was that, if she felt like this, she ought to examine herself and find the reason why "nobody wanted her" instead of blaming people and retiring into sulks and self-pity, but the effect of the scene on Twice seemed to have been the reverse of the effect it had made on me. Through it, she seemed to have made some pathetic appeal to him so that, since it happened, he had given her even more of his time in the evenings, allowing her to sit with him in his study which was mainly a drawing-office and where I myself did not go unless he invited me to look at some piece of work he was doing. I was not jealous of the time Twice gave to her, but I could not understand the appeal she had for him, and her whole personality lay between us like a barren wilderness in the realm of our emotions, a wilderness in which I was afraid to set foot by any talk, other than of the most casual nature, about her.

"But, Twice," I said now, "why? Since the nobody-wants-me carry-on last week, I thought everything was merry as a marriage bell! There have been no moods or anything and she is going down to the Bay again and — "

"Do you know what she has been doing

in the Bay?" he interrupted, his voice shaking with suppressed rage. "Borrowing books about sugar-processing from the Chamber of Commerce library and reading them and spewing their contents over me in the evenings until I think I am going out of my mind! Does she think I want to spend my day in a sugar factory and then have Madden's theory of crystallisation rammed down my gullet all evening?"

Sometimes I think there is a chance that I am not the most tactful woman in the world, because at this moment I began to laugh, causing Twice to throw his shoe with a bang on to the floor and glare at me with blazing eyes.

"I am happy that you find this funny!" he said.

"Darling, don't be so angry. It's rather pathetic, really. She needs so desperately to reach common ground with somebody. Don't you think that's it?"

Even as I spoke, it struck me as odd that, little as I liked Dee and little as I could understand her appeal for Twice, there was never a time that he criticised her that I did not feel constrained to take her part. We could never be together about her, it seemed. Twice glared at the shoe he had thrown to the floor and I went on: "I agree that it is pretty inept to try to get close to you through a sea of molasses or something but her sheer ineptitude is one of her dominant characteristics."

"You pointed that out away back on the ship, and you also pointed out that she was destructive and you were right on both counts. Janet, how do you come at these things about people?"

"I don't know, Twice. I think it is the Reachfar in me. I have an animal instinct for danger to things I value. I don't come at things, as you call it, with everybody. I am as blind as a bat about most people, as you well know, but I think I have an instinct about anyone who constitutes a threat to you and me and she seemed to do that right from the start."

"What sort of threat? You can't mean that you ever thought that I would fall in love with her?"

"No. Not that." I sat down and picked up my hair-brush with the dent in its back and held it between my hands. "It seemed to me that you regarded her as a potential daughter of ours," I said, looking down at the brush, "and I didn't like that. I couldn't imagine the union between you and me producing a leaden lump of introspective ineptitude like Dee, and if you could see her as a daughter it meant that she was between us like a destructive wedge. I think you did have a bit of a fatherly thing for her, didn't you?" I asked quietly.

"Yes, I did, but there was something else in it too. When we met her in London I simply didn't believe in all this stuff about how difficult she was and how impossible to deal with. I have always found, even with the toughest conscripts in the Army during the war, that anybody can be dealt with if one is prepared to take a little trouble. I simply didn't believe in the born outsider, if you like."

"No man is an island," I said.

"Huh?"

"John Donne," I explained and quoted: "'No man is an island, entire of himself; every man is a piece of the continent, a part of the main . . .' I can't remember how it goes on."

"Well, Donne could never have met anybody like Dee," Twice said. "With that nature of hers, she will never be a piece of the continent or a part of the main."

"But it seems to me that that is what she is trying so hard to become, Twice, with her study of the sugar industry and all that. I agree that it is pretty inept to try to approach you through a sea of molasses, as I said, but surely that is what she is trying to do — to approach you?"

Twice has an unremarkable face except for his strikingly blue eyes, but it is a firm face and I always find it somehow incongruous that, when he is very much moved, his lower lip slackens and begins to tremble like the lip of a child who is about to cry. This happened now, and I sat waiting for what he would say, and I saw his teeth bite at the lip as if to steady it before he said:

"I feel as if somebody had died, as if a child of ours had died. Oh, I know it isn't true — I know the child did not exist, that I moulded Dee in my mind after my heart's desire, I suppose." His speech gathered speed now that he had begun to say the thing that was so difficult to express. "When we met her in London, I saw her as part of you, as someone who had known you in the long time before I met you and as someone who had sought you out and needed you — needed *us*. I thought she knew about *us*," he said on a note of protest, slamming his hand down on his knee, trying to say the unsayable, "that when I took her round the factory it was really *you* and I who were doing it — that in everything I do or you do, the other is implicit in it." He paused before he added in a low voice: "But it isn't like that. She doesn't know about us." He then looked up at me. "Do you know what she said last night in the study? That she didn't know how I had ever come to marry anyone as light-minded and silly as you and that she didn't think you had much moral sense, really."

Quite unconsciously his voice had adopted something of Dee's prim censorious manner, and this time I began to laugh and could not stop until I saw Twice glaring at me angrily and realised that if I did not pull myself together I would lose this opportunity of bridging the gulf that had lain between us since we left London. "I'm sorry," I panted, "but I can't help it. It *is* funny, Twice. I know that she has hurt you and disappointed you terribly, but seen from where I stand, this thing that she said is funny."

I knew as I spoke that Dee had hurt Twice so much with her silly remark because his affection for her had made him vulnerable and that I, who felt no affection for her, was invulnerable and quite impervious to her opinions.

"I can't see it funny from any standpoint," he said, "that she should criticise you to me of all people. Don't you see what it implies? It means that she simply doesn't know me!"

"That's true, but then she probably formed her own vision of you just as you did of her."

"But she has been with us for weeks now! She has seen us together!"

I suppressed my desire to start laughing again, a desire which came from a deeper source than Dee or anything she had said. The laughter was coming as much from relief and gratitude that the wilderness of Dee between Twice and myself had disappeared as if it had been swallowed by an earthquake.

"Twice, don't you see that this is some

more of this cursed ineptitude of hers? I am sure most of the people we know regard me as light-headed and silly and probably amoral too — I'll be annoyed and disappointed if they don't because this is how I would like to be regarded. One has to have some privacy, after all, and what I really am is nobody's business except yours and mine. But only Dee is inept enough to say that she thinks this about me, especially to you."

"Inept or not, why did she say it?"

"That I don't know. Maybe she meant it as an oblique compliment to yourself — that someone as serious-minded and intelligent as you should be so patient with someone as light-minded and silly as me."

"It struck me as merely disloyal, destructive and bitchy," he said, "and, in Sashie's phrase, it has made me utterly disenchanted with our Dee. Even if it was intended as a compliment to me, it augurs either a malice or a stupidity that is almost past belief."

"No. I don't see it as either malice or stupidity. It is simply that she has no idea of the relationship between you and me or any idea of relationships at all. She cannot see that a remark by her to you about me can affect the relationship between you and *her*. It's from this that her ineptitude springs. It's odd that away back aboard the ship Roddy Maclean said she hadn't a clue about relationships. He was right."

"Anyway," Twice said next, "if Dee has gone off back to England in a huff by the time I get back, I won't be sorry." He looked at me angrily. "I feel I have made a middle-aged fool of myself over her and I dislike her all the more for that."

"I think you are taking the whole thing far too seriously," I told him, but I knew that he had been more deeply involved emotionally than I had been aware and that his hurt and disappointment were deep.

"Maybe I am. Anyhow, don't have any nonsense while I am away. She has done enough harm. She is a destructive little brat, as you said long ago and you were quite right."

"No. That isn't true. Roddy is nearer the mark. It is this cluelessness about people and their feelings that is at the bottom of it."

Twice went to the window and looked away across the dark valley to where the chains of lights about the factory resembled the lights of a ship on a night sea.

"Whether he was right about that or not, I don't like that youth. I don't trust him."

I recognised that by thus dismissing the subject of Dee, Twice was putting his hurt disappointment and his embarrassment at feeling a "middle-aged fool" behind him, but that he should make a new departure by beginning to carp about Roddy again annoyed and irritated me.

"I wish you would stop croaking that out without any explanation of what you mean," I said. "It's just like Cousin Emmie, as I told you before. And I simply don't understand you. If Roddy isn't a fanatical engineer as yet, he is young and has time enough to grow into it, and in the meantime he is a charming boy."

"He has far too much bloody charm," Twice said, staring away at the factory lights. "I hate the thought of him in that power-house up there. He is shifty, shiftless and bone lazy, and he'd try to lie his way out of the back kitchen of hell," he ended viciously.

"Twice, is this a straightforward opinion you have formed of the boy as himself or is there any jealous rubbish about his liking for me and mine for him mixed up in it ?"

He turned to face me. "Honestly, Janet, you don't come into this at all. I admit that in the first days at sea there was a bit of suspicion about you in what I felt about him, but it isn't like that now. I am talking of him as a young man like Mackie or Christie or any of the other youngsters up there."

"Then how did you come to think like this about him ?"

"In the ordinary course at the factory. You simply can't rely on him to do what he is told or take the trouble to do it properly. Dammit, you can't rely on him to *stay* in the power-house — he's as likely to be in the office drinking tea with the typists. And there are a couple of hundred thousand pounds' worth of new turbines in that power-house and the whole plant depending on them, but he is just as likely to forget to open or shut a valve as the sun is to rise in the morning. And then he gives one a charming smile, as if one was a woman he'd bumped into accidentally and says: 'I'm awfully sorry. I am entirely to blame.' Charm, you know. The attempt to oil his way out when he's been too lazy to check the oil in his lubricators!"

"Twice, does Rob know any of this?"

"I haven't told him, if that's what you mean. I'm too big a coward to look old Rob in the eye and say: 'Look here, that son of yours is a stinker!' But I pitched a tale to Sir Ian. Young Mackie is mad about those turbines, so I asked Sir Ian to let him stand watch in the power-house four hours on four off round the clock while I'm away. Mackie has been doing nights up till now. And Mackie jumped at it because the distillery is more active on the day-shift and it's all more exciting. Mackie would eat and sleep in the power-house if he got a chance, so I know things can only go to hell for four hours at a stretch."

"This is all terribly worrying, Twice. The factory staff has always been so trouble-free except for the odd professional breeze between you oily engineers and Cranston and his white coats in the lab."

"Well, that young slob is trouble in my book, but maybe it won't be for long. He's not really on the contract staff, you know. There's a queerness about the whole thing, to tell the truth. Rod is very cagey about him, somehow."

"I'm terribly sorry about it all, Twice. He has been so very good about Dee, too."

"That's another thing. I wouldn't trust him not to marry Dee — not because he is fond of her but because of her money."

"Aren't you being a little far-fetched there?" I asked.

"Maybe I am, but I am not as starry-eyed and trustful as you are. Heaven knows, I don't like Dee very much today, but as long as she is here we are in some degree responsible for her. I've seen Maclean in the office with the typists — there's a little new girl up there called Lucy Freeman, coffee-coloured and very pretty — and he gets the old come-hither look very, very easily, but I've never seen him get it over Dee. You are not going to tell me that a hot-arsed bloke like that runs about with our Dee out of the goodness of his heart. I just don't believe it. But he hasn't many scruples. He might try to marry Uncle Archie's money."

"Well, you and I agreed at one time to differ about Dee. We have come together on that, but we'll still have to differ about Roddy," I said. "I just don't see him as you do, Twice."

"I think he gambles too," Twice said, frowning. "I've seen him coming out of Sloppy Dick's bar in the Bay. I don't feel that the Maclean sons are given allowances big enough to stand up to the stakes at Sloppy Dick's."

"No. That I don't like the sound of," I admitted.

The next morning at eleven o'clock Dee and I watched Twice's plane soar away to the north, turn in a wide circle and climb away out of sight, southwards, over the mountainous backbone of the island, and then we came back to the waiting car. I had an unreal feeling, as if my feet were not quite on the ground, as if I were being pulled upwards in the slip-stream of the aircraft by an invisible, in-tangible cord that was attached to me some-where in the region of my heart. Groping for reality, I tried to think myself back to the time before I knew Twice, to the time when an attachment like this did not exist so that I might be again as I was then, but one cannot go back through time. One can make an evocation of the past, but inevitably that evocation has something of the colour and texture and feeling of all the time that has been experienced since. My relationship with Twice was the most important experience of my life, the experience that coloured and altered the texture of everything so that, in the moment when the aircraft disappeared, I knew that I could never be as I was before I met him. I was a different person now, the person who loved Twice and I must live with this tugging sense of loneliness until he came back. To part is to die a little. . . .

I do not think Dee and I talked very much on the way home from the airport, and when we came into the house I went straight up to my bedroom. On my dressing-table a dozen roses stood in a tall vase, and from the stem of one of them hung a card on which was written: "Flash — with love — Twice." I sat down on my bed and began to cry.

"Miss Jan, I'm going out to — " said Dee in the doorway and then: "What's the matter? Don't you feel well?"

I pointed at the roses.

"Don't you like them? They were terribly expensive. I fetched them last night, so I know. Twice said I wasn't to tell you and he gave them to Clorinda. They've been in the laundry all night. I'll take them away if — "

"Leave them alone!" I snapped at her, irritated beyond bearing by this dreadful ineptitude of hers or inability to feel or whatever it was.

"But why are you crying?"

I drew a deep breath and bit my lower lip. "I don't feel very well. I am going to lie down for a little. I'll be downstairs by lunch-time."

"Can I get them to bring you some tea or something?"

"No, thank you, Dee. Are you going out?"

"I was going round to the club."

"That's splendid, dear. Off you go."

She did not come back until lunch-time and by then I had pulled myself together. Twice was not mentioned between us. For the rest of that day and most of the next Dee was very silent altogether, as if she were mystified and at the same time a little afraid of me, but as the days followed one another she became more normal and very agreeable and companionable. Everything was quietly routine. Cousin Emmie called once or twice; the factory hummed on and the cane fields were turning one by one from emerald green to Cousin Emmie brown as the crop was cut and the chopped-off blades withered to trash in the heat of the sun. On the eleventh day after Twice's departure, at nine in the morning, there was a cablegram: "Please meet me Thursday noon love Twice."

I showed it to Dee.

"But that's tomorrow!" she said, and it seemed to me that her brow clouded.

"Yes," I said.

"But that's two days too soon!"

"Too soon for what?" I asked, puzzled.

She opened her lips to speak, closed them again and then, after a pause, she said: "Not *for* anything. It's just that I wasn't thinking of his coming until Saturday."

She left the room without further explanation, and a moment later I saw her car go down the drive. It was only then that it occurred to me that for the last eleven days Guinea Corner and I myself had more or less revolved round Dee. What she had wanted to do had been done. If she wanted me to go to the club with her, I had gone; when she went somewhere and did not invite me to go with her, I had stayed at home. When I thought now of those days, I thought that well might she have been content, and when she returned for lunch I said carefully: "Dee, are you free to meet Twice tomorrow at twelve or shall I ask Sir Ian to take me down?"

"Oh, I'll take you down to meet him," she said, but she did not smile and obviously she did not share in my joy at his return.

The next morning, before we left the house, I said to my cook: "No lunch today, Cookie. The plane may be late and we'll have lunch in the Bay."

As Dee drove out of the gates of Guinea Corner she said: "Are you going to the Peak for lunch?"

"Yes, I thought so."

"I'm not coming," she said. "I'll drop you and Twice and call back for you."

"Dee, what is all this about the Peak? If you feel like this, I'd much rather have got Sir Ian to come down with me."

"There isn't any all this. I'm just not going to the Peak, that's all. . . . I suppose you would have preferred Sir Ian to drive you, anyway."

"Dee, please don't be silly. We'll all have lunch at the Palace, then."

"No, we won't." Her mouth tightened into a little button with a vertical line at each side as it used to do when she was a child. "I'm not interfering with what you and Twice want to do. We don't have to have lunch together."

In an exasperated way I wanted to tell her that she had already "interfered" by this refusal to go to the Peak, but instead I said: "Oh, very well, Dee. Of course, I don't understand in the least what is going on, but I suppose it is none of my affair, anyway."

"Don't be angry with me, Miss Jan!"

I drew a deep breath, hoping that it would crush my exasperation down, and it did, packing it into a tight knot in the region of my solar plexus.

"It is very difficult for me not to get impatient, Dee. It would be easier if you would explain a bit."

"There's nothing to explain. They just don't want me around the Peak and I'm not going there."

"Oh, all right," I said wearily. "You don't have to go to the Peak if you don't want to."

We met Twice. Dee dropped him and me at the Peak Hotel and drove away.

"Dee not staying for lunch?" he asked.

"No. She has something to do in the Bay — I don't know what and I didn't ask. She'll be back for us at two-thirty."

"What you mean is that she has still got what Sir Ian calls a fit o' the pique at the Peak?"

"Well, yes."

"What's she been like these last two weeks?"

"Splendid. Not a pout or a glower," I said, but I was not going to spoil his home-coming by telling him what I thought was the reason for the more amenable mood. "Not a word until today when I suggested coming here for lunch. Oh, the devil with it! Darling, I *am* glad you are back!"

Twice and I had a pleasant two hours, chatting to Isobel, Don and Sashie and other friends until shortly after two, when Lionel Somerset, Twice's colleague from the office, came in and he and Twice went off into a corner to discuss some matter of business. Isobel, who had been superintending the busy patio bar where I was finishing my coffee, came towards me between the tables in her pale-green shirt and slacks, and I watched with pleasure her free stride, the long legs swinging from the hips, which were so narrow for her height and width of shoulder, and I wished that Dee had some of this forthright air of easy self-confidence.

"How did you come down?" she asked. "Sir Ian or Dee aren't here?"

"Dee brought me. She is coming back for us. She had things to do in the Bay."

"It seems like weeks since we've seen Dee. I wondered if she was sick, but that Maclean type was in here the other night and he said she was all right."

I noticed the phrase "that Maclean type", which had obviously been adopted by Isobel from Don, and in her accent it had a curious ring. "Dee has been taking her job of nursemaid to me while Twice was away very seriously, I am afraid," I said. I thought of telling Isobel that Dee had the idea that they did not want her at the Peak, but I then thought that it would infuriate Dee if she were to find out that I had been "interfering", as she would call it, so I said instead: "What Maclean type did you mean?"

"You know the one I mean, I guess. Roddy, they call him."

"And what's wrong with him?" I asked.

"Oh, nothing much, I suppose. I just don't happen to care for him, that's all." One of the waiters appeared beside her. "Yes, Peterkin, what's on your mind? Okay, I'll come. Excuse me, Janet. Come down again soon, huh? And tell Dee to come and see us, for goodness' sakes!"

While I sat in the bright noisy bar, waiting for Twice to be free and for Dee to come with the car, I felt that in a few hours the peace that had prevailed over me and Guinea Corner for twelve days had been torn to shreds. The world would be a splendid place, I thought unreasonably as I had often thought before, if it were not for the people in it, but at the back of my mind I knew that what was nagging at me was the climate of adverse opinion that seemed to be building up round Roddy Maclean. My loyalties to the people I like cause me more trouble than any other one thing.

We arrived home at Guinea Corner about mid-afternoon and Twice at once changed out of what he referred to as his "city slicker suit" into shorts and a shirt, and intimated that he was "just going up to have a look at the factory".

"That flippin' factory!" I said. "I don't believe you came home to me at all. The lure is the heap of junk up there!"

I said this upstairs in our bedroom where the door stood open, and I did not know that Dee also was upstairs, but after Twice had driven away she told me that she had heard and added: "Miss Jan, I don't think Twice can like it very much when you call the factory a heap of junk."

She was painfully solemn and earnest, as if she had screwed her courage to the sticking place in order to give me this gentle advice on how best to handle my husband; and although I wanted to laugh at her, I did not because I knew it would hurt her mortally.

"You think not, Dee?"

"I'm sure he can't like it. After all, he helped to build it and he is terribly interested in it."

Now this was the year 1952, and since the end of 1948, more or less, I had suffered at close quarters the prolonged birth-pangs of the new Paradise Factory. I had seen the plans drawn, I had heard the oaths when a lay-out would not "lie down", I had seen a T-square go through the study window and accidentally and incidentally clout the yard boy on the skull when it was discovered that the planned sugar-cane elevator would not "come in", and I myself had been hit on the face with a thrown cushion when I said that if the boiling-floor was my kitchen I would have that door there instead of here. Twice will always hit me in the face with a cushion first before admitting that I may be right about an engineering matter, but I do not mind and it does not happen very often.

I now stared solemnly back at Dee and wondered if she seriously believed that I had lived down these years with Twice and had not yet discovered that he had helped to build the factory and was interested in it. For a moment it seemed to me that my decision made long ago to meet life with a light-hearted smile wherever possible had been almost too much of a success, if this was what made Dee think that I, or any woman indeed, could be as stupid as this, and at first I could not think of anything to say, but after a moment I said: "Dee, have you ever thought that it is possible to make love obliquely?"

She frowned and her face flushed a little. "Love? Obliquely?" she repeated.

"Yes. When I call the factory a heap of junk, it is a way of telling Twice that I love him and want him to stay with me instead of going up there."

"And he understands that?"

"Oh yes." I felt embarrassed now. There was something indecent about this ineptitude of hers.

"I don't know anything about love and obliqueness," she said and drifted away from me out into the garden, where I saw her pause by the hibiscus clump and begin to pick at the leaves, and, suddenly depressed, I went upstairs to do Twice's unpacking.

Just before I finished, I heard Roddy's voice downstairs and Dee's car drive out, and as I was silently giving thanks for this in my mind, my maid came into the room and said: "Tea in de drawin'-room, Ma'am, an' Miss Emmie from de Great House in de drawin'-room too," and thinking that life never brings a good without an evil, that it always carries a sting in its tail, I went downstairs.

Cousin Emmie was in her usual chair in a corner of the drawing-room, with the parasol on one side of her and the bag on the other.

"And so your husband came back all right?" she greeted me.

I would not have minded so much if she had said "got back", but the use of the active "came" seemed to imply her belief that Twice was only awaiting the right opportunity to run away from me for good.

"Yes. Two days sooner than we expected," I said rather pointedly.

"I see that that little girl is off with that young man Maclean in her car." She now contrived to convey that they had eloped, probably taking with them the Paradise pay-roll.

"Only round to the club, I suppose," I said.

"That young man is no good to that little girl."

"Nonsense! He is an ideal companion for her."

"I don't like him."

"Dee apparently does and so do I."

"I don't trust him."

"Why not?"

"There's more in that young man than people think and not what they think either."

"What do you mean?" I asked.

"Another thing I don't like," she went on, not replying to my question but changing the subject in her exasperating way, "is this party they are going to have at the end of Crop round at the club. It is a lot of nonsense. These negroes don't want parties. They would rather have the money it costs to buy fancy clothes and cheap jewellery. My cousin doesn't look facts in the face."

This was one of those truths which, at Paradise, we preferred to keep submerged, and this public airing of it did not make me like Cousin Emmie any better.

"Why do you distrust Roddy Maclean?" I asked as she helped herself to a piece of cake.

"I can't see to the bottom of him," she said in a sinister croak, and I would have pursued this further but that at that moment Sir Ian strode into the room.

"So here you are, Emmie! What the blazes you doin' round here again? Mother has six women at the house all waitin' for *you* so they can play bridge!"

"They can't play bridge," she said in her monotonous, unemphatic way that yet had its own deadly emphasis. She had not even jumped when Sir Ian came shouting in as I had done. "None of the people here can play bridge. If they played like that in Kensington I don't know what would happen."

"This ain't Kensington an' they call it bridge an' the car's outside."

Cousin Emmie got up, took a biscuit and popped it into the bag and took up her parasol. "I am ready," she announced like a shabby French aristocrat on the way to the tumbril and the guillotine.

Twice, on his way home, passed the car with Sir Ian and Cousin Emmie on his way across the park and came into the house laughing. "Was Sir Ian round here retrieving Cousin Emmie again?"

"Yes. Madame has a bridge party and she ran away round here. She is as much of an anxiety to the Dulacs as Dee is to us. . . . Did you remember to cash the house-keeping cheque?"

Twice nodded, opening the flapped breast-pocket of his shirt and taking out his wallet. "Except for going round to play chess with Cranston now and again, she doesn't go to any other house on the estate. I think that old dame must like you, Janet."

"I don't think she likes anybody much. I think it's because we were on the ship together. She would say that that makes a difference — she always sees differences where other people don't see them and not where they do if that is what I mean."

Twice, smiling, opened his wallet, but suddenly became rigid and frowned sharply. "Good God!" he said.

"What's wrong? Oh, Twice, you didn't forget about the cheque?"

I have always been the family banker because Twice has an active dislike of money, a dislike so strong that, in spite of his very good memory, it creates some kind of psychological action that makes him do what my father calls a "willing forget" about anything connected with it. "This is the vegetable woman's night and — "

"I didn't forget, darling, honestly! But the money's gone!"

"Twice, it couldn't get out of that buttoned pocket even if you were hanging upside-down!"

He dropped his eyelids and looked guilty.

"You've had your shirt off!" I said.

He looked more guilty still. Since his attacks of bronchitis, one in Scotland and one on board ship, I had been laying down the law about his habit of discarding his shirt at odd moments when he went into one of the hotter or messier parts of the factory, for he had a trick of forgetting to put it on again.

"Only for ten minutes when I went down under the boilers."

"Twice, I've told you till I'm sick that

we have a laundress and it doesn't matter if your shirt — "

"Twenty-five pounds, wasn't it?" he interrupted me. "Well, we've had it, chum. I'd heard there was pilfering going on in the office, but twenty-five quid is quite a bit."

"In the office? You left the shirt in the office?"

"Yes. On the hook behind the wash-room door." He suddenly stood up, turned his back to me and stared across the valley at the factory.

"Twice, what is it?"

"When I came out of there to go to the boilers," he said, "Roddy Maclean was coming in, on his way to the typists' tea session." He turned round. "He was good enough to stop me, ask me if I had had a good trip and assure me that Mackie was on duty in the power-house."

"But, Twice, do you realise how monstrous this is — this thing that you are implying?"

He turned away. "I don't trust that youth. I never have. There was never anything like this in that office until he joined the staff. Write another cheque and

I'll go up and cash it. The office will still be open."

When he had driven away I sat thinking about Roddy. It was rare for Twice to form a strong dislike for anyone or, indeed, for him to form a strong liking. This was partly why his attachment to Dee had been important to me because it had been an unusual thing, for as a rule Twice was one of those equable people with an ability to "get along" with nearly everybody without becoming deeply involved with anybody, quite unlike myself, who am always in a frenzy of enthusiasm for somebody or in an uneasy state of irritation with somebody as I was now with Cousin Emmie. Now, Cousin Emmie affected Twice not at all. He disliked her less than he had done on the ship, and now regarded her as more of an eccentric figure of comedy than anything. Nor was he affected by Dee, even, to the extent or in the same way that I was. When Dee was gloomy and miserable, I tended to become gloomy and miserable too, whereas Twice would do what he could to help her, and if he failed would become impatient and irritated, but she could not inoculate him

209

with her gloom and misery as she could me.

Only once before had I known Twice to take the kind of dislike he had for Roddy to anyone, and in the former case the dislike had been for a colleague called Pierre Robertson, who, in the end, turned out to be a petty criminal, and it was distressing that a similar pattern seemed to be taking shape in the case of Roddy Maclean, worse than distressing because Roddy was the son of a man well-known and much respected throughout the Caribbean, and, that apart, Roddy was much involved with Twice and myself through Dee. But between the case of Roddy and that of Pierre Robertson, however, there was a major difference, major in my eyes at least. In my relations with people I work largely by what I can only call intuition, and I had disliked Pierre Robertson in the first moment that I met him, whereas my first reaction to Roddy Maclean had been the very opposite of dislike.

However, Twice worked by logic and reason much more than by intuition, and I respected this. His attachment to Dee, even, had been formed on the practical basis that I had known her as a child, that she was unhappy and at odds with her family and that a few months with us in a different milieu might be of help to her. Meeting her in London, he had not looked at her as I would have done were I meeting her for the first time, as Dee Andrews, a fairly dull-looking and unattractive girl of not much interest. On a generous impulse of trying to help, Twice had approached her and had then become attached to her. I respected this logical and reasonable way that Twice had of going about things although I could not approach people in this way myself, so I began to try to think of Roddy in a manner detached from my intuitive liking for him.

Twice spoke the truth when he said that Roddy was unlike most engineers. This was the first thing I had to admit. Roddy had not about him the air of a scientist of any kind. In an age when people are growing standardised, when it is possible in the London subway, for instance, to look round at the passengers and divide them into "banker types", "saloon bar types" or "good husband and father types", it was difficult to fit Roddy into any category. It was difficult, even, to fit him in as the son of Rob and Marion Maclean, somehow, and difficult, too, to fit him into his own day and age. There was about him something archaic, something of a time when the world was younger and more adventurous, of the days when the Caribbean was richer in pirates than in engineers, and at the same time his air of gay, reckless courage gave him a forward-going feeling as if he would be the one to stride ahead of the rest of us into the future.

Another thing that I had to admit about Roddy was that he differed from the other young men who came to the house in that he came only when Twice was out, and very often when Dee was out too. Most of the young men who came to Guinea Corner were young engineers who came to sit at the feet of Twice. Without self-flattery, I had little doubt that Roddy came to talk to me; but, in spite of Twice's earlier suspicions, I was certain that Roddy had no interest in me of a male-female kind. Also, I now recognised, when he talked to me he differed from most people of his age that I had met in that he did not talk about himself. Indeed, one of the most attractive features I found in him was his genuine and vibrant interest in almost anything, be it the book I was reading, the letter from my father in Scotland, the embroidery I was working on or what Glasgow University had been like when I read English there twenty years ago. Roddy, I discovered now, was a past-master at the art of drawing one out, of making one talk, and this probably explained why Dee felt so comfortable in his company, while I, of course, found him a relief after some time spent in the company of the introspective Dee.

But in spite of all this calm logical examination of Roddy, I could not see him as a petty thief, creeping into the office wash-room and stealing the housekeeping money from Twice's wallet. I could visualise Roddy as the master-mind and action-leader in an attempt to rob the Bank of England, but I could not visualise him going through the pockets of odd garments left in lavatories.

When Twice came back with the twenty-five pounds, he handed the notes to me, and there was a tense silence between us for a few moments.

"Where is Dee?" he asked then.

"She and Roddy went off in her car. I suppose just round to the club."

"Janet, do you think she is fond of him?"

"I doubt if Dee can be fond of anybody, Twice. She seems to want to rely on people, have them there when she needs them but without her giving anything in return. I think the trouble is that she *can't* give anything. She does not seem to feel anything about anybody really — all her feeling is engaged with herself and, like the rest of us, she thinks that everybody is as she is. When you went away she did not seem to miss you and she could not imagine that I was missing you. She was unspeakably — well — inept."

"It may be a blessing she is like that. I'd hate her to get involved with that bloke."

"Twice, I simply cannot see that boy as a petty thief."

"Why not?"

"I can't explain it. Pilfering is too small for him somehow. If Roddy is going to sin, he'll do it on a grander scale."

Twice narrowed his eyes, frowning, looking into my face. If I respect his rationality and logic, he also respects these intuitions of mine.

"I agree with you," I said, "that there is something unusual about him. He isn't run of the mill, but I'd bet my Sunday boots he didn't steal that money."

"For Rob's sake, I hope he didn't, but I wish I felt as sure as you seem to do," Twice said.

7

"RELATIONSHIPS ARE ALWAYS COMPLICATED"

IN Crop or out, Twice and I always got up with the sun, which was about six o'clock in these early months of the year, and this was the best part of the day. Paradise, like all the upland valleys of the island, was subject to a heavy night dew which made the early morning cool and also gave them an almost sophisticated beauty as if, during the night hours, Nature had become discontented with her appearance and, rising in the morning, had put on every decoration of lace, coloured ribbon and jewel that she possessed. The red, pink and yellow rosettes of the hibiscus, with their long golden tassel of stamens, blazed between the dark-green velvet of their leaves; the pinky-mauve clusters on the Pandora vines swayed among their feathery leaves like ostrich plumes, and the orange and purple papery-textured flowers of the bougainvillaea rustled in the dawn breeze with the dry whisper of stiff silk. And all the spiders had left the results of their night's labours in great webs, some of them two feet in diameter, between the branches of the trees, some of them great looping festoons of fine thread that went from leaf to leaf and shrub to shrub. And, on top of all this, the dew had left a shower of jewels. The drops hung from every web and festoon, some like pearls, some catching the sunlight to become diamonds, and others taking on, too, the red and blue of the flowers to become rubies and sapphires among the millions of emeralds that were drops that had borrowed their colour from the leaves and the grass.

A little after six we had breakfast on the veranda, and on what I thought of as her "good" days Dee would join us, while on what I thought of as her "bad" days she would decide she was a nuisance, in the way, and that we did not want her, and would not appear downstairs until after Twice had gone out.

By the beginning of March, when she had been with us for well over two months, we had given up all attempts to argue her out of these attitudes of hers and had begun to take the days as they came, although, to be honest, I have to record that the "bad" ones, when she came down late and drooped about the house and garden picking at things, rendered it difficult for me to keep my temper below what, in engineering parlance, Twice called its flashpoint.

On this morning in early March, however, it seemed that we had a good day before us, for she appeared at the breakfast-table bright and pretty shortly after six and ate the meal with us, chatting of the goings-on at the club the night before, where Cousin Emmie, less than an hour after the lavish dinner at the Great House, had eaten four ham sandwiches and drunk a bottle of stout.

"She says you have to keep your strength up in these hot climates," Dee explained.

"Awful old woman," I said. "Dram, bring Charlie for his milk."

The dog and cat had just come back from their morning mongoose steeplechase through the sugar cane and Dram picked Charlie up from the lawn by the scruff of the neck, bore him to the veranda to the saucer, sat down and watched him lap with besotted pride as if Charlie were the only cat in the world endowed with this astounding ability to lap milk from a saucer.

"Cats!" said Twice sharply.

"Gr-r-r!" said Dram, springing up to stand guard over Charlie, every hair bristling while he looked about him for the hated enemy.

"None!" Twice said. "All gone! Sit down, you fool." Dram sat down and put on his besotted look again. "I wonder what, in the name of goodness, he thinks Charlie *is*?" Twice asked.

"Charlie is his well-beloved with whom he is well pleased, isn't he, Dram?" I said, and Dram wagged his tail.

"Twice," Dee said, "may I come up to the factory this afternoon? I want to watch the crystallisers."

"Not today, Dee. I'll be at the Bay office all the afternoon," said Twice, and, as if he were behaving in the most reasonable way in the world, he planted a kiss on my cheek, went down the steps into his car and drove away.

I am not, I think, a very nervous or timid woman, for, after all, I was in the Women's

219

Air Force during the 1939–45 war and did not have my buttons torn off for cowardice or anything, but I sat looking down at Dram and Charlie and felt Dee growing bigger and bigger and blacker and blacker and more and more frightening round the corner of the table to my left. Without words, after what seemed like the year between when you first hear the whistle of a bomb and hear the "ker-lump" as it hits the earth, she rose from the table and went away upstairs, but so slowly that I felt she had time to pick at the carpet on every tread with her toe-nails.

All morning, as I went to and fro about my household jobs, I felt that a black cloud was hovering at the top of the stairs and might come rolling down upon me at any moment, but no sound was heard, and at about eleven o'clock I came through from the kitchen and stood guiltily in the hall, feeling that I ought to go up to see Dee, but at the same time afraid that, if I did, I might lose my patience and make the situation worse than ever. Still feeling guilty, I turned towards the drawing-room, deciding to write a few letters instead, and as I went in the voice said:

"That Nurse Porter is round to have coffee with my cousin this morning," and there was Cousin Emmie, ensconced in her corner, with the bag and the parasol in position about her chair.

"Good-morning, Miss Morrison," I said and went back to the kitchen to ask for coffee to be brought in.

"I don't like to listen to my cousin and that nurse going on about illegitimate babies and syphilis," Cousin Emmie said, dipping a piece of shortbread into her coffee and sucking it with a sloshy noise.

It may be remembered that I indicated earlier, when telling of our shipboard days, that Cousin Emmie had something of a gift for silence, so that she could pay a visit lasting for about an hour in the course of which she could eat and drink a prodigious amount while making no more than three of her raven's croaks. On this morning, however, unlike Dee and as if to impress on me that life is full of variety, she seemed to be in an unusually chatty mood.

"My cousin is a fool," she told me, and then, after a conversational lull during which she ate half of a biscuit and put the other half in the bag, she continued: "My cousin thinks you can stop people having illegitimate babies and getting syphilis, but you can't."

There was another lull while I refilled her cup. "As long as there are men and women there will be illegitimate babies and syphilis," she said.

"Don't you believe in social advancement or the progress of medicine at all, then, Miss Morrison?"

"Oh, they'll advance as they call it," she said, answering a question for once. "There aren't so many people like the Borgias now and we don't have the Black Death, but there are people like my cousin and we have the atomic bomb and that's just as bad."

"Madame Dulac does a great deal of good among the people in the island and especially on the estate here, with doctor and nurse and the clinic and everything."

"No she doesn't," Cousin Emmie said flatly. "Not good. She calls it doing good, but she is only trying to get her own way. And she won't change anybody. People are as they are. I know them."

With this last sinister croak, she withdrew under the carapace of the felt hat by bending down her head and concentrating on a piece of cake, which she dismembered and ate raisin by raisin with a clicking of false teeth, and I sat on, fascinated, as if I were a rabbit in the presence of a weasel, until I nearly jumped out of my skin when Isobel Denholm walked into the room. I had not even heard her car come up the drive.

"Hi, Missis Janet," she said. " 'Morning, Miss Morrison. Is Dee around?"

"I think she is upstairs, Isobel."

"Work has started on the house up at Mount Melody. I thought maybe Dee would like to come up there with me."

"Perhaps she would. She must be writing letters or something. I'll call her."

"Don't you bother, Janet. I'll go up if that's okay. Which room?"

"First on the left at the top of the stairs," I said, gratitude welling in me like a mountain spring but tainted with some nervousness about Isobel's reception. However, after a few seconds I could sigh with relief, for I could hear Dee's voice, light and seemingly carefree, floating down the stairs, and soon they arrived in the room together.

"We're going up to Mount Melody, Miss Jan. Is that all right?"

"Of course, Dee, but it is nearly twelve. What about lunch?"

"I've got it in the car," Isobel said.

"Splendid. Off you go."

They went out, and Cousin Emmie, chewing her last raisin, reached for the bag and the parasol and rose to her feet.

"She is sensible, that big red-haired girl," she said. "She is better company for that silly little thing of yours than that man Maclean," and without further words she drifted out through the hall, across the veranda and down the steps, the draperies of her beige foulard hanging about her like bedraggled plumes.

During the afternoon I sang around the house and garden, so carefree was I now that Dee was employed and off my hands, and in the belief that Cousin Emmie, in the way that lightning never strikes in the same spot twice, would not call again that day, except that lightning is not at all an apt analogy for Cousin Emmie. There was in her something elemental, it is true, but nothing of the nature of lightning. She made me think more of some static yet mysteriously powerful force like the law of gravity which holds people to the earth even in the Antipodes, where they are hanging upside-down, for I have never been out of the northern hemisphere and this is the view I have of people in Australia.

Twice arrived home from St. Jago Bay about six o'clock and said: "Is Dee in?"

"As I indicated at lunch," I said, "you have a damned cheek to ask, after putting her into that Ishmael of a mood this morning. No. They are not back yet, or maybe she has gone down to the Peak with Isobel. Do you realise that this could be a break-through to peace between her and the Peak?"

"Never mind that now. Janet, a queer thing has happened." I looked hard at him. "Somerset has hired Roddy Maclean as his assistant. He starts in the office on Monday."

I sat down with a bump. "Mr. Alexander, this is so sudden!"

"Yes, isn't it? That's just what I thought."

"You hadn't an inkling of this before today?"

"Not the smell of an inkling. Of course,

225

Rob's been away in Jamaica this last week, but it seems to me that nobody here on Paradise had much inkling either. If they had, it would have been mentioned, don't you think?"

"One would think so. Twice, I don't suppose you like this very much, do you?"

"Well, I wouldn't have walked down the street and have picked Roddy Maclean to work in our office, but I would rather have him down there messing about with a few papers than up here messing about with those turbines, and I suppose the poor blighter has got to be somewhere. In Sir Ian's words, let's have a tot. I'll get them."

We sat on the veranda and stared out through the mesh screens at the rapidly falling darkness.

"Although I still think that some of your suspicions are quite unfounded," I said, "Roddy's way of going about this seems to me to be unnecessarily devious. I mean, why the secrecy?"

"Exactly. Somerset wasn't cagey at all, you know. He just said: 'By the way, you'll have heard —' quite airily and told me he had engaged him on six months' probabation. I knew he was looking for somebody who knew the basic difference between a wheel and a lever for the office, and he just came out with it in the natural course."

"What did you say?"

"I told him I hadn't heard, actually, but that I'd been crawling round the underworks of the factory here and hadn't been talking much to anybody. I don't think he realised I had been hit amidships. Somerset is pretty dumb that way."

"Well, I hope everything will be all right."

"There's one good thing. There is no currency lying about down there — everything is by cheque, even typists' screws. You know, when you think of it, it may be just the place for that youth. He is much more a collar-and-tie type than a greasy engineer, and Somerset obviously likes him."

"And what of you?"

"You know how seldom I am in that office. He is nothing to do with me. He is Somerset's pigeon, and as long as they keep some control between them on the tide of bumph that's rising round our ears down there I'll be quite happy. By the way, I'll have to go to Trinidad about the end of this month. There's a good few hundred thousand about to be spent down there on some bulk-loading plant and we have been asked to quote. It's a nuisance, but there it is."

"The first time is always the worst," I said. "We'll get by." But as I did not wish to think about the trip to Trinidad, I continued: "Have you contrived to inoculate Somerset with that cross-index filing system yet?"

Twice and I had first met in the office of an engineering works in Scotland in 1945, where I, as secretary, was responsible for what Twice called "the bumph", and he had been much impressed by the filing system that I had worked out to meet the specific demands of the firm. Lionel Somerset, the colleague who had recently been sent out from England to organise the newly-established office of Allied Plant Limited in St. Jago Bay, was a young man with no qualifications for the post, as far as Twice and I could see, other than that he was the son of one of the directors of the firm, had spent two years playing cricket without distinction at one of the older universities and had a social manner which led him, after meeting for the first time men of wealth or influence such as Sir Ian, to refer to them ever afterwards as: "Dulac of Paradise? Oh yes, a great friend of mine", and which led him to refer to Twice as: "Alexander, my oily wallah". Twice and I referred to the first form of reference as the conferring of the "GFOM" and to the second as "Somerset's subordinates", so that men like Sir Ian were "Sir Ian Dulac, GFOM", while Twice, ten acres of plant near Birmingham, with some three hundred acres of satellite plant scattered throughout Britain, and the Board of Directors of Allied Plant Limited were all referred to by Twice and me as "Somerset's subordinates". This, of course, was private parlance and we really got along very well with Somerset when we met him at cocktail parties and things.

During recent weeks, however, Twice had been worrying a little about the muddle in the office at St. Jago Bay, had described to me the nature of the enquiries which were flowing in in such numbers, and I had planned a filing system with which he was attempting to "inoculate" Somerset, or, in other words, Twice was attempting to persuade Somerset that the system was all Somerset's own idea and that the sooner it could be installed in St. Jago Bay, the less likelihood there would be of Allied Plant Limited going bankrupt.

"He announced today that he had accepted the system in principle," Twice replied to my question now.

"What does that mean?"

"It means that Somerset doesn't understand it, that it is too much effort to study it, but that as soon as his PA — short for Personal Assistant, meaning Roddy Maclean — starts work he will be instructed to implement it forthwith," said Twice.

"Roddy is to be known as his Personal Assistant?"

"So I gather."

"The things that bloke thinks of!" I took thought for a moment. "You know, Twice, Roddy Maclean is going to make rings round that poor Somerset."

"That had occurred to me. Roddy has already charmed him out of his back teeth practically," Twice said and laughed.

"You laugh? I thought you despised Roddy's charm?"

"Not at all. Charm is a bit like a loaded gun — one's opinion about it alters according to where it is pointed. When Roddy pointed his charm at me over his neglect of the turbines up at the factory, I began to think of some of the less refined holds in all-in wrestling, but when he points it at Somerset by reading through your instructions for that filing system and then saying: 'This is a marvellously organised system that you have worked out, sir', as I gather he did, my opinion alters completely. He absolutely convinced Somerset that the thing was all his own work although you and I know that Roddy knows that you worked it out. That means that he had the measure of Somerset inside half an hour."

I giggled. "Good for Roddy!"

"I simply don't know what to think about that youth," Twice said thoughtfully. "He has obviously got his head screwed on, as Sir Ian calls it. Somerset was near to raving about him. I suppose he was just misplaced up there in the power-house." He gave vent to one of his mischievous chuckles. "Somerset has a new word, by the way."

Like the Greeks, albeit I imagine that this was his sole resemblance to that classic race, no matter what the subject, Somerset had a word for it, but the thing that fascinated Twice and me about Somerset's words was that on many subjects of quite wide range he had only one word and made it suffice for all occasions. Thus, on any accountancy matter, Somerset said: "A mere question of a journal entry"; on any horsy matter he said: "She has a very nice action behind", regardless of the fact that sometimes the "she" happened to be a gelding, while on any political matter he always said in a secretive way: "They know at the top" as if to imply that he himself was included in the "they". These phrases were of endless delight to Twice and myself, so that, now, it was almost with held breath that I said: "No! What?"

"Constructively-minded!" Twice told me triumphantly. "It was about the new letter-headings — the samples he got were blue printed on brighter blue, and when I sort of objected — "

"In what words precisely did you sort of object ?" I asked.

"I asked him why he didn't have SWALK for 'Sealed with a Loving Kiss' printed on the backs of the envelopes while he was about it. It was then that he said I was too conservative and not constructively-minded, but I said, con-structively-minded or not, I preferred to write engineering stuff on white paper headed in black."

"And what paper are you having ?"

"White headed in black of course!" said Twice, as if I had asked some entirely unnecessary question.

"Pity. I think the blue on blue with a few forget-me-nots quoting for a sewage disposal plant would have looked very sweet."

"But, anyway, he says that Roddy is constructively-minded, so that should off-set me and my old-fashioned ideas."

We began to talk of other things, and Dee in particular, and suddenly, seemingly apropos of nothing, I said: "You know, Somerset was right about Roddy Maclean."

"Right ? In what way ?"

"With his constructively-minded. Oh,

I know it is a mere claptrap cliché with Somerset and means nothing, but accidentally it is true about Roddy. Do you remember that night when we had that hair-tearing row aboard the *Pandora*? And I kept saying Dee was destructive?"

"I'm not likely to forget it. I don't know what got into us that night, but go on."

"I can't," I said. "I don't know what I am trying to say, really. But Dee strikes me as being against — well, life, I suppose — *de*structive; and Roddy strikes me as being *for* it, on the side of life, *con*structive."

"He is certainly for it if the look in his eye at the typists' tea-session is anything to go by," Twice said.

"Do the office girls like him?"

"Like isn't quite the word. When he comes into the office, I always expect a serpent to wriggle in through the air-conditioner wearing an ugly leer and with the apple of discord hanging from its fangs."

"I know what you mean."

"I know you do," Twice assured me.

"If the girls didn't like him, they wouldn't be normal," I said defiantly. "In fact, everybody likes him except you and Cousin Emmie. What company you choose!"

"It's in the power-house I dislike him and nothing to do with Cousin Emmie. And, anyway, he is not all that universally popular. Isobel Denholm doesn't like him either."

"That's probably sour grapes. Roddy doesn't like red hair," I said.

"Never mind. Yours is getting greyer every day."

"But seriously, Twice, Roddy going into the office down there is not going to worry you?"

"No." He frowned. "But I wish it were easier to know what one thinks about people. Such a little thing can tip the scales. Up there in the power-house, when Roddy neglected those turbines that day, I was prepared to believe that nothing was too low for him. I suppose it is absurd, but that is really how I came to connect him with the pilfering."

"It is absurd. Extremism is always prone to the absurd and you are an engineering extremist. We agreed about that long ago."

"Then, today, when I heard how he

had bent Somerset so beautifully and painlessly to his will, the pendulum swung the other way."

"It really boils down to the fact that you like turbines and don't want them bent and you don't like Somerset and would like to see him bent into a figure eight," I said: "and in the light of turbines you don't like Roddy and in the light of Somerset you do."

"Complicated, isn't it?"

"Relationships are always complicated. And the corollary of the whole theorem is that you like turbines better than Roddy and you like Roddy better than Somerset."

"That's not saying much. I like most things and people better than Somerset."

"And I like Roddy better than turbines," I said.

"I like *you* better than turbines," said Twice.

"And I like *you* better than Roddy," and at this we began to laugh, for, on the whole, Twice and I find a great deal to laugh at although lots of other people would not consider that great deal to amount to very much. Dee was one of those other people, for she now came in while we were laughing and, of course, said: "What are you laughing at?"

If you are one of two people who has been laughing at, with and to one another, it is very difficult to explain to a third person just what you were laughing at, so I answered feebly: "Oh, nothing much, Dee."

"I suppose you were telling Twice about me being in a temper this morning about not going to the factory?" she accused me, glowering at us.

I at once had an urge to rush upstairs and lock myself in the bathroom, but before I could move or speak, Twice said: "Dee, I gather you have been out with Isobel being absolutely bloody about Janet and me all day, jeering and laughing about us until your heads nearly fell off!" and he glowered back at her, his face an absurd parody of her own with its sullen brows and pouting lower lip. For a long second she stared at him startled before saying gravely: "Oh, Twice, who told you that? Honestly, Isobel and I didn't — " I found it frightening that she was what I can only call so far out of human touch that she could not at once see that Twice was not being himself but a parody of *her*self. She paused, looking from one of us to the other, the suspicion growing in her eyes that he was not to be taken seriously, and her voice trembled as she then said: "Oh, I see. I'm sorry."

"So well you might be," Twice told her. "As a matter of fact, Janet did tell me you spent half the morning sulking, and it's damn' silly of you, too silly to laugh at even."

Her lip began to tremble and tears to gather in her eyes.

"Janet didn't tell me about it so that we could laugh. She told me by way of persuading me to take you up to the factory as soon as I could, and as soon as I can I will take you."

Listening, I began to feel sorry for Dee, who stood there with the tears beginning to flow now. I felt sorry for her as one feels sorry for the insect in the path of the road roller, for Twice seemed to me to be deploying far more force than the occasion demanded.

"I'm sorry," she quavered at him.

"You are not a damned bit sorry," he

told her, "except for yourself, Dee, and it's not good enough. . . . Where are you going?"

"Upstairs."

"Then be down for dinner in half an hour and looking pleasant."

She stared at him while he stared back at her, while I gripped my hands together in my lap, looked down at them and let Twice and Dee stare one another out.

"Twice, would you like me to go away back to England?" she asked.

"No, I should hate that, Dee. It would mean that you, Janet and I have failed to get on together, and I don't like to fail, especially at getting on with people I like."

She was sobbing now. "What do you want me to do?"

"Nothing except try to look past yourself and straight at other people and then you may see that Janet and I aren't complete hypocrites."

"But I didn't say you were, Twice!"

"You implied it and it's extremely insulting."

"I hadn't thought of it like that, Twice. I just thought — " She paused.

"You just thought about nothing but

239

Dee Andrews, isn't that it?" She hung her head. "It's a lousy bad habit," Twice told her. "I'd get even more miserable than you if I thought about nothing but me all the time, for I feel I would be even worse thinking matter. Stop crying, Dee. Run upstairs and get ready for dinner."

As soon as she had gone, I said: "But, Twice, you were terribly rough on her! You were like a steamroller going over a fly."

"Yes, maybe, but all that has happened is that the fly has gone into the crevice in the road for a bit and will emerge in due course as large as life and twice as ugly. You said earlier that relationships are complicated, but this one with Dee is a Chinese puzzle. In spite of everything, I still want to get her sorted out, but I'm afraid only she herself can do it. It's rot to think that anything we can do or say will make any difference."

However, from my point of view, the fly that was Dee's touchiness was better hidden in a crevice in the road than flaunting itself all the time on my sight, for, as I had said to Roddy on board the ship, maggots that I cannot exterminate

240

are more bearable if hidden from me, and for quite a time after Twice's outburst Dee had at least the appearance of more equable temper. She and Isobel spent a lot of time at Mount Melody, frequently ending their day at the club or down at the Peak, so that when Roddy left Paradise for his new post in the Bay Dee did not miss him as much as I had at first feared that she might.

On the last Saturday evening that Roddy spent at Paradise, Dee came home from Mount Melody at about six o'clock, and I said: "Why didn't you bring Isobel to dinner? Isn't she going to the Club Dance tonight?"

"Yes, but she had to go down to the Peak to dine with some kitchen-equipment-selling man and she is coming up again afterwards. We have been at the club until now."

"Many people there?" Twice asked.

"Not many. Roddy and the Cranstons and Vickers, and Nurse Porter was there but not for fun. Joe the barman cut his hand on a beer bottle yesterday and she came to give him a scolding for not going to the clinic to get it dressed again today. She is a nice sort of person, isn't she, Miss Jan?"

"Very nice," I agreed, although I felt that this was hardly an adequate description of the redoubtable Nurse Porter.

She was not at all redoubtable in appearance, but this was deceptive. She was a charming young St. Jagoan of half-African, half-East Indian blood which gave her the fine Aryan bones of the latter and the large liquid brown eyes and fluid voice of the former, but she became very redoubtable indeed against the background of the clean white concrete clinic where she held sway, doing, with equal calm, anything from stitching up cutlass wounds to setting broken bones or extracting bougainvillaea thorns from the large pads of Dram. The estate also maintained a doctor, but one of Nurse Porter's favourite phrases was: "Tchah! We won't bother Doctor with *that*!" whereupon she would set to work. Every day of the week was programmed for specific treatments, and every Saturday morning the door of the clinic was closed for an hour while Nurse Porter went to the Great House to make her weekly report to Madame, and in this hour Madame caught up with all the news of her coloured employees as well as their medical situation. "Mr. Cranston was talking about this pilfering that is going on in the office, Twice," Dee said next in the manner she adopted when she spoke of the technicalities of sugar-processing, as if she were embarking on a subject of which I knew nothing and expected me to maintain a well-bred silence in the presence of my more knowledgeable betters. Now, although it may not be my place to say it, I am extremely good, unlikely as this may seem, at maintaining silence when it pleases me, although I will not go so far as to say that it is a well-bred silence. Indeed, I think I am silent only when I have the hope that by listening to other people I may learn something that I want to know, and now, as I stared vacantly in front of me, Twice's glance moved over my impassive face before he looked at Dee and said: "Oh?"

"Whoever is doing it got away with the badminton money out of Miss Freeman's desk today," Dee told him. "Eleven pounds fifteen it was." She became suddenly censorious. "Roddy is quite awful sometimes, Twice."

I felt myself grow tense as Roddy's name came so patly behind the news of the fresh pilferage, and Twice was looking at me as he asked: "Awful in what way?"

"When Mr. Cranston was wondering who the pilferer could be, Roddy said it was probably Cousin Emmie!"

This was too much for me, and my solemn demeanour gave way before a gust of laughter which caused Dee to look at me not entirely pleased and ask solemnly: "Did you know there was pilfering going on at the office then?"

Ever since the loss of the housekeeping money had been reported to Sir Ian, Twice had been carrying a marked five-pound note in his shirt pocket in common with most of the other members of the staff, but I was not going to reduce Dee's thunder to a fire-cracker by mentioning this.

"No, I didn't know," I told her, "but I was laughing at Roddy's suggestion about Cousin Emmie."

"I don't think it was very funny of him," Dee said disapprovingly. "Do you think it funny, Twice?"

Twice smiled a little. "I think the absolutely unlikely is always a little funny, Dee," he said.

"Unlikely or not, I don't think Roddy should have said it," Dee said, glowering at us. "It might make people start to think things about Cousin Emmie, people like Mrs. Cranston. I mean, people can very easily be made to think things about people."

"Yes, that's true," I said, looking at Twice. "Relationships between people are always complicated, and quite silly remarks can matter, but I don't think what Roddy said will matter in the case of Cousin Emmie, Dee. That she should pinch the badminton money is too absolutely unlikely altogether."

"I still think that Roddy shouldn't have said it," Dee persisted in her sullen censorious way.

After dinner was over and she had gone back round to the Club Dance, Twice looked up from his book and said: "I wish I knew what to think about that young devil Maclean."

"Me too," I said, "but what brought him into your head just now?"

"It's that crack about Cousin Emmie.

245

It is exactly the sort of thing *you* would say."

"I ?" I frowned at him. "What in the world can you mean ?"

"It is," he assured me. "I can imagine the talk round the table at the club and you suddenly saying it was probably Cousin Emmie who took the badminton cash. It's not the remark of someone trying to divert suspicion from himself to someone else — it's the attitude of someone like you who loathes petty pilferage and escapes out of even talk of it into absolute nonsense."

"I've always said the odd few pounds in desk drawers and pockets was too petty for Roddy," I told him.

"I know, but there is still something odd about that bloke. Oh, well, we'll see how things go at the office in the Bay."

There was an awkwardness of silence about Roddy's departure for his new post, an awkwardness which I felt more keenly, perhaps, than I had any justification for feeling it, but, none the less, I was disappointed that, from the time that Twice told me of the projected move until Roddy left Paradise, he did not come to see me.

It seemed to me that we had been good enough friends for him to come and tell me personally of his new plans, and, in my foolish way, I was hurt that he avoided the house and then left Paradise without calling to see me.

It was Rob, Twice told me, who had informed Sir Ian that his son had taken this new post at the Allied Plant office, but between Rob and Twice themselves there was a constraint of silence about the boy. Shortly after Roddy's departure Twice went on his trip to Trinidad, and when he returned to Paradise Rob behaved as if Roddy had never been in the employ of the Estate and as if he was not now in the service of a firm with which Twice had any connection. It would have been natural, Twice felt, if Rob had enquired how the boy was shaping in his new post, but Rob did not mention the subject, and Twice, consequently, did not mention it either, but he felt a little hurt and mystified, just as I did, when Marion Maclean made no mention of her son to me either, although she knew that I was interested in the boy and he had spent a fair amount of time with me.

When I was alone in the house I thought a great deal about Roddy; and the more I thought of him, the more uneasy I became. Twice is very fond of saying that I go about with my head in the clouds and my feet never quite on the ground, but I do not think this is true, or maybe it is that, just as everybody is different in every other way, so do all people have different clouds for their heads and different ground for their feet. Be that as it may, it seemed to me that nobody at Paradise other than myself was at all astonished at the fact that Roddy had established himself in a bungalow at the Bay complete with cook and houseboy, or at the fact that from four in the afternoon onwards, after he had left the office, he seemed to spend all his time gambling in Sloppy Dick's bar or at the expensive Peak Hotel, pursuing a way of life to which his salary from Allied Plant could not possibly aspire.

Twice was inclined to the view that Roddy was an unusually lucky gambler who might also pilfer a few pounds as and when required, so that after one or two near-quarrels we had ceased to discuss the subject, for I had to concede that when

Roddy left Paradise the pilfering at the office stopped immediately and I can never make a concession that I do not like to make without at the same time losing my temper. Dee, although unusually acute about financial matters, was in a country with whose cost-of-living index she was not acquainted, and, of course, she probably thought that Roddy was in receipt of a generous allowance from his parents as she herself had been until she inherited her fortune from her Uncle Archie. But I thought I knew Rob and Marion Maclean well enough to be certain that, now that they had educated their son, he would be expected to stand on his own feet, for Rob and Marion were people of a background similar to my own and it seemed reasonable that they would have the attitudes normal to that background and its tradition.

In a very short time Roddy as a personality retired from the forefront of life at Paradise, partly by his own volition, for he did not come up from town to visit us, and partly because it was more convenient for us all not to mention him. On one occasion, about four weeks after he had left Paradise, there was a minor flare-up between Twice and myself because Twice came home and reported that he had seen Roddy emerge from one of the cafés in Victoria Court, which was the main brothel area of the town, and on another occasion there was some speculation between us when Twice, as if paying duty tribute to the goddess of fair play, told me that Roddy was doing tactful wonders in the organisation of the St. Jago Bay office in the teeth of the inefficient yet position-conscious Somerset, but that was all. From every point of view Roddy might never have come to Paradise and might never have left it so suddenly and secretively.

8

SHIPS PASSING IN THE SUNLIGHT

A T Easter it was traditional to stop work at about midday on Maunday Thursday and not resume until six o'clock the following Tuesday morning. This was the only time during Crop that the factory was deliberately closed down and processing suspended. A "shutdown" for mechanical, weather or other reasons was regarded as a tragedy, but the voluntary "shutdown" for Easter was hailed by everyone as a junketing half-time interval in the hard monotonous work of Crop. And this year it was a particularly joyous pause, for even Rob Maclean and Twice could not think of any part of the equipment that was working badly and would have to be put right during the short holiday period.

At Easter, in St. Jago Bay, the Yacht Club held its annual regatta and every young man and most of the young women had appointments to "crew" in one or another of the yachts, so that Mackie and the other young engineers and chemists all left Paradise on Thursday evening to put in some practice before the regatta on Easter Monday, and the rest of us looked forward to a few days of non-routine, crowned by the regatta as a finale to the holiday. Dee had been invited to sail in the Peak Hotel yacht *Amaryllis*, which was skippered by Don and had Roddy, Isobel Denholm and young Mackie as her crew, but Dee preferred not to go, and Twice and I did not press her, for she was not a strong swimmer and, in the words of Cousin Emmie, "anything might happen" in a sea where a squall can come up with the sudden viciousness of a tiger's paw. Nevertheless, in the contrary way of human nature — or human nature as manifested in me, at least — although I was relieved that she was not sailing. I was annoyed at the reason for the non-sailing.

"They don't really want me," she said, her lips tight, at breakfast on the morning of Maunday Thursday. "They only asked me to be polite and because of you and Twice and things. I shouldn't be any use, and four is all they need. Five is too many."

"Nonsense!" Twice said. "There is nothing all that real and earnest about the racing — it's just a nice day's sailing, that's all."

"Well, anyway, I don't want to go in *Amaryllis*."

"All right, Dee," I said. "You don't have to go if you don't want to. Is Roddy a keen yachtsman? I know that Don and Isobel and Mackie are."

"Roddy can do a bit at most things," she said. "He is a very good joiner-in. He wanted me to go. He was very nice about it."

Twice and I made no comment, and after a moment she went on: "But I said I wouldn't." She looked from one of us to the other. "I didn't make a fuss or tell him and Don and the others that they didn't really want me or anything. I just said I'd be too nervous to be of any use."

She now had an apologetic air, as if she were begging us to understand that although she felt unwanted she was trying, for our sakes, not to make a parade of it in the local community. She was exasperating and, at the same time, pathetic.

After breakfast Twice went up to the factory office, and Dee went off somewhere with Sandy Maclean, whose Easter vacation from lessons had now begun, and when I came out of the kitchen in the middle of the forenoon Cousin Emmie was depositing her bag and parasol by the chair in the corner of the veranda, and without preamble she said: "Are you going to this regatta on Monday?"

"Yes," I said, my voice sounding defiant even to myself. "I'm looking forward to it. I missed it last year because there was trouble at the factory and Twice was working over the Easter weekend. Are you going?"

"I don't want to, but I'll have to go now if you are going because my cousin is going, and the servants are getting a holiday and there will be no food."

"I am sure you will enjoy it once you are there. The yachts have coloured sails and it is all very gay and beautiful."

"I don't like yachts. Miss Murgatroyd's cousin was drowned off a yacht at Cowes. I don't like the Peak Hotel either. I don't like that man de Marnay."

This, of course, raised my hackles, for

Sashie is a special friend of mine. Indeed, he has my equivalent of Somerset's GFOM and a great deal more. "Why don't you like him?" I demanded.

"He is a foreigner and he looks as if his legs were one person and he were another," said Cousin Emmie and took a large bite of scone.

I was flabbergasted and also infuriated that this silly-looking old woman should have come so close to — should have arrived at the very essence, indeed — of Sashie's complexly guarded secret.

"He and his legs are all one person!" I snapped.

"They don't look it," she said and took another bite of scone.

We were sitting in a hostile silence when Dee came back with Sandy, stopped her car at the bottom of the steps, and, with a look at me that almost spoke aloud the words: "I am trying to be a good girl and a great help to you," invited Cousin Emmie to go for a drive.

"No," she said. "I am all right where I am."

In Dee's suddenly sulky little face I thought I could read a world of meaning —

the feeling that she liked Cousin Emmie and I did not, and yet in an unjust way Cousin Emmie preferred to stay with me instead of going with her for a drive and a hundred other things — and for the millionth time I wondered with exasperation why human nature has to be so complex.

"Are you going down to the Peak to swim?" I asked Dee, but it was Sandy who answered: "No, Missis Janet. We're goin' up to Mount Melody to see Miss Isobel."

I turned to Cousin Emmie: "Have you ever been to Mount Melody? It is a most interesting old house."

"I've seen it," she said. "That Denholm girl has sense turning it into a hotel. It's not fit for anything else except perhaps a lunatic asylum."

Mentally I shrugged my shoulders and watched Dee and Sandy drive away.

There was a silence until the car was out of sight, and then: "That girl made a great mistake bringing that car out here — a great mistake," said Cousin Emmie.

"In what way? She is a first-class driver — even Twice can sit beside her without squirming. Young people here wouldn't have much fun without some form of transport."

"It gives things away," she said, pursuing her own train of thought as she always did.

"Gives what away?"

"It lets them know she is wealthy — a car like that."

"Who?"

"The men," said Cousin Emmie, her voice low and sinister. "I don't approve of young women being wealthy. It puts them in a difficult position. You never know what might happen."

"Then I don't agree with you," I said. "When I was young I had nothing but the small salary I earned and that wasn't much fun. I like to see young people having a good — "

"Aha," she interrupted me on a particularly raven-like note, "but you got married to a fine hard-working man. If you'd had a fortune, some adventurer would have got hold of you. I know them."

"Oh, nonsense! Any intelligent young woman would — "

Staring past me at nothing at all, she interrupted me again: "Intelligence doesn't come into it. Young girls just get led away into ways they don't want to go. I know them."

I could think of nothing to say so we sat more or less in silence until Twice came home for lunch, fortunately very early, and drove Cousin Emmie back to the Great House.

"Darling, she *is* just about the end!" he said when he came back.

"What did she say to you?"

"She said she was very disappointed to learn that you were going to this regatta, that she thought you had more sense. Janet, I think in her grudging way that old woman must be fond of you."

"Well, I am not fond of her! Besides, she isn't fond of me or of anybody else. She is just annoyed she can't come here for lunch on Monday, that's all. I think myself it's *you* she likes — she said you were a fine hard-working man."

"Cheeky old cow," said Twice.

About ten o'clock on Monday morning every car on Paradise except that of the Yates streamed out of the south gates on the way to the regatta, with Cousin Emmie sitting beside Madame in the Rolls, her face wooden both in colour and expression.

The pregnant Dorothy Yates did not feel like the long day in the Bay and she and her husband had volunteered to look after the younger Compound children who were being left behind in the charge of their nurses, but Sandy Maclean was in the Bay party, regarding this regatta day as an opportunity for a longer swim than usual from the Peak beach.

The Peak Hotel had formerly been the Great House of an estate that specialised in the raising of cattle and polo ponies and whose lands had covered much of what was now the fashionable new hotel district of the Bay as well as the flat coastal plain which was now the airport. The Peak House, now the main building of the hotel, stood on the summit of a cliff promontory, on the west of which lay a wide bay with the commercial port and the old town, and to the east of the promontory was a smaller bay which was the yacht harbour. The Yacht Club buildings were tucked into the bottom of the cliff below the hotel, and it was possible to descend, by winding paths through the hotel garden, to the gate in the high fence that led into the back yard of the Yacht Club.

Sir Ian was a senior member of the Yacht Club in much the same way that he was a member of the Chamber of Commerce, a Justice of the Peace, an important voice in the Jockey Club and Custos Rotolorum of our parish, and today he was wearing what he called his "sea-goin'" hat, and in a very genial frame of mind as he inspected Sashie's and Don's arrangements for the Paradise party which consisted of a long table under a row of sun umbrellas and a row of chairs as close to the railed seaward edge of the cliff as was safe. The position on the northward curve of the cliff was a little like the prow of a ship and became very much more so when Madame selected the centre chair, a straight-backed one provided by the thoughtful Sashie, for Madame never lounged, arranged herself quite upright and looked out to the far horizon where the blue sky met the bluer Caribbean.

"Figurehead!" Twice whispered to me.

"Very nice indeed, Mr. Sashie, thank you," Madame now announced. "And a splendid day for the regatta, not too hot and the breeze not too strong."

"We did our best, Madame, my sweet," said Sashie.

She looked him firmly in the eye and he looked as firmly back at her, his expression a mixture of mischief and deference.

"Marion," she said next, "come and sit by me, please. Janet, you on this side and keep in the shade. I suppose you young people are going down to the beach? That's right. And when you are called to lunch, come at once. Mr. Sashie and Mr. Don have a great deal on their hands today and have no time for dawdlers. Emmie, sit down and don't stand there like a wooden image!"

Madame now looked about her, appeared satisfied with her dispositions and turned to her son. "Very well, Ian, when are you going to begin?"

"Regatta began ten hours ago, Mother, when the big boats went off on the Round-the-Island race."

"I know that perfectly well, Ian. I have been to regattas here before you were born. As you know perfectly well, what I wish to know is when is the race that our Mr. Mackie and Roddy and the others are sailing in?"

"Our class isn't until after lunch, Madame," Don said.

"Oh. In that case, we shall all have a cool drink," said Madame, and, standing up, she began to turn her chair round to face the table instead of the sea. Rob Maclean arranged it to her liking and she sat down again. "Ian, attend to the drinks, please." As far as Madame was concerned the regatta did not begin until after lunch, and very soon, having called to the table every acquaintance that passed — and she knew all the Europeans in the island — she was presiding at a morning drinks party that might as well be taking place at Paradise.

Dee stayed beside me, by years the youngest person at the table, for all the others of her age were involved in some way in the sailing. I was conscious of her there, in the party but not of it, but I had no time to devote to her, for on a day like this Marion Maclean and I were more or less in the capacity of ladies-in-waiting to Madame. Madame invited everybody who passed to sit down and have a drink, but beyond that she did not lift a finger. Sir Ian had his duties as a member of the Yacht

Club Committee; Twice and Rob had disappeared with a group of acquaintances, and Marion and I were kept busy. As I dispensed drinks and chatted to plantation wives, business men's wives and the wives of government officials, I was conscious all the time of Dee, a silent withdrawn presence, and although I introduced her here and there and did my best to include her, her conversation did not pass the initial "How d'ye do" with anyone.

After about an hour, when there seemed to be a lull in Madame's informal party, I withdrew from the table and made for Sashie's bedroom to wash my hands and have a quiet cigarette in peace, and I did not invite Dee to come with me. I was just coming out of Sashie's bathroom when he himself arrived, followed by a waiter with a tray on which stood a brown teapot and two cups.

"Tea!" I said. "Sashie, you are a pet! I just came in here to get away from the tomato juice and orange juice and all the sticky mess."

"So I felt, darling. Sit down. You look worn out already. Is it the heat? Do you feel unwell?"

263

"No, Sashie, I'm all right. Sashie, it's Dee!" I burst out. "She is sitting on my spirits like a leaden weight. She is out there and she won't take part in anything. What the devil is the matter with her?"

Sashie poured tea, looking down at the pot. His face was closed and inscrutable, and I had another surge against Dee because it seemed that she was driving a wedge between my friend Sashie and me, causing a disruption in our relationship as she had caused a disruption between Twice and myself in the early days on board the ship.

"I have never been so defeated by anybody as I am by that girl!" I said angrily.

"Not even Cousin Emmie or young Maclean?" he asked mischievously, looking up for a moment from the tea he was stirring.

"I don't have to live with Cousin Emmie or Roddy Maclean!"

"True." Sashie returned his whole attention to the tea-cup, and there was a prolonged silence until I said pleadingly: "Sashie, you are smarter about people than most. What do you think about Dee, really?"

"Thank you for these words of praise." He looked away out across the crowded lawn. "If I knew what I thought, my sweet, I should give tongue, being always ready to assist my chums in any way I can, but, like you, I have never been so defeated. And then there is something that is a little unusual about it all — unusual for me, I mean." He paused for a moment before he said: "I really dislike the child more than I can say." He turned to me with his self-mocking smile. "I am seldom affected by real dislike of people, so uncomfortable and generally unhelpful."

"What is it in her that you particularly dislike?"

"That is the annoying thing, my sweet. I do not really know. She makes me feel uncomfortable, which is probably reason enough for disliking her. The world is uncomfortable enough without people like Dee in it."

"Uncomfortable in what way?"

He wriggled his slim shoulders. "As if I were in the presence of an anachronism, rather. It is this thing she has of wanting to be all-in-all to someone and yet having no aptitude to achieve what she wants. She

265

has been born in the wrong time or the wrong milieu perhaps. If she had been born in the Middle Ages, she would have become a nun — had a vocation, you know. A vocation, in a way, is merely a conviction that one is of supreme importance — is all-in-all to the Almighty, a conviction that for some specific purpose God cannot get along without one's services. Born in a different milieu, she might have chosen to work in service to humanity — missionary work or nursing spring to the mind and she would have been a devoted member of some sisterhood and have ended up sharing a flat with her friend Jonesy that she had trained with and they would have all sorts of little private jokes of their own and be all-in-all to one another."

"Like Cousin Emmie and Miss Murgatroyd!" I said, as if a great white light were breaking over my mind, as indeed from my point of view it seemed to be.

"Who *can* Miss Murgatroyd be?"

"Cousin Emmie's friend that she shared a flat with, but never mind that now. Sashie, I believe you've got something. When Twice goes away and Dee and I are alone in the house, she is quite different. There are none of these moods and nonsense. Sashie, you *are* clever."

"I wouldn't say that, my sweet. Besides, even if one is right in what one thinks, it is a little pointless. There is nothing much one can do to bring her over to the side of life, for I think that is what one dislikes so — her air of being against the main flow, as it were. She ought to be doing a job of some sort with her temperament, preferably in business of some kind. She has a good brain in that way — she has twice the acumen of Isobel, for instance."

"She probably inherited that. Her people have been in the money-making racket for generations."

Sashie laughed. "Darling, I adore your scornful attitude to big business. So rare and refreshing."

"I am not scornful of it exactly," I said and then added: "or maybe I am. After all, what's the good of all the big business and wealth if you are in a muddle like Dee? At her age I never had a penny, but I was never as damn' miserable as she is. Well, thank you for the tea, my pet. I suppose I'd better go back to the tomato juice."

"The gin will soon be coming up,

darling. It's after twelve. Gin isn't so sticky. I'll come out with you. I can possibly be of temporary help with Dee, anyhow."

"How ?"

"I'll get her into the wine store. I am not being self-sacrificial, my sweet. Don and Isobel have nothing in their heads but sailing today and I could do with Dee's help."

"That is if she will oblige," I said doubtfully.

"Darling, next to being all-in-all to somebody, Dee likes to make money, and money is positively minting itself in the bars today," and as we emerged into the crowded patio bar this was obviously true.

When we reached Madame's table Sashie's approach to Dee was absolutely direct in the light of what he had said about her character.

"Dee, darling, I hate to do this on regatta day, but *do* you think you could give me an hour in the wine store ? Even if you only do lunchtime ? Don and Isobel have nothing in their heads but bowsprits and foresails, and we are losing money hand over fist because I can't keep the bars supplied."

Her face brightened for the first time

that day. "Oh, Miss Jan, do let me! I'm just in the way here really." She looked along the chattering table. "Miss Jan, let me help Sashie. I'd like to. I think these yachts are just a bore!"

"Just little ships passing in the sunlight," said Sashie mischievously, but Dee was too busy trying to overcome my imagined disapproval to notice this.

"Goodness, if you'd like to spend your day like that, Dee, off you go, but don't let Sashie slave-drive you!"

"Oh, nonsense!" she said, and, light of foot and face, a different person from the sullen lump who had stood beside me all the morning, she went off with Sashie up the lawn.

Much lighter at heart, I returned to my duties at Madame's side.

"Darling," said Twice, coming up behind me when I was alone for a moment, "have you any money on you? I've ordered some drinks for a few people and I've got nothing but that marked fiver."

"But, Twice, I put money beside your hairbrush this morning!"

"I know but I came away without it."

"You are a pest!" I opened my handbag.

"I've got nothing but this fiver, but here you are. And put it in your wallet. If you lose it, you'll have to scrounge your drinks for the rest of the day like Martha's aunt!"

He took out his wallet and, suddenly becoming still, he swallowed jerkily and noisily. I looked at him.

"The marked fiver's gone," he whispered.

I got up and we both moved away from the table and, involuntarily, we both looked down at the Yacht Club slipway where Roddy, Don and a group of yachtsmen were gathered.

"When did you check it last?" I asked.

The note had lain undisturbed for so long that we had become careless, no longer bothering to look in the wallet each evening as we had done for the first day or two after the theft of the housekeeping money.

"I don't know. Wait a minute. It was there last Tuesday when I tested that diesel locomotive after the railwayman was killed. The police had to see that I was licensed to drive a locomotive and the fiver was there when I showed them my licence. Since then I haven't looked."

"But, Twice, it couldn't have gone today. You haven't had your shirt off here!"

"He was up at the office on Thursday morning to arrange with Mackie about the sailing," he said, looking down at the slip-way.

"You had your shirt off?"

"I took it off to have a wash and they called me to the telephone."

We both went on staring down at the Yacht Club, and then my gaze shifted to Marion where she sat still, calm and digni-fied beside Madame. "Oh well, darling, this isn't the place to talk about it. Let's forget it for now. You had better go back to your chaps — they will be thinking you've welshed and left them with the bill."

"Don't let it spoil your day."

"It won't do that."

But it did, of course. The colours of the sky, sea and yacht sails seemed to be less brilliant, the people seemed less carefree, the brightness had fallen from the air.

After lunch, Miss Poynter, who had owned the Peak House before Sashie and Don bought it to turn it into a hotel, took Madame, who was an old friend of hers, and Cousin Emmie away to her little house in the grounds to have a rest from the sun and glare and also a good gossip. Isobel Denholm, who was now occupying one of the tourist bungalows in the grounds, had made the Paradise party free of its facilities for the day and we also had the use of Don's and Sashie's bedrooms. I naturally gravitated to Sashie's bedroom again and stayed there for quite a long time, he and Dee buzzing in and out in the course of their duties.

Shortly after lunch I had seen the start of the race that Don's *Amaryllis* was sailing in, and very beautiful she had looked, with her black hull and flame-coloured sails, with the magnificent Don wearing nothing but swimming trunks and the red-haired Isobel in a brilliant jade-green bathing dress, looking like two creatures come forward through time from the dawn of the world when all was flawless. Roddy Maclean and young Mackie were also fine-looking boys, but no male had a chance of drawing a glance when Don was about, especially in a near-naked state, and, in any case, I had no wish to look at Roddy Maclean.

I watched the launches go out towards the buoys that were the check-points, I watched the coloured butterflies of yachts get under way, and then retired to Sashie's bedroom where Twice would fetch me in time to see the finish.

"So wise of you, darling," Sashie said as the afternoon wore on. "By the time the evening is over, we'll all be stretcher cases."

"How is Dee, Sashie?"

"In splendid form and being a marvellous help. All the bars are pulling it in like crazy and not a bottle unaccounted for. When the bars get out of hand the whole place goes mad."

Dee now arrived, her wine store keys tied firmly to the shoulder-strap of her playsuit. "Badge of office," she said, flicking them at me. "Having a nice day, Miss Jan?"

"Yes, thank you. And you?"

"Simply splendid! We are really in business today, aren't we, Sashie? I've sold all twenty-three bottles of that doubtful champagne now. There's a bunch of tourists having nothing but champagne cocktails."

"Yes and they are from the Palace, thank Heaven," Sashie said, "so one won't have to see what they look like tomorrow."

"The two of you are no better than a couple of Caribbean pirates," I told them.

"Darling, don't be nasty. I'm going to ask them to bring us a nice cup of tea — so much more wholesome than that champagne."

We had just poured out a second cup of tea all round when Twice appeared at the bedroom window and shouted excitedly: "Come on *out*, you lot! The first two are rounding the last buoy and *Amaryllis* is *there*!"

He ran away across the grass, and Sashie put down his cup, saying: "Bless my soul!" and hurried out, with Dee and myself behind him.

The cliff-top, which had been sprinkled with chattering groups of people, many of them not watching the yachts at all, was now bare and everybody was clustered at the rail at the cliff edge. There was a tense excited silence. The bars were empty and untended, for the negro barmen had joined the crowd at the cliff rail. Sashie whipped the cloth from a table.

"Come," he said. "Up here!"

Dee and I got up and looked to the east like the rest of the crowd. Nearer and nearer came the two boats, white feathers of spray flying from their bows, *Amaryllis* on the shoreward side, her flame-coloured sails almost parallel with the surface of the water and, a little to seaward but bow to bow with her, another boat rigged in brilliant green and white.

"Well done, *Amaryllis*," said Sashie's cool unexcited voice, dropping with a tinkle like ice into the vibrant air, to melt away on the hot wave of rising excitement as the two boats cut along to come level with the prow of the Peak Rock. Even Madame, now, was out of her chair like all the others and clinging to the rail as the boats swept past, and in a brilliant flash my eyes photographed Don at the helm of *Amaryllis*, like sculptured bronze, every muscle seeming to strain forward to push more wind into the already full sails, while Isobel and Mackie lay away out over the water, seeming to be attached to the hull by no more than their toes. The boats swept on, the silence seemed to be sucked after them in their wake as the heads turned to follow them, until suddenly the air was shattered by the shot of a pistol.

"That's it!" said Sir Ian, turning from

the rail. "Dammit, who won?" and he took off his sea-goin' hat and mopped his forehead.

"I'm damned if I know, sir," Twice said.

The air was full of the same question and the same answer while the people turned from the rail, chattering, as the tension broke down and I watched the other boats of the race come straggling along with a loss of urgency that seemed to have reached out to them from the cliff-top.

There was a louder rumble through the chatter and Sir Ian's parade-ground bellow came: "Quiet, everybody!"

" — class race which has just ended," came the voice from the amplifier on the Yacht Club tower. "First, Number Five, *Amaryllis*, St. Jago, Captain Don Candlesham. Second, Number Two, *Sea Wing*, Bermuda, Captain Druce Whiteman — "

The voice rumbled on, announcing the third and fourth yachts placed, but was lost in a wild babel of voices that rose into violent cheering from all over the Peak lawns, the Yacht Club and the shore of the bay beyond.

I am one of those people who are never up with the hounds of local affairs, and it was only now that I became apprised of the knowledge, through listening to the talk around me, that the Bermudan yacht *Sea Wing*, owned and manned by the four sons of an American oil magnate and the race terror of the Caribbean, had arrived in St. Jago Bay the day before. Over the weekend and during this morning I had heard the name *Sea Wing* being bandied about, but only now was it borne in on me that it was regarded as a great piece of luck that the Whiteman brothers should arrive in St. Jago for our regatta and that the race in which their boat was entered was regarded as an exhibition of seamanship in which the other boats only "went along for the ride". It was *Sea Wing*'s habit to go everywhere about the islands, break all local records and sail away with her sun-tanned crew, leaving a wonder and a dream behind, and today, although the Whiteman brothers were popular heroes, there was among the St. Jagoans that satisfaction of the utterly unexpected coming true, the satisfaction that a circus audience feels when the clown suddenly springs at a bare-backed horse and gives an astonishing exhibition of trick riding.

I sat watching the happy people as they all relived again and again the moment when the boats swept past the prow of the cliff, and Sashie said: "Well, well, just fancy our little boat and her comic crew going and doing a thing like that!"

"I didn't see Roddy as *Amaryllis* went past," Dee said, and, now that I thought of it, I had not seen him in the boat either in that thrilling moment.

Dee and Sashie were turning away when Don came striding up from the Yacht Club, breaking quickly away from group after group of people who gathered, laughing, round him, and he broke into a run as he reached the summit and would have gone straight past us up to the hotel had not Sashie said mischievously: "I *told* you to go to the bathroom before the excitement began, dear!"

Don halted and gave Sashie that look of half-amusement, half-exasperation that so often passed between them.

"Congratulations, Don," I said. "I gather that it was a splendid victory."

Don's handsome face darkened. "*Amaryllis* won the race," he said shortly. "We sailed her like a dodgem car at a fun fair!"

and he strode away across the grass and into the hotel.

"Dear, dear," said the irrepressible Sashie, "temper!"

Young Mackie now came up the cliff, his shoulders bright pink and sparkling with salt crystals. "Sashie, could I possibly have a bath? I'm not the bronze Apollo sort."

"But of course, dear," said Sashie in the voice of an old family nannie, "and then you will come to me and I will paint those shoulders with my nice cool lotion. You look like a parboiled lobster. Come along."

We all repaired to the hotel, Dee disappeared, presumably to her wine store, and Sashie, Mackie and I went to Sashie's room, where he put Mackie into his bathroom and shut the door. "And just you stay there, Janet, like a good girl. You have had enough sun today too. Nannie will be right back when she has seen what all those naughty servants in the kitchen and the bars are doing." He bustled out, and by the time he reappeared, followed by a waiter with a tray of drinks, Mackie had come out of the bathroom and I was anointing his shoulders with sunburn lotion from Sashie's big bottle which was an old and valued acquaintance of mine.

"That's right," said Sashie comfortably, still in his nannie's role, "and you are not too badly scorched, Mackie, dear, and you will feel much better in a little while after a nice little drink. Now, be a good boy and confess everything — but everything — about the race. Don is locked in his bathroom in the naughtiest temper and won't come out and I simply cannot have the nursery getting all out of control like this." He handed Mackie a whisky and soda. "Come now, what happened?"

Mackie was a shy inarticulate young man with bright dark eyes that always tried to look round corners to right or left of him when his shyness overcame him, which was fairly frequently.

"Oh, nothing much," he mumbled.

"Of course not, dear," said Sashie. "One doesn't suppose it was anything *much*. The point is, *what* was it?"

"Well," said Mackie, taking a deep breath as he realised that Sashie would not free him until he had answered, "we were rounding the outmost buoy, you see, and we all — Roddy and Isobel and I, I mean

— well, the boom came round and we got in a bit of a muddle; that is — well, we got in a bit of a muddle."

"Yes. And?" Sashie interrogated inexorably.

Mackie's dark eyes flicked shyly from one of us to the other and then sought the corners of the room. "Well, I don't know what happened," he said hesitantly. "Roddy must have — must have done something — it was Isobel — he must have tried to kiss her or something, but she took a swing at him — gosh, that woman's as strong as an ox!"

"Of that we are aware," said Sashie. "Yes?"

"Well, he went overboard."

"Shiver my timbers! Do I understand that you three left young Maclean in the Caribbean?"

"Oh, the launch took him aboard," Mackie said and suddenly gave a giggle.

"You laugh?" Sashie enquired mock sternly, and Mackie at once looked apologetic.

"It was Don and Isobel," he said.

"Yes?"

Mackie looked from one of us to the

other. "Don said, was Roddy at the regatta for sailing or sex, and Isobel said — she said — " Mackie dissolved into a fit of laughter, recovered a little and added in a Scotticised version of Isobel's drawl: "That one? He don't think of anything else! It's my guess he'd do it with a yak!" Again he looked at each of us in turn. "I thought that was funny," he ended apologetically.

"Yes, indeed, Mackie," Sashie said. "Very funny and quite extraordinarily true."

Mackie laughed, more at ease now. "So we lost a little way rounding the buoy, you see. That's why it was so tight at the finish. Don could sail these Whitemans out of the water, given a decent crew."

"Don't be over-modest, my sweet. You all did very well in spite of your unseaman-like antics and I am very pleased with you," said Sashie, now in the character of Madame Dulac.

When Mackie had gone out, leaving us alone, I said to Sashie: "Do I understand that Roddy Maclean is coming into com-petition with Don as the local parish bull?"

"My dear," Sashie said, regarding me with solemnly rounded eyes, "compared with young Maclean, poor Don is an utterly broken-down old man. Maclean is in Victoria Court even at lunchtime!"

Sashie's manner of saying this, while making me laugh, brought a picture of Victoria Court into my mind. It was built originally by the newly risen merchant princes of St. Jago Bay as their fashionable residential area, but had degenerated in the course of some eighty years into the red-light area of the town. In a British city, it would have been called a square rather than a court, for it consisted of some twenty large, three-storey houses enclosed in gardens and forming four sides of a square, with, in its centre, a statue of Queen Victoria, seated plumply on a throne and holding in firm hands the sceptre and orb. Eighty years ago I could imagine the wives and daughters of the wealthy dockside importers and exporters languishing in crinolined propriety at the windows of the upstairs drawing-rooms behind their slowly moving fans or being driven by carriage round the statue to attend a garden party on the other side of the square while the Queen looked out with approval over their stately activities.

In the early 1950s it was one of my constant treats to be driven through Victoria Court when Twice brought me to St. Jago Bay. I found a piquant enjoyment in visualising this place as it once had been and comparing it with how it was now. The gardens, long untended and unwatered, had turned into dusty deserts with a few broken trees, under which lay abandoned wrecks of cars and rough shacks round which a few chickens bathed in the dust among empty cigarette cartons and rusty sardine cans. At the windows, where the ladies had once sat coyly behind their fans, there were now the black and yellow faces of cheerful bawds who called their greetings and invitations to all that passed, while from rooms where, once, the melody of the "Lost Chord" had tinkled across the air while some miss prepared her piece for that evening's party, there now came the brazen voice of a juke-box, playing the latest importation from New York. And, still, in the centre of it all, plump, unsmiling, impervious to heat or noise, Queen Victoria sat on her throne, the waste-paper and debris blowing around her, her nose chipped, the top of her sceptre gone, an abandoned car tyre hanging like a displaced nebula round the orb in her other hand.

"Roddy may be like me and be morbidly fascinated by the atmosphere of Victoria Court," I said to Sashie now.

"Well, I have heard it said that there is often common ground between people where you would least expect it," Sashie said.

Now that the regatta was over, the crowds in the grounds and round the bars of the Peak Hotel began to disperse, the visitors from the other hotels, who had spent the day at the Peak because of its advantageous position for watching the sailing, going back to their own places for dinner. The Yacht Club Dance was to be held in the Peak ballroom, but this was confined to members of the club and their guests, and very soon the Peak had settled back into its normal atmosphere of spacious luxury. As the dusk began to fall and the fairy lights came on in the trees outside, Dee came to me where I sat with Twice in the patio bar and said: "Miss Jan, will it be all right if I stay for the dance?"

"Of course, Dee. We'll be delighted if you will stay."

"Are you glad now that Janet made you bring your dress this morning?" Twice asked her, smiling.

There had been a near-scene that morning when we left Guinea Corner, for Dee, like Cousin Emmie, had not wanted to attend the regatta at all, and in the end it was I who put the suit-case in the car with a change of clothing for her.

"I am sorry I behaved badly this morning," she said gravely now in response to Twice's laughing remark. "I am sorry I have said horrid things about Don and Isobel, and Sashie too. I have had a really lovely day. Are you two staying on?"

"No, only for dinner," I told her. "Twice will have an early start tomorrow to get the factory working again, you see."

She pouted. "That flippin' factory!" she said.

It almost took my breath away, and Twice smiled at her broadly before he said: "You couldn't be more right, Dee. That flippin' factory! Run away and change."

We watched her go away across the lawn to be joined by one or two other young people, and all of them made their way to

Isobel Denholm's bungalow where the younger people were dressing for the evening.

"Can it be that somebody is learning something?" Twice said to me quietly.

"Could be. Somebody is learning something every minute, I suppose," I said, but I was not thinking of Dee.

I was thinking of this anomalous person Roddy Maclean who seemed to live a life of comparative luxury on next to no income, whom Twice thought could be a thief, whom Dee said was not "all sexy and things", and whom Isobel Denholm said "would do it with a yak", which Sashie said was true, and whom Cousin Emmie "did not trust and could not see to the bottom of". And I was thinking that, in Roddy's own words, nobody gets all of anybody and that none of us, with our various opinions, had managed to get all of Roddy.

9

"SHE KNOWS NOTHING ABOUT DEE ANDREWS"

ABOUT three the following morning I heard the door of Dee's bedroom close as she came in from the dance; at five Twice and I got up, and shortly before six the headlights of Twice's car went raking down the drive, turned to the right and headed for the factory, while from all round the Compound other headlights gleamed across the park, converging on the same spot at the factory gates. Very shortly the siren blew, the orchestra of the machinery began to hum once more across the valley and Easter and "halftime" were over.

It was about ten o'clock when Clorinda came out to the garden to tell me that Dee was awake and was asking me to come to her bedroom, a request that made me hesitate, after the maid had gone back to the house, while I wondered what could have happened the night before, and my heart sank down into my gardening shoes.

It is typical of the attitude that Dee had induced in me that I could not think of any pleasant reason why she wanted to see me in her room, that I made up my mind at once that we were in the midst of another social and emotional crisis and that this one, which could be discussed only in the privacy of her bedroom, must be much more violent than any that had gone before. Low of spirit and dragging my feet, I made my way upstairs.

When I went into the room, Dee was not in bed but at the writing-table, very busy and with a letter addressed to her father already completed and standing against the table lamp.

"Hello," I said, doing my best to hide my relief, "you are very bright and lively after dancing till two in the morning."

"I woke you when I came in, Miss Jan? I'm sorry. I tried to be quiet."

"I was awake, anyhow — a bit anxious about getting Twice out in time."

She rose from the table, went to the window and stood with her finger at her lip, looking out into the garden. I sat down on the chair she had vacated, lit a cigarette and waited.

"I asked you to come up so that we shouldn't be interrupted by Cousin Emmie or Sir Ian or anybody," she said, speaking with her back to me.

"Yes, Dee?"

She turned round, interlaced her fingers in front of her, looked down at them and said: "Miss Jan, Roddy and I have decided to get married."

I could not have been more astounded if she had told me that Cousin Emmie had spent the previous evening dancing the Can-Can in the Peak ballroom, and I could at first think of no word to say, but Dee helped me out by continuing: "I suppose you are going to be like the rest and not be pleased, but there it is," whereupon her face, which had been composed and pleasant when I entered the room, took on its familiar look of sullen defiance.

"Why in the world shouldn't I be pleased?" I said at once. "Dee, darling, I'm delighted! I've liked Roddy since the moment I met him and I can think of nothing I could like more for you. I simply couldn't speak at first, I was so pleased!"

"Truly, Miss Jan?" she asked, her eyes round, her lips tremulous with anxiety.

"Truly and truly, Dee! And you mustn't have this silly idea that people aren't pleased. Why shouldn't they be?"

She drew away from me, turned away a little. "Isobel Denholm isn't pleased, and neither is Sashie. I could feel it last night when we told them. And Twice will be angry, but I don't care!" She was all defiance now.

"Dee, this is nonsense, you know," I said, wishing that I had more conviction of speaking the truth. "Why in the world should Twice be angry?"

"He doesn't like Roddy."

"Oh, that! That was only annoyance because Roddy didn't fall flat on his face in worship of his blooming old turbines! Twice is quite different about Roddy since he began to do so well in the office in the Bay."

"Is he really, Miss Jan? Really? I don't want Twice to be angry, but I've got to do something, and Roddy is nice and kind and understanding and people are horrid to him just as they are to me so often and we got engaged last night and I've written to tell Father," she said with a rush, pointing to the letter that leaned against the lamp.

Now that the first shock was over, my faculties began to work at their not very bright best, and I felt a slight inward chill at the words "people are horrid to him just as they are to me" and remembered that I had always thought it a grim idea that the males and females in a leper colony married one another for no better reason than that they both had leprosy.

"Who is horrid to Roddy?" I asked.

"Everybody. His parents and everybody — even Twice; even if it *was* about the turbines, it is still being horrid. And Don and Isobel were absolutely filthy to him yesterday during the race."

"Oh? What happened?"

"Roddy made some mistake, pulled the wrong rope or something and they threw him overboard. He might have been drowned!" she said indignantly, while I smiled inwardly at the difference in the nature of Roddy's "mistake" as recounted by Dee and as recounted by Mackie. "I know Don and Isobel are friends of yours, Miss Jan," she went on in the disapproving, censorious manner that came to her so readily and tended to make me feel like a particularly backward child, "but I think it is childish and disgusting of people to be horrid and despising to somebody all because of a game going wrong. Sailing is only a game, after all."

"That's true, Dee, but maybe Isobel and Don did not mean to be horrid and despising as you call it. Maybe they were over-excited with the race and everything. Excitement does distort the vision a bit."

"It wasn't excitement during the dance," she argued, "and Isobel was simply horrid to both of us all evening."

I thought privately that Dee would find her life incomplete if it did not contain someone who was being "horrid" to her, just as her engagement to Roddy would be less real to her if nobody was being "horrid" about it, but I said: "I should not worry, Dee. I imagine that you and Roddy can get along without Isobel's approval. Do you think your father will be pleased?"

"I don't see why not," she said indifferently. "I should think it will be all right. He has always wanted me to get married and the Macleans are quite a good family, aren't they? Not that it matters. I am going to marry Roddy and that is all there is to it."

Again I thought that no action was real for Dee unless she made it in defiance of somebody or something, and when she turned back to the writing-table and picked up her pen I gladly left her and went downstairs.

With my head in a whirl, I went out to the veranda, and when I saw the brown canvas bag in the corner of the drawing-room beside the feet of Cousin Emmie I regarded her arrival at this moment as a predestined and integral part of my mental turmoil, and quite automatically I turned back, went to the kitchen and asked for some coffee to be brought in.

"My cousin will be round here this forenoon," she announced without preamble when I joined her.

"Sir Ian? Good."

"No. Lottie."

"Madame Dulac? Why?"

"She has heard about this engagement between that little girl of yours and that man Maclean," Cousin Emmie said as if this were a lugubrious eventuality which I ought to have foreseen. "You know what people like my cousin are like."

"No, I don't," I contradicted her snappishly. "There are times when I don't know what anybody is like."

"My cousin thinks that engagements are causes for congratulations and funerals are occasions for condolences."

"And aren't they?"

She picked up a biscuit, examined it doubtfully, returned it to the plate and chose another. "No," she said then. "Only some of them — not many."

She left me to ponder this, making no other remark until she had drunk two cups of coffee and popped the last biscuit, the one she had formerly discarded, into the bag, whereupon she took up the bag and parasol, rose to her feet and said: "I don't like that woman Maclean."

"Marion?" I said, my hackles rising at once.

As if I had not spoken, Cousin Emmie pursued her train of thought, looking past me and out to the garden. "She is the ambitious sort. I wouldn't be surprised if she put that son of hers up to proposing to that silly little girl."

"Really, Miss Morrison, I have never in my life heard such malicious rubbish — " I had begun, preparing to pay off all my scores against Cousin Emmie in one furious tirade ending by forbidding her to set foot in my house again, when the Rolls drew up outside to disgorge Madame, Sir Ian and Marion Maclean.

"There they are, just like I told you," croaked Cousin Emmie, and she drifted out through the french window into the back part of the garden leaving behind her the impression, as she so often did, that she had not been humanly present at all but was a manifestation of some superhuman agency such as Fate or one's conscience.

By the time Twice came home for lunch all my guests had gone, Dee had left to meet Roddy for lunch in the Bay, and I was sitting alone in a state of utter bemusement in a corner of the veranda. When Twice came leaping up the steps and said: "Big news, what?" I regarded him dully and did not speak.

"Where's Dee?" he asked then.

"Gone to lunch in the Bay with her intended."

"Does one gather that you are displeased?"

I raised my hands and let them fall again, saying nothing.

"Janet, what has happened?"

"Apart from my being stunned by the unlikely then bombarded into pulp with congratulations, nothing."

"You are uneasy about this?"

"Very. Aren't you?"

"No. It seems to me to be quite a good answer. Roddy is the only one of us who can make any shape at handling her and I believe they'll be happy. He seems to me to be — "

"No longer a petty pilferer and gambler whom you don't trust?"

"Oh, I thought you'd heard! It wasn't Roddy who was pilfering. It was that little girl Freeman in the office — they caught her red-handed on Thursday afternoon."

I sagged in my chair. "Why I don't rise up and murder you all I don't know. When did you hear they had caught the Freeman girl?"

"This morning. I thought the news would have got here by grape-vine by now. I suppose the engagement put it out of all their heads." I stared straight in front of me, making no comment, and Twice went on: "I feel like apologising to Roddy for the things I thought about him. I

297

believe the boy has a lot in him and probably he and Dee will — "

"It seems to me," I broke in, "that you, in common with a lot of other people, have got your feet 'way, 'way off the ground, Twice. I think that having become disenchanted, as you call it, with Dee yourself, you are jumping at this as a solution. I have never seen Roddy as you did, and I still don't see him as you do — as a potential and suitable husband for Dee. I don't like this thing at all. In fact, I think it stinks!"

Over the pre-lunch beer we became very heated indeed while I adduced all my reasons for distrusting the situation between Dee and Roddy, from the fact that they seemed to have come together primarily because of other people's "horridness" to both of them, through Dee's opinion that Roddy was not "all sexy and things" as opposed to Sashie's knowledge of his intimacy with Victoria Court down to Cousin Emmie's suggestion that Roddy had been "put up" by Marion to marrying Dee for her money. At this last, Twice became really angry and said: "I might have known it was that bloody old woman who put this blight on you!"

"She didn't. The blight was there the moment that Dee told me about it."

"But why, for heaven's sake? Up to now you have been Roddy Maclean's chief advocate, but now that he's in the clear you have to start getting doubtful!"

"It simply doesn't *feel* right, Twice. I have never believed that Roddy was a thief or lazy or shiftless or any of these things, but I *do* believe that Isobel Denholm is right when she says he would do it with a yak. And Dee is so frigidly cold — it simply feels all wrong," I repeated.

"Oh, you and your feelings!" Twice said, exasperated, and then added more calmly: "Anyway, what can we do?"

"Nothing, nothing at all, except let things take their course, but I wish to heaven we had never brought her out here in the first place!"

Aware that he was originally and entirely responsible for the fact that Dee was at Paradise, Twice became furious and lashed out at me with: "It's my belief that you are just plain jealous of that girl!"

"Twice Alexander! You should be ashamed of yourself!"

For the remainder of that day and during many days that followed the atmosphere in the house was as uneasy as if a monkey playing with a cocked and loaded gun were amongst us, but, as often happens in such situations, Dee, who was the monkey with the gun, was for once at ease and oblivious of any strain at all. She, who had been so sensitive hitherto to every change of voice tone, to the most fleeting facial expression, went along from day to day, gaily unconcerned, very much the happy daughter of the house, accepting all the congratulations that flowed in from St. Jago and England, looking forward with a confidence she had never before shown in herself or the future to her wedding in London in the autumn and a lifetime of blissful happiness. Roddy, her now formally affianced, came to Guinea Corner only once, to attend the celebration party which Twice and I gave, and, whether or not it was my morbid imagination, he seemed to avoid me as carefully as most people avoided Cousin Emmie.

As is well known, however, humanity is not so constructed that it can look hard facts in the face for very long at a time, and life connives at this weakness by offering all kinds of avenues of escape, and I, mentally, am endowed with an escape mechanism as instinctive and efficient as that which, physically, characterises the stag or the fox. Quite soon my uneasiness about the engagement was lulled to sleep by the lapping waves of the congratulations and pleasure of all our acquaintance and I began to see myself as a cross between a successful match-making dowager and Cinderella's fairy godmother and to feel, indeed, that but for my heaven-inspired intervention Dee might have turned into an old woman like Cousin Emmie. And so everything rolled along very happily. Dee went to the Bay most days, and she often went up to Mount Melody with Isobel, where the alterations to the house were now in full swing, for all the "horridness" about Roddy after the regatta had now, like many other things, been smoothed away.

About three weeks after Easter Twice went away on another trip, and Dee, who had been going to Mount Melody or the Bay every day, began to hang about the house again. On about the third afternoon I took her firmly to task about this.

"It is ridiculous! Most days I have to go to some meeting or another of Madame's, the Clinic Baby Show is coming up and it is working out that you are hanging about here alone half the time, Dee. You and Isobel haven't quarrelled, have you?"

"Gracious, no! I told Isobel about Twice going away and wanting to be with you and she quite understands. Isobel is a very understanding sort of person, although you mightn't think so."

"Why mightn't I think so?"

"Well, she looks so big and abrupt and sort of careless, striding about like a fugitive from a cattle ranch, as she herself says." Dee laughed. "But she really understands awfully well about all sorts of things. I don't think she likes Roddy very much, but we just never talk about him."

"Doesn't it annoy you rather that she doesn't seem to like Roddy?" I asked, for, of course, had I been Dee such a thing would have annoyed me so much that I probably would not even speak to Isobel, but it seemed that Dee had much more tolerance, not to say sense, than I had.

"Why should it?" she asked. "Everybody can't like everybody. And Isobel doesn't like any men much — she is almost like Cousin Emmie about them. She distrusts them."

"Oh? I thought she and Don were great friends."

"Only for things like sailing and water-ski-ing. That's because they are both good at the same things. Isobel says that marriage is a game for mugs, so we don't talk about that either."

"There seems to be an awful lot of things you and Isobel don't talk about. Isn't it all rather a negative business?"

Dee smiled. "No. There are a million things we do talk about. Getting married is the only negative and that is just really because she doesn't like Roddy and I don't like Don and Don is the only man Isobel has any use for. But she is an awfully comfortable person to be with and we get on very well together. I mean, we can *do* things together, like this Mount Melody thing. You ought to see it, Miss Jan! You would never recognise that dark old dungeon of a house. I say, come up there with me this afternoon! We can take a picnic tea."

"No, not this afternoon, dear," I said. I had never liked Mount Melody, and the drive over the tortuous jungly road that led to it I liked still less. "Some other day, perhaps. I have some writing to do this afternoon."

Dee pouted a little. "You and your writing! You seem to me to be always writing. Are you writing a book?"

"A book? Me? Are you off your head?"

I felt angry with an anger I did not dare to show, for her careless question was an invasion of a strict privacy and a privacy whose very existence I wanted to hide. Ever since I was about eighteen years old I had thought that to write a book must be the most splendid thing in the world, but I had never had any conviction that it was something that I could do. Lack of conviction, however, did not stop me from trying, and most of my free moments were spent at my writing table scribbling away, and the fact that nothing I wrote ever pleased me did not stop me either. This scribbling, it seemed, was something I had to do, and in a guilty secretive way I did it, as if I were practising some furtive and disgraceful petty vice. I could not bear that anybody, even Twice, should know about it, because it seemed such a terribly overambitious thing for someone like me to do. I myself was not ambitious about it; I knew my scribbles had no future, but I felt that no one would believe that I could spend hours doing a thing which I knew to be futureless. People, even Twice, would think either that I had literary ambitions or that I was mad, and either idea was unbearable.

"What in the world made you think that?" I asked.

"It just came into my head."

"Well, open your skull and let it out again. Crumbs, do you really think me conceited enough to have literary ambitions?"

"Not really."

"I am afraid my writing is very mundane — mostly letters home and Madame's reports on her various charities and things. I get all that to do because I can type and Marion Maclean can't."

"Actually it wouldn't be conceited for somebody as old as you to try to write a book. I mean, you are old enough for things to have happened to you and to have seen

a lot of things and places. It's for somebody of my age that it is conceited and
silly."

"I don't agree with you there," I said.
"I don't think age has much to do with it.
It is more a question of the sort of vision
a person is born with. Look at Keats, for
instance."

"Oh, Keats! Poetry!"

"Don't you like poetry any more? You
used to like it when you were small."

"Oh, that." She frowned out at the
garden. "I mean, when you're grown-up
— well, it's not much use, is it?"

"It depends on what you mean by use.
For me, poetry has a lot of use. It makes
me feel happy for one thing, and I can't
think of anything more useful than that."

"You are lucky." There seemed to me to
be a faint sneer in her voice and it irritated
me. "I am afraid I need more than a few
lines of poetry."

"Then you do need quite a lot," I said.

She frowned discontentedly and I had
the impression that she was as irritated with
me as I was with her. We had come accidentally to the basic difference between
us, for there are people who are prone to

happiness and people who are not so. I belonged to the first category and Dee to the second, it seemed, and the people of those two categories always act as irritants to one another. But I did not want, at this stage, to quarrel or even argue with Dee on even the most abstract of subjects, so I went on: "But you are truly happy in your engagement, Dee?"

"Oh yes." The faint frown and discontent left her face. "I am really happy, Miss Jan."

A few days later I did allow myself to be persuaded to go up to Mount Melody, partly because Dee was so anxious that I should see the alterations and partly because Sir Ian, bored with this second half of Crop, wanted to go himself and bullied me into it one day when Dee mentioned the trip in his presence. Mount Melody was approached by a tortuous and precipitous road that followed the gorge of the Rio d'Oro and a little over a year before Isobel's grandmother had been killed when her car went over the edge and crashed to the river bed below. Mount Melody, as I remembered it, was linked in my mind with this accident and therefore coloured in my mind by the associations I had made for it. I remembered an old grey stone house with an imposing pillared entrance that led into a dark mahogany-panelled hall, out of which the mahogany staircase led away up into further panelled darkness. I remembered it as a forbidding haunting sort of house where the river, away down in its gorge beyond the terraced garden, sent its voice echoing upwards while the reflection of the water rippled over the ceiling of the vast drawing-room with a horrid uncanniness. It was from the sound of the water that the house had taken its melodious name.

Today, the grey stone front was the same as ever, but when we went in through the portico to the hall the old black mahogany of the panelling shone in brilliant sunlight.

"My goodness, what have you done?" I said to Isobel.

"We tore the inside wall out of the library on the first floor hall," she said. "The library is going to be the main bar. The tourists that come to this island aren't interested in libraries, anyways. It was Dee's idea. Dee is terrific at this game, Janet." And, as an idea, it was a good one, for the bar-ex-library was at the back of the house and led out through french windows directly and at a higher level than the front entrance to the top terrace of the garden above the river gorge.

Seeing Dee and Isobel together like this, interested in the same project, brought out the difference between them which could not have been more marked in two girls of approximately the same age. Physically, they were as different as two members of the same species could be, for Isobel must have been about twice the size and weight of Dee, and added to this there was the difference between Isobel's flamboyant red hair and vivid blue eyes and the sombre pale browns of Dee. Yet, Isobel did not have the effect of making Dee look colourless and dull, as Roddy, for instance, with his deeply tanned skin and flashing eyes, tended to do, nor did Dee's dainty neatness make Isobel look coarse or clumsy. It was more that they complemented one another and threw each other into relief as the brown sturdiness of the stem complements the delicacy of almond blossom while the fragile curves of the petals complement the angular strength of the stems.

"This is quite an undertaking you have gone in for, Isobel," I said, when Dee had taken Sir Ian away to show him something in the sun-bright garden. "You are going to have a big job running this place."

"I know. I'll have to get help. Not servants, I mean. That will be easy. I am beginning to wish that David wasn't so set on being an architect or that Dee wasn't going back to England. That's a bright kid, Janet. Any time you want a testimonial as a governess, just you come to me!"

"I am afraid I had very little to do with her education, Isobel. It was more a question of getting her over a difficult patch when she was a child."

"She's made a bit of a hobby of difficult patches, hasn't she?"

"No more than a few others I could mention, Isobel," I said with a smile.

"Okay, I admit everything!" She laughed and quickly became grave again. "But I had more fighting equipment than that little kid," she added.

"Yes, I think perhaps you had."

"Janet — "

"Yes?"

"No. We'll skip it. I'm probably prejudiced."

"Come now," I said, "is it about Roddy, Isobel?"

"I said we'll skip it."

"What is worrying you?"

"She's just so — so darned young!"

"She is older than you are."

"That's true. In some ways, she can give me ten years. But in other ways — "

"Yes?"

"Forget it, Janet. As I said, I am prejudiced and I am not being fair, like as not. You see, I've come a long ways since last year, when I was hitting it up with Don down at the Peak there. I've found out a lot of things about myself since then — I found them out the hard way. That's where I feel that Dee is a kid — she knows a slew of stuff about planning a hotel and wines and business — her head is bursting with brains and knowledge and hard sense — but — but she knows nothing about Dee Andrews!"

"The things about Isobel Denholm, Dee Andrews and Janet Alexander are all things we have to find out for ourselves, it seems to me," I said, "and quite often what you call the hard way is the only way of finding them out." I paused. "I understand that you don't care for Roddy Maclean?"

"No, I don't."

"Can you tell me why?"

"No, I can't. That's being honest, Janet. It's one of those things like a mongoose and a rat, and I am not saying Roddy is the rat, either. It's just that there's something in him that — that — " Suddenly she shuddered convulsively before she went on: "Do you ever get the feeling that somebody — somebody just doesn't belong to the same — the same *species* as yourself? Do you ever get a queer feeling, for instance, when a negro does something typically negro?" she asked.

"Yes," I agreed a little unwillingly, for I found no pleasure in admitting this, for I imagined that I must make the negroes shudder when I did something that they found typically white and it is not pleasant to feel that one can induce shudders.

"And if there was something about them you would never catch up with in a million years and it makes you half-scared of them, half-mad at them?"

"Yes," I said. "I can get that feeling

coming up that awful bush road of yours between here and the gorge. I am afraid of that bush overpowering me and yet I want to attack it with an axe."

"That's it. That's the way I am about Roddy Maclean. It's hell in a way. I like Dee. I like Dee a lot, Janet, and I want her to have everything she wants, yet I don't want Maclean to have her. Oh, let's forget it. I suppose I am sorta jealous or something. I don't know."

I gave a good deal of thought to what Isobel had said, but I came only to the banal conclusion that there was no accounting for people's personal reactions to other people. Dee did not like Don Candlesham, but I found him a pleasure merely to look at in addition to being quite a pleasant companion. Isobel did not like Roddy, but I still found him a very likeable young man, as I had always done.

10

"PEOPLE ARE NEVER SETTLED UNTIL THEY ARE IN THE GRAVE"

IN the first few days of June Twice made another quick trip to Trinidad, and on his return, after a short visit to the factory, he said: "Well, we are into the last week of Crop."

"Are we? I had no idea we were so nearly through. Twice, that's marvellous!"

From that moment onwards, it seemed, one could hear the orchestra of the factory losing volume and momentum, as if its daemon knew that the time had come for this frenzy of activity to slow down towards a stop. The broad acreage of cane-fields was now like a patchwork quilt made of squares of bright green, Cousin Emmie brown and velvety black, for the cane pieces that had been cut when Crop started had now put on their first new growth; those more recently cut were

314

still covered by the withered blades, and those that were to be replanted had been turned over by the heavy ploughs into a rough black tilth.

In a day or two the engine-noises of the haulage tractors began to die away, which meant that, one by one, as the cane to be hauled grew less, they were being taken off duty and into the transport yard for overhaul for the next year. And then came the day when the last tractors on duty went past Guinea Corner with bunches of flowers tied to their radiators while the drivers and loaders on top of the trailers wore flowers in their hats and sang as they made this last journey of the year to the factory. "Two and a half days to go now," Twice said, as he came in that afternoon. "We'll grind off the last cane in the yard by tomorrow morning, if all goes well, and the sugar should be in the sacks by midday on Friday."

"And then the siren will blow for Cropover," I told Dee.

"And when do we have the party?"

"The next week, probably on the Friday," Twice told her. "It takes about a week to get the food organised and so on."

Exactly as Twice had foretold, with the good fortune that had attended the entire Crop, the siren began to blow its long final blast for the year at about a quarter to twelve on the Friday; on that evening Sir Ian called to tell us that Madame had set the celebration of Cropover for the following Friday, and from that moment we all fell into a frenzy of food. There were no catering services in St. Jago in those days, and as the week went on nobody spoke of anything except how So-and-so could not deliver that dozen chickens after all, and how the turkey that had been sent to Mrs. Grey would not go into her oven, and would somebody else cook it and give her some chickens instead. I am a reasonably competent plain cook for a small household, but food in the tropic heat on the scale provided for one of Madame's "entertainments", as she called them, simply nauseated and appalled me, and all I could do was to lapse into my childhood state under the command of my grandmother and "do what I was told". Marion Maclean was the officer in charge of the food operation, and she knew that she could rely on me to have a bird or two cooked in my kitchen and bake a cake or two, but apart from this my only function was to receive notes from her, brought by Sandy on his bicycle: "Try to rustle up three more large dishes to hold trifles", or "Send Mrs. Murphy your egg-beater. She has lost hers", or "Send Dee or somebody to the Great House store-room for that hideous china basin with the purple roses and send it to Mrs. Cranston for the fruit salad". Sandy, it now being the summer holidays, tore to and fro on his bicycle or his pony; Dee and Isobel swept from one house to another with car-loads of pans, basins and roasting tins, and round to the club with baskets of china and glass; and Sir Ian and Madame, in the midst of it all, were in their element.

On the morning of the Cropover party everything worked up to fever pitch. By seven o'clock all the Estate lorries and all the cars were ploughing up the white dust as they converged on the club with loads of everything, from teaspoons to forms and trestle tables, and every oven in every house was sizzling with cooking meat while every refrigerator was oozing with trifles and jellies. At two in the afternoon the heavens opened, split asunder by a long streak of blue lightning which was followed by a cannonade of thunder that rolled and reverberated round the valley, and then down came the rain in what seemed to be a solid block of water. By three o'clock the roads where the white dust had risen in clouds round the cars an hour before were running like rivers or spreading into lakes, and when Twice's car came up our driveway, followed by the Rolls, wakes formed behind them as they turned in the inland sea which was our gateway.

"This is just about the end," I greeted them when they jumped from the cars on to the veranda.

"Not at all, me dear," said Sir Ian, shaking a shower bath from his pith helmet all over Dram, who, with a hurt look, picked up Charlie and carried him into the drawing-room. "Just a little electric shower — it'll cool things down an' lay the dust. We'll have a splendid evenin'."

Looking out at the wall of water that hung between me and Dram's hibiscus clump, it was difficult to believe him, but I had had enough experience now of St. Jago's sudden violence of climate to hope that we might have our party that evening after all.

"What about havin' tea, Missis Janet?" Sir Ian said next. "Can't do any more work until the rain stops."

"Where is Dee?" Twice asked me as the tea was brought.

"Down in the Bay having her hair done," I told him.

Sir Ian, of course, was perfectly right about the weather, for shortly after four the rain stopped as suddenly as it had begun, the clouds parted like grey curtains to show a slit of blue sky, they parted a little more so that the sun came through, and at once turned them from heavy grey to fluffy white and then the wind rose and began to drive them away over the hills in impatient little gusts, like a dog sending home straying sheep.

Twice and Sir Ian had just risen to return to their duties at the club when Nurse Porter drove up in her little black car.

"Hello, Nurse," I said; "come in and have some tea."

"No, thanks, Mrs. Alexander. I have a call. May I borrow your Land-Rover,

Sir Ian? I have to go away up into the bush behind Mount Melody, sir."

"Certainly, me dear. It's round at the house and the keys are in it. What's wrong up there?"

"Some woman is sick — haemorrhage of some kind, it sounded like, but you know what people are on the telephone. It was her brother that called from the box at Running Cut and we were cut off — the storm likely. But they are our people all right, sir. Freeman is the name. Probably connected with Tony the Millman."

"You don't want someone to go away up there with you, Nurse?" Twice asked.

"Certainly not, Mr. Twice!" She turned her car about efficiently, looking a little like Boadicea in a starched white cap. "It isn't far, only a bit rough. See you at the Cropover later. 'Bye." She drove away and Twice and Sir Ian went back to the club.

From my point of view the preparations for the party were now over, the last salad bowl and fruit dish requisitioned and despatched according to Marion's orders, and the turkey in my oven cooking to schedule, so I went upstairs to lay out

Twice's evening clothes and my own. Twice came back at six o'clock, saying that everything at the club was organised, and began to pour drinks.

"Dee isn't back," I said.

He turned from the tray and looked at his watch. "It's after six."

"I know. Still, we are not due at the Great House until eight and she takes no time at all to dress. That's one thing."

We went upstairs, carrying our drinks, had leisurely gossipy baths and dressed, but by a quarter-past seven Dee had still not appeared.

"She is cutting it a bit fine," Twice said, looking over my shoulder into my face in the glass.

"Go on," I said, "say it! You hope to God nothing has happened to her!"

"You are quite right. I'll say it. I hope to God nothing has happened to her! I hope she hasn't run into a landslip on that gorge road after that downpour this afternoon."

"Twice!"

"Wait! What's that?" I could hear nothing but the croaking of the tree frogs, the chorus of the crickets. "Yes, that's the

Daimler." He went to the window. "Yes. She's coming down the south approach like a bat out of hell. I must say she can handle that car."

In a few moments the car door slammed outside and Dee ran upstairs. I met her on the landing.

"What happened, darling? Did you mistake the time or have a puncture or what? I'll turn on your bath."

She stopped dead and stared at Twice and me in the bedroom doorway.

"I don't want a bath. I hadn't a puncture. I'm not going to this party."

"Dee!"

"I'm not going!" she said, her voice rising and cracking as it rose.

"Steady now, Dee," Twice said.

"I'm not going!"

"But, Dee, why?"

"I'm not going! You can't make me! I don't want to go! I'm not going!"

"Dee," Twice said quietly, "nobody is going to *make* you do anything."

Her eyes looked from one of us to the other and round the landing as if she were afraid that we would close in on her and drag her to the party by main force.

"People are always making me do things!" she almost screamed.

Twice ignored this and went on in a flat calm voice that made me think of the voice of Cousin Emmie. "But I think you must give us some excuse to take to Madame. Don't you feel well?"

He moved a little towards her, and she backed sharply, hitting the wall behind her. Twice stopped moving.

"I'm all right," she said in an eerie whisper now, and then gave a loud sneeze.

She had moved to a spot where the light struck directly upon her face, and I now saw that she was excessively pale, with a high flush burning on her cheek-bones.

"Dee," I said, going towards her, "you've got a chill! You have a temperature!"

"Leave me alone! Don't come near me!" She pressed back against the wall.

"But, Dee, you must let — "

"Leave me alone!" Her teeth began to chatter, she shivered violently and her voice rose now to a shrill cracked shriek. "All right! I've got a cold! I'm going to bed, but *leave me alone!*"

"Now, Dee — " Twice began sternly.

The high cracked voice now became a throaty husky whisper that to me sounded savage and full of hatred.

"Leave me alone! I don't want you! I'm all right!"

"You're not," said a flat voice from the staircase. "You are hysterical."

Dee drew a sharp breath broken by a sob and spun round, and Twice and I also turned with a jerk to look at the staircase. At the bottom of it, in the dimness, for the hall light had not been switched on, stood Cousin Emmie in the panoply of her old gold velvet, and her little fur made of the two sad, dead little animals, the parasol in one hand and the canvas bag in the other.

"Where did you come from?" I asked.

"I have been here for the last hour. My cousin is in a temper so I came over here. I was in there," and she pointed with the parasol at the drawing-room door.

"Oh — oh — oh!" shrieked Dee on a piercing note.

"Stop that," said Cousin Emmie, beginning to climb the stairs. "You don't have to go to this party if you don't want to. Go to bed."

All three of us watched as if transfixed while she slowly climbed the stairs, but when she brought her foot from the top step to the landing, Dee, with a jerk like a coiled spring suddenly released, darted into her room and closed the door with a bang. Cousin Emmie stopped in front of Twice and me where we stood side by side like part of Stonehenge, fixed her colourless expressionless eyes on us and said: "You had better go down there and drink something and get along to my cousin's. I'll see to that little girl. I was a nurse once." She gave a peremptory rattle on the heavy panel of the door with the bone handle of the parasol. "I am coming in," she said. To my amazement, amazement that made me clutch at Twice's arm to convince myself that this was real, the door opened about six inches, Dee gave a gulp and said: "All right. Come in, Miss Morrison."

The door closed; Twice and I stared at one another for a blank moment, and then, speaking no word, we went to the drawing-room and Twice picked up the whisky decanter.

"What in the world is going on?"

I whispered after taking a sip of whisky and water.

"Heaven alone knows," Twice whispered back.

As a rule, I think that he and I have a reasonably developed sense of the absurd, but it did not strike us as odd that we should be talking to one another in frightened whispers in our own house. At least, while we were doing it, it did not strike us as absurd, and for what must have been about twenty minutes we stood there, in the light of a single lamp in the big room, staring at one another and daring, now and then, to pose scared questions to one another. In the end Cousin Emmie came downstairs and switched on the main lights at the door of the room, and this was as if she had freed us from the spell which, at the top of the stairs, she had cast upon us.

"It's quarter to eight," she said in her toneless voice. "If you are late, my cousin will be in a worse temper than ever."

She sat down, took off her fur and disposed it on the back of her chair. "I don't want to go to this party. I don't like parties, especially my cousin's parties. I'll

stay with this little girl. Is your cook here?
To bring us supper?"

"Yes. Yes, of course." I felt quite
helpless. "I'll go and — "

"Look here," Twice said, "if Dee is ill
we just can't walk out — "

"She is not ill. She has a bit of a cold
and she is in a state, but it's no use you
people staying here. That will only make
her worse."

"Now look here, Miss Morrison . . ."
Twice began in a hectoring voice. "If Dee
is ill we must get the doctor — "

"You can send him round from the club
if you like," Cousin Emmie said, not in the
least intimidated or moved in any way.
"There is not much he can do — probably
more harm than good. The fewer people
there are fussing round that little girl,
the better."

"But what is *wrong* with her?" I almost
shouted. "She was all right this morning.
Now it's as if she hates us all!"

"She does hate you all," Cousin Emmie
told me flatly. "She made a mistake saying
she would marry that young man, and she
hates herself, and so of course she hates
everybody."

"Made a mistake?"

"Yes. She has found out now it was a mistake. I knew it was a mistake from the start. I have never liked that young man."

I clenched my teeth and stared at Twice, who, with teeth clenched, stared back at me.

"There is no use going on like that because all your plans have gone wrong and she is not going to marry this young man," Cousin Emmie told us in her flat way. "It is none of your business if she has broken her engagement to him, and don't you go bothering her about it. You'd better just get along to that party of my cousin's. I am going to see about supper for that little girl and me."

She drifted out of the drawing-room and turned towards the kitchen, and, having glared at her back, I then glared at Twice before flying upstairs.

"Dee!" I called out when I discovered that the bedroom door was locked. "Dee, I want to see you."

"Go away," said the voice from inside. "Go away. I don't want anybody but Miss Morrison."

I did not plead any more. I turned away, but by the time I reached the bottom of the stairs the tears were threatening to run down my cheeks. Cousin Emmie was emerging from the kitchen. Not wanting her to see my face, I called to Twice: "Twice, we'd better go. We are late now. Dee seems to be all right." Reluctantly, Twice came out to join me. "You'll be all right, Miss Morrison?" I called back from the darkness of the veranda.

"Yes," came the expressionless voice. "Just tell my cousin that little girl has a chill and I'd rather stay here with her than go to that party."

I am not going to pretend that I enjoyed Madame's Cropover dinner. Indeed, I had the greatest difficulty in persuading myself, at times, that it was taking place at all and that I was among those present. My mind was split into two distinct parts, one being the part that was with me here in the Great House in its party atmosphere, the other part having remained at Guinea Corner in the aura of Cousin Emmie.

Twice and I were the last to arrive, and when we told Madame and Sir Ian that

Dee had contracted a sudden chill and was unable to come there was an immediate crowding round of the guests with kind enquiries, and, to me, the strangest thing of all was that Rob, Marion and Roddy Maclean were in the forefront of the anxious enquirers. Explaining to them that she had a slight temperature but was not seriously ill, I found that I kept rubbing against Twice's shoulder to assure myself that the scene at Guinea Corner had really taken place and that Cousin Emmie had actually said that Dee was no longer engaged to Roddy. It would not have surprised me in the least if Dee had suddenly popped up beside me in her new yellow evening dress, thereby convincing me that I had dreamed the events of the last hour. Quite obviously, if Dee did not intend to marry Roddy, Roddy did not as yet know of her non-intentions. As if through a swirling mist that dazzled my eyes and caused my ears to hum, I heard Twice say: "So if you will excuse us after dinner, Madame, Janet and I will go home and not come round to the club. It is very kind of Miss Morrison to let us come away like this."

"Tchah! Emmie will be perfectly all right," said Madame; "but I quite understand your anxiety, Twice. These sudden chills can be extremely nasty."

On the whole, I suppose that we carried the thing off quite well, but I found it very difficult to keep my mind on the conversation at dinner. As soon as it was over and Twice and I were preparing to leave, Isobel cornered me on the dark veranda.

"Just what *is* the matter with li'l Dee?" she demanded, her vivid eyes catching the light from a window and seeming to bore into me.

"It's nothing much, Isobel. Just a chill and a shivery temperature, you know."

"She was all right this morning at the beauty parlour. When did this start?"

"Just after she came home," I said, and strode past her, away from her suspicious eyes, to the waiting car.

When Twice and I reached Guinea Corner, Cousin Emmie was sitting in her favourite corner of the drawing-room, a tray with coffee and biscuits on a small table beside her, the canvas bag and the parasol also beside her chair. This gave her the transitory air that always characterised her and I found it difficult to believe that, about two hours ago, Twice and I had gone out and had left her in charge of our household.

"You needn't have hurried back," she said. "That little girl is asleep."

"How is she?"

"She has a bad cold in her head, that's all. She got caught in that rain this afternoon, with no clothes on as usual. I don't like this climate. You never know what's going to happen."

I sat down firmly in a chair opposite to her and said sternly, prepared to stand no nonsense with my way of it: "Look here, Miss Morrison, what is all this about Dee not going to marry Roddy?"

"I don't see what you mean by all this," she said, breaking a biscuit in half. "She is not going to marry him because she doesn't want to."

"*Why* doesn't she want to?" I felt that I was shouting with exasperation.

"She doesn't like him."

"Did Dee tell you this?" Twice asked.

"Yes. If she didn't tell me, how would I know?"

"She didn't say anything to *us*!" I

snapped. "And she doesn't seem to have said anything to Roddy either!"

"She is afraid," said Cousin Emmie and swallowed a mouthful of coffee. "Oh, not of that young man — she will probably tell him tomorrow. But she is afraid of you," and she looked from one of us to the other before beginning to pour herself some more coffee.

I was so exasperated that I wanted to shake her. "Afraid of *us*?" I said, springing to my feet. "What the devil has she got to be afraid of?"

"She is afraid of you going on the way you are going on now because all your plans are upset." She looked up at me, a teaspoon held over her cup. "But I am not afraid of you and you might as well sit down and control that temper of yours," and she took a spoonful of sugar, put it into the cup and began to stir the coffee very slowly and deliberately.

In a flabbergasted way I sank back into my chair, and Twice took refuge by going to the tray in the corner and beginning to mix a glass of orange juice and soda for each of us. Into the silence Cousin Emmie began to speak in her flat toneless voice. "As a rule, I never interfere in anybody's affairs, but when I was sitting in here tonight, waiting for you to come down and she arrived home, I heard all that went on up there, and when I heard her getting hysterical I thought it better to — " She suddenly stopped speaking, the coffee cup on the way to her lips. "She is awake," she said, put the cup on the tray and went out of the room and upstairs, hardly seeming to disturb the air as she went.

"I didn't hear anything!" I said angrily to Twice, who merely shook his head.

In two minutes Cousin Emmie re-appeared in the doorway and stood looking at Twice. "She wants to see you," she said.

"Me?" Twice looked from Cousin Emmie to me and back to Cousin Emmie again.

"Yes, you." She sat down again behind her coffee tray. "You are hurt, of course," she said to me, fiddling about with cup and spoon after Twice had gone upstairs. "You are hurt because she hasn't asked to see you. You are a fool. You pay far too much attention to other people. She is a silly little thing, but no sillier than most people," and she then took a sip of coffee.

"You think people can help people, but they can't — not in important ways. It is a mistake to interfere at all."

"You interfered tonight and it was very helpful," I said. "You stopped her having screaming hysterics."

"You can stop people having hysterics and you can set their legs if they break them, but you can't help them not to be silly. I have watched you doing your best with that little girl ever since we were on that boat and she was being silly about your husband. You should have been your natural self and have given her a good smacking. I would have done."

"I bet you would!" I thought, but I said: "What good would that have done? She would probably have run away."

"If she had run away she would never have got engaged to this young man," Cousin Emmie countered. "If she had been her natural self she would never have done it. She only did it because you had been nice to her, as she calls it, and she knew it would please you."

"Please me? *I* didn't want her to get engaged to Roddy Maclean!"

"Oh yes you did. Not that young man

335

Maclean specially, but you wanted her to get engaged to somebody and get settled in life and all that sort of thing. So did my cousin, and so did Ian — so did everybody, except me. I am not silly enough to think that anybody can get settled in life. People are never settled till they're in the grave."

To listen to her was an odd sensation. There she sat, dipping biscuits in coffee and chewing the mess with her false teeth and making a sloshy, all-too-human and fleshy noise, and yet her toneless expressionless voice had an inhuman detached quality as if the words were issuing from the Sphinx or some other unworldly oracular source.

"This is nonsense!" I said forcibly, struggling free of the spell she seemed to be casting over me. "*I* didn't want her to get engaged — "

"Yes you did. You wanted her to get settled in some way, and marriage is the way people always think of for settling young women. Everybody wanted it, whether they think they did or not, for her and for that young man too. And all that builds up an influence with people like her. She is still silly enough to think she can please other people. I'm not. I know you can never please everybody, and it is far better just to please yourself."

"Are you sitting there telling me that Roddy Maclean proposed to Dee just to please Twice and me and Madame?" I asked.

"No, I'm not, and well you know it. In the first place, that young man probably proposed because she is wealthy and he knew he had the influence of all the rest of you backing him up. That young man has a lot of brains and a lot of determination. He has the sense to know what he wants, not like that silly little girl."

"I thought you didn't like him?" I was silly enough to say.

"Why should I like him just because he has brains and determination and knows what he wants? Hitler had brains and determination and knew what he wanted," she pointed out, dipping half of a biscuit into the coffee cup. "That little girl is not in the least interested in men or in getting married."

"Have you any idea what she *is* interested in?" I asked rather sourly, but I was at once ashamed of the sourness when

I remembered that, tonight, this old woman was being helpful albeit her manner made it difficult to appreciate that helpfulness, so I added: "Miss Morrison, you seem to know more about Dee than any of us and I am grateful for anything you can tell me."

She looked flatly at me for a few seconds before beginning to fiddle with her coffee again. "She has talked to me a lot," she said. "She talked to me because she is the same sort of person as I am although she does not really know it" — if she heard my sharply indrawn breath she did not show it, " — that is, as far as any two people are the same sort. I can't be bothered with men, and neither can she. Men are always bores like my cousin Ian with all his rubbish about India and this island, or smug bullies like my old father was, or they think that women are only for running a house or going to bed with like that man Maclean."

With a sudden inner shock, I realised that this last was a crystallisation of something that I myself had long felt about Rob Maclean. "That little girl upstairs doesn't like men either," Cousin Emmie was going on. "It's probably because of

338

this father of hers she has told me about, but it's partly just her nature — the way she is made. That little girl likes women better than men, and another thing is that she likes that big red-haired American girl. And she likes making money, and what she really wants to do is go into that hotel business up at that lunatic asylum place with that girl, and I told her she should just go ahead and do it, but she is afraid of what you are going to think."

With my mind in a whirl, I caught at the nearest straw. "I can't understand all this rubbish about her being afraid of me and what I think."

"It is because she likes you. She likes you more than she likes your husband even, so she is more afraid of you than of him. People are never afraid of people — not really afraid in a deep way — unless they like them."

And with another little shock I felt that this must be true, for Cousin Emmie herself seemed to fear nobody and she also seemed to like nobody.

"Did she tell you why she isn't going to marry Roddy?" I asked after a moment. "What I mean is, did she tell you what

she is going to *say* to Madame and everybody her reason is? Just that she has
changed her mind?"

"I suppose that is what she will say.
But quite likely she caught him at some
nonsense that brought her to her senses
and made her come back here in that state
she was in."

"What sort of nonsense?"

"His sort of nonsense," said Cousin
Emmie uninformatively and pushed the
little table with the tray to one side. "She
will probably tell you all about it now
that she has come to herself," she said,
standing up and popping the last biscuit
into the bag. "Will your husband drive
me home to my cousin's?"

"Of course, Miss Morrison. And thank
you for being so helpful tonight."

When I went upstairs to fetch Twice,
he was just coming out of Dee's room,
and I waited till he came down to the hall.

"Dee says you are to come to see her
if you would like to," he said.

"Did she tell you anything?"

"About Roddy? No. And I didn't ask.
She did nothing but apologise for that
carry-on when she came home tonight."

"Oh well, I'd better go up," I said. "Miss Morrison is ready to go home. Will you take her?"

"Of course."

He turned to the drawing-room door as Cousin Emmie emerged, the bag in one hand, the parasol in the other, the fur about her neck.

"You have given us a lot of help tonight, Miss Morrison," he said, but she merely looked at him in her blank way. "I still don't know what happened between Dee and Roddy, but I suppose it's best if we say nothing to anybody for the moment."

"My cousin, you mean?" she asked. "I never say anything to her, anyhow, except what has to be said. She would only get angry." She pulled her fur more closely about her neck with the hand that held the bag. "I expect my cousin will give herself a stroke one of these days, always losing her temper the way she does. You never know what might happen at her age. We'll go now," she ended, looked at me and went down the steps to the car.

Dee was sitting up in bed, her nose red, a flushed fever spot on each cheek, her whole face drooping and lugubrious. All her becoming suntan seemed to have disappeared in the course of a few hours; her skin looked dully sallow against the white pillow behind her, and the hair that had been dressed that morning lay about her head in dank greasy tufts.

"How do you feel, Dee?" I asked.

I felt unsure of myself, as if Dee were someone I no longer knew. It was not like meeting a stranger, which one does with an open mind — it was like meeting someone who had undergone a sudden metamorphosis which one had been told about but which was not outwardly apparent.

"I've only got a bit of a cold," she said. "Miss Jan, I am very sorry about when I came home tonight."

"That's all right, Dee. You were very upset."

I was very nervous, feeling that I was facing something that I did not under-stand, and I was also exasperated with myself for being nervous.

"I should never have got engaged to Roddy," she said. "It was just like when I got engaged to Alan Stewart. I didn't really want to do that either — yet I just did it."

"Because Roddy and all of us here on Paradise seemed to want it?" I asked, working on Cousin Emmie's theory.

"Yes. That and — well — everybody gets married. At least, most people do."

"But you would really rather run a hotel with Isobel?" I plunged.

"Cousin Emmie told you?"

"Yes."

"I am glad she did, Miss Jan." She looked down at her small hands on the sheet. "I suppose you think I am — I am queer." She looked up, and there was something like a smile on her face as she spoke the word.

I shook my head. "No. I'll be honest, Dee. If I were in your place, I am the sort that would rather marry Roddy than go into business with Isobel, but then I haven't much of a head for business." I felt monstrously awkward and tried to smile as I ended.

"I don't know if you'd have married Roddy though," she surprised me by saying, "even if you didn't like Isobel better and feel more comfortable with her as I do. Miss Jan, these Macleans are friends of yours and I am going to tell you about Roddy, just so that you will know and maybe be able to help Missis Marion. I like Missis Marion."

I felt suddenly cold in the warmth of the tropic night as I sat waiting without speaking.

"Roddy isn't what his mother and father think he is," she said. "He didn't do any engineering at the university. He didn't do anything except mess about with literature and poetry and things. He hasn't got his degree in engineering or anything."

"But Dee! I — this can't be — I mean what — " I heard myself making no sense and fell silent.

"It is the easiest thing in the world to cheat your parents about things," Dee told me calmly. "One's parents never know anything about one — they see one as an embodiment of their wishes or something. Most of Roddy's brothers have studied engineering as their father and mother wanted, so Roddy just let his father and mother think he was doing engineering too. He is the most frightful liar, anyway."

"I see," I said, semi-stunned.

"He lies as a matter of course about anything that suits him, like while he has been engaged to me he has been carrying on with coloured girls down around the Bay and everywhere."

I at once suspected Isobel of making mischief here and I said: "You can prove this about the coloured girls? Or is it hearsay, Dee?"

"Oh, I could prove it if I wanted to," she said and her plain little face showed disgust. "That's why I was in a state when I came home. When I left the Bay this afternoon I took a run up to Mount Melody to see if the rain had done any damage to that part where the wall is down. Roddy was up there with a coloured girl. They were arguing about money. He was saying he had given her enough already. They were in the old coach-house, sheltering from the rain, I suppose."

"Oh, Dee!"

"It's all right, Miss Jan. I don't care a bit really — not now, anyway — but it was sort of horrid at the time. I knew he was a bit like that. Since we got engaged he was always wanting me to go to bed and do things with him and so on. And I think

345

he must have done something to Isobel too, although she has never said anything." She had been looking down at her hands and now she looked up again. "I am only telling you about all this because Missis Marion is probably going to get a bit of a shock about Roddy some day, and if you know now what he is like you will be over your shock by the time hers comes along and be able to help her a bit, maybe. I like Missis Marion," she repeated. "You see, Roddy is just different from her other sons, like me being different from the sort of daughter Father would have liked to have. Roddy is a sort of artist or something instead of being an engineer like the Macleans wanted. He wrote that book you were reading on the boat, something about love."

"*But Not For Love?*" I squeaked. "Rubbish! That is by somebody called S. T. Bennett!"

"That's right. That's the name he writes under."

"But that book is *good*!" I said stupidly.

"Is it?" Dee asked without much interest.

I stared at her. She was away beyond

346

my comprehension. Here was a young woman who had been engaged to a young man who had written a most distinguished novel and she had not even bothered to read it. My mind became side-tracked.

"Dee, when you were small, you used to read a lot. You hardly read at all now. Why?"

"It doesn't get you anywhere," she told me flatly, and I suddenly seemed to see an actual physical resemblance between her and Cousin Emmie. "Look at Roddy. He has spent five years at the university, and he has nothing to show for it except for knowing a lot of stuff about poetry and this one book. He isn't even qualified for a decent job."

I felt that we were getting into deep water. There was no doubt, I told myself, there were deep differences between Dee and me, but this one was deep enough to drown us. Dee considered that Roddy with "this one book" had nothing to show for his five years, and I considered that with *But Not For Love* Roddy had more to show for his five years than all of us at Paradise could show for all our lifetimes. This is the sort of difference between two people that is beyond all discussion and resolution; there is no bridge that spans this gulf, and there is no explosive that can destroy this barrier.

"Do his father and mother know about *But Not For Love*?" I asked.

"No. He is scared to tell them because they would find out how he wasted his time at the university. That's what I meant when I said he was such a liar. He lives by lies."

"When did he tell you about the book?"

"Only yesterday when I told him that we ought to ask Twice to help him to get promotion in Allied Plant."

I rose to my feet, feeling excessively tired and also, in a strange new way, out of sympathy with Dee who seemed with each second to be growing more like her cold, distant clever father, a man whom I had never liked, but at the same time that this seemed so, I knew that it was not so. It was not Dee who was changing. This cut-and-dried young woman in the bed was Dee as she really was and always had been, but she was stripped now of the attempt to be what I and her family had tried to make her be, just as my own eyes had been stripped of the distorting lens through which I had looked at her.

"It is long after midnight, Dee. You must go to sleep," I said. "Have you everything you want?"

"Yes, thank you. And, Miss Jan, I really know what I am doing about going to Mount Melody with Isobel — it is truly what I want to do. You are not angry about it? We are still friends?"

"I am not angry, Dee. About going there with Isobel, I am glad you have found what you really want to do, but on the business side of it I hope you will let your father know what you are doing and have a proper agreement about shares and things."

"You needn't worry about that side of it," she told me lightly, and I felt that she spoke the truth. "You like Isobel, don't you?" she asked.

"Yes, I do, Dee. I have always liked Isobel," but I did not say that Isobel, like Dee herself, seemed tonight to be a different person and that all my feelings about her were in a state of suspension.

I left her, and instead of going straight to my bedroom I went downstairs and took

But Not For Love from the bookshelf, and while I sat with it unopened in my hand I heard Twice come in the back way from the garage and run upstairs. When I went up, he had taken off his shoes and socks and was sitting on the edge of the bed watching himself wriggling his toes, a habit he has when he is thinking. He looked up at me and then down at the book in my hand.

"Men have died from time to time and worms have eaten them," I said, "but not for love!" whereupon I threw the book on to the bed and, to my own disgust, broke down into tears. "I'm sorry," I said after a moment. "I am sorry to make one more scene tonight."

"Go ahead," Twice said. "I wish males weren't conditioned from near-infancy not to seek relief in tears. I only took my shoes off to stop me from kicking the furniture to bits."

"Unfasten this dress for me, please, darling," I said, and when he had undone the back of the long dress I stepped out of it.

"What happened in that room along there?" he asked. "What's the score? I gather from that old woman that you and I and Sir Ian and heaven knows who else forced the unwilling Dee into the arms of Roddy Maclean."

"I suppose we did in an unconscious sort of way. Being honest, I did hope in a vague way that she would get married and be off one's hands, I think."

"Do I gather that she is homosexual — a Lesbian ?"

"I wish I were quite clear in my mind just where the borderline lies between what we call normality and Lesbianism," I said. "I wouldn't know. I am away out of my depth. But it seems to me that Dee is more of a neuter with a slight tendency towards homosexuality — if the tendency had been strong, surely she would have discovered it in herself long ago." I took the pins out of my hair. "Lord, I'm tired, but not sleepy tired."

"Nor me neither forbye and besides," Twice said in imitation of Tom at Reachfar, and I smiled at him before I picked up the copy of *But Not For Love* from the bed beside me.

"Anyhow," I said, "my worries about Dee are over. Having discovered herself tonight as she seems to have done during her session with Cousin Emmie, she has turned into a different person already. Did you feel that?"

"Yes, I did. All that dreadful touchiness seems to have gone."

"I know. Twice, this has been a night of queer things, and there is something even queerer that you don't know about yet." Holding the book between my hands, I looked at him across it. "Do you know who wrote this?"

"S. T. Bennett, isn't it? Why?"

"S. T. Bennett is Roddy Maclean."

"You're off your nut!"

"Maybe I am, but that is what Dee said and she should know."

He stared at me, frowning, before he took the book from me and let it fall open between his hands. He read a line or two.

"It could be," he said wonderingly. "Yes, it could be."

"It definitely is, I think. If all that Dee says is true, Rob and Marion are in for a bit of a shock and something of a very pleasant big surprise too."

When I had repeated to Twice all that Dee had told me about Roddy, I ended:

"It all seems quite fantastic, and in a queer way it makes me feel terribly old. When I was at the university it would never have entered my head to tell people that I had passed the degree exam in Physics when I had never even attended the class let alone sat the exam, but that's what Roddy has done — he has been doing it for five years. I wonder if he has even got a degree in Arts ?"

"That hardly matters at this stage when I think of the sort of degree he is going to get when Rob finds out about this," Twice said. "Rob Maclean is not the sort of bloke you can fool like that and get away with it."

I began to laugh. "Roddy's got away with it for five years and I must say I can't help admiring him for it. And he has made a success of what he set out to do — that will make a difference with Rob, as Cousin Emmie would say. Of course, I'd admire the man who wrote that book no matter what he did, I think."

"Well, Roddy seems to do plenty, what with his sex life and all."

"I always liked Roddy and I still like him, sex life and all. And I admire him too. He has got all the guts I never had."

"How do you mean?"

"I wanted to write once, when I was his age, but I let people turn me into a nursemaid instead. Cousin Emmie is right. People can be influenced out of their very natures by other people."

"Maybe you made your people happier than Roddy's will be when the light breaks over them. The Macleans would rather have an engineer for a son than S. T. Bennett, I bet, especially Rob."

"Maybe I did make my people happy," I agreed. "And, anyway, I could never have written anything half as good as this."

I picked up the book again, put it on my pillow, took off the rest of my clothes and got into bed.

"You probably couldn't have," Twice said. "You're not ruthless enough. I have always thought that one can't set the Thames or the heather on fire unless one is ruthless enough not to care about burning out the city of London or all the wild life on the moor."

"I hadn't thought of that," I said, "but I suppose you are right."

11

A BLOWN OSTRICH EGG

THE next morning Dee still had a slight temperature and was quite happy to stay in bed, and when I went up to see her after breakfast she was just finishing the writing of a letter. With deliberation, she addressed the envelope, folded the sheet of paper, picked up her engagement ring from the bedside table, dropped it inside and stuck down the flap.

"Could Caleb go over to Olympus with this, please, Miss Jan? Roddy won't have left for the Bay yet."

"Yes," I said. "Of course."

During the night, it seemed to me, Dee had grown very like her father, and the longer I stayed in the room, the stronger the likeness became. She had withdrawn into herself and obviously wished that her engagement and all the events of the night before had never happened, but, this being impossible, she was doing the next best thing, the thing that her father would have done — she was ignoring completely the fact that these things had ever taken place.

"Isobel is moving up to Mount Melody on Monday," she said after I had called the yard boy and had despatched him with the letter. "It will be all right if I go on Monday too?"

I felt that this was the merest outward form of politeness and that if I had said that I did not wish her to go on Monday she would merely have smiled faintly at me for being unreasonable and have gone in any case.

"Of course," I said, "if your cold is better and you feel well enough."

"I shall be all right now that — all that is over and done with . . ." and over the writing paper and the envelopes on the bed she made an impatient dismissive gesture with her hands, a gesture like one I had seen her father make many years ago.

There was an awkwardness between us which, I was aware, was emanating largely from myself. I did not as yet know this new Dee and I felt strange in her presence while she had broken through into some new self-knowledge and the confidence that came with it and was thus in complete control of the situation. I also felt depressed at the element of distance that had developed between myself and someone I had known — or thought I had known — since her childhood.

"You must do as you please, Dee," I said, "but I hope you will stay in bed for today at least."

"Yes, I'll do that. I want to write to Father, explaining everything and telling him about Mount Melody, and I can write in bed as well as anywhere else."

As she spoke, she picked up her pen from the bedside table, and I felt that I was dismissed, as her father used to dismiss me in the days when I was his secretary.

When I went downstairs, Twice was sitting on the veranda and I said to him: "Dee is so like that stick of a father of hers that I can hardly believe it."

"I suppose she is more likely to be like him or her mother than anybody else."

"But she seems to have turned into a replica of him overnight!"

"I wonder. I don't believe that people change overnight. Since I saw her an hour ago, I have come to the conclusion that our bringing her to St. Jago has been a complete success." He grinned at me. "Our object was to take her away from the influence of her family and let her be herself. We seem to have achieved it. That the self she is is not what we imagined is beside the point, after all."

"I suppose that is true. It's all rather dreary though, like Cousin Emmie saying you never know what might happen."

Dram and Charlie, having finished their morning mongoose-hunt in the nearby cane-piece, came into the garden through a hole in the hedge and prepared to settle under their hibiscus clump. I thought of the *Pandora*, of the sailors giving us Charlie, of the first time I saw Cousin Emmie in the smokeroom and, finally, of the moment on the deck before the ship sailed when I discovered that I really did not want to come back here to St. Jago at all. I have noticed that when one is feeling depressed one tends always to think of things that depress one still more.

"I suppose it would have been better if we had never brought Dee out in the first place," Twice said, contradicting what he had said a moment before, "but how can

358

one know? It seemed like a good idea at the time. I suppose I had a rush of blood to the head that night I suggested it, but our leave at home had been such a success that I think I felt that we couldn't put a foot wrong and all that."

"I know." I stared out at Dram and Charlie now stretched out under the hibiscus. "Twice, that leave at home last year was a sort of turning point. When I came back here with it behind me, I felt that things would never be the same again. Actually, every single little thing that happens is a turning point. No second is ever the same as any second that went before and what happens in each second alters *us*, but it is all so minute and gradual that we don't notice it. It takes a great big thing like a birth or a death or the sort of rediscovery of home that I made during that leave to make one realise this constant process of change. That rediscovery of home was like being born again with better sight, and it put this island into perspective for me. Before we went on leave, this place had the upper hand of me, but when I stood on Reachfar hill and looked at St. Jago from there I put the darned thing in

359

its place and it has never regained control of me. And I see now that Cousin Emmie has helped."

"Cousin Emmie?"

"By always being in complete control of herself and everything around her. I couldn't get my feet off the ground and get airborne on the atmosphere of St. Jago with Cousin Emmie about. She wouldn't let me."

I went to the mosquito mesh of the veranda and stood looking out over the garden, over the wall that bounded it, over the cane-fields to the large clump of eucalyptus and mahogany trees on the slight rise where the Great House stood. To the left of the rise with the trees, on the flat plain, lay the sugar factory, its tall smoke-stack an incongruous symbol of modern industrialisation against the primeval bush of the surrounding hills.

"Cousin Emmie is right about this island, Twice," I said quietly.

"What does she say about it?" he asked from behind me, equally quietly.

"She says we white people shouldn't be here. She says the island doesn't want us and the negroes don't want us. She said the negroes didn't want a Cropover party —

that they would rather have the money it cost to have a spending spree on their own." I stared hard at the black exclamation mark that was the factory smoke-stack, which, as well as being a symbol of modern industrialisation, was, for me, the symbol of Twice's aspirations as an engineer. He was a young man for the position he held and it was in this green valley that he had proved himself. "Cousin Emmie was right," I said and turned round. "The workers were not one damn interested in that party last night. Eighteen months ago, when we did the Varlets play at the Great House, the people were *with* us but they are not any more. Eighteen months is a long time in this island. Yesterday the people weren't with us any more. You see, I know what it feels like when people are really with you and not apart as the servants were yesterday about the Cropover. I danced at a Harvest Home once when I was a kid of eight and everybody was welded together in one feeling. I know what it feels like to be in the place where one really and truly belongs." I felt tears gathering in my eyes and blinked as I said: "Oh, it's all silly, all these associations and memories that one drags through life, and all these influences from the past that flow in on one."

"It's not silly," Twice said very quietly. "These associations with similar things that happened before and the recognition of influences and responses that flow towards us are the only guides we have. It seems to me that you and I are arriving at the same point by devious routes as usual. It is true that the negroes don't want the Cropover any more — they want a cash bonus on the Crop instead. And you, although you hesitate to say it, are right about you and me and this job here in the islands. The job is all right — this industrial expansion that is going on is a real thing — but the way we white people live, especially here at Paradise, that's no good to you or me, darling. It's gimcrack. It makes me think more than anything of that blown ostrich egg in Madame's drawing-room. It's brittle with age, it's hollow, and at the slightest rock of the table it will fall to smithereens."

"Twice — " I began, and then I found myself at a loss for words, while tears began to flow out of the corners of my eyes. "Oh, God, I don't know what's the matter with me! This is the second burst of tears in twelve hours!"

"I know what's wrong with you," Twice said, "but the only words I can think of for it are the old Army ones — you are bloody well fed-up."

"That's it. I am bloody well fed-up." I dried my eyes. "I have no right to be. I've got everything in the world any woman could want, but I am fed-up."

"Heavens," Twice said, "what a relief it is to have got all this out into the open. I have been thinking about it ever since we came back, and then I would see you here in this house with the servants and a way of life that we can never achieve at home and I'd shove my discontent aside. You see, you are very good at this thing of being mistress of a small but dignified house, Janet."

I smiled at him in a watery way. "And you are very good at being Caribbean representative of a British firm, Twice, but what's the point if neither of us really likes it?"

"Exactly. Well, all we have to decide now is what we are going to do."

"I leave that entirely to you, darling. I think I have made enough trouble for now."

"The thing to do is to complete this tour of duty, of course, if we can bear it at all. The point of this meeting is that a conclusion has been reached in principle, as Somerset would say, the principle being that we want a job at home and are finished with foreign parts. That's right, isn't it?"

"Oh, Twice, it's so terribly right!" Tears once again began to run out of my eyes. "This lot are sheer relief," I told him.

"I am going to ask Clorinda for some coffee," Twice said and disappeared into the house.

When he came back, I had stopped weeping the silly tears and felt as if I had made a turning out of some endlessly long road, glaring with sun and dust and bordered by twisting jungle into a cool winding track that led over a wide wind-swept moor.

"I can't get over the interconnectedness of things," I said. "All this is bound up in some strange way with Dee and Cousin Emmie, especially with Cousin Emmie. It is as if she had forced me, against my own will, to look at the truth, just as she forced me, last night, to see Dee as she was and not as I wanted her to be."

"Then it looks as if you are about to be

forced to look at some more truth," Twice said from where he stood by the table that held the coffee, "for here she comes."

"I don't care. Not now. And you'll have to entertain her, anyhow, if she wants to stay. I have to be round at the Great House by eleven. I say, one of us ought to go up and see Dee."

"She's all right. I went up while Cookie fixed the coffee. Good-morning, Miss Morrison."

"You are just in time for some coffee," I said.

She sat down, disposing the canvas bag on one side of her and the parasol on the other. "How is that silly little girl this morning?"

"A lot better. She is sitting up writing letters."

"My cousin is in a temper again. She is too old to stay up all night at parties, as I told her. She said you were going round there this morning." She looked at me accusingly.

"It's the appeal for the new TB Ward," I said and my voice was apologetic.

"A lot of nonsense. These services should be in the hands of the government and my cousin shouldn't interfere. She could give money if she wanted to, but that isn't what she wants — she just wants to interfere." She turned to Twice. "Are you not round at that factory this morning for once?"

"No. We are on holiday until Monday."

Cousin Emmie made a noise between a snort and a grunt, broke a biscuit in half and dipped a half into her coffee.

"Does that young man know yet that that girl is not going to marry him?"

"She sent a letter to him early this morning," I said.

"I thought something like that had happened. I met that Mrs. Maclean in her car in my cousin's avenue when I was coming out. She would be going to tell my cousin about things being broken off. That means my cousin will be in a temper at lunch again."

Amid all that had happened, I had given no thought to Marion Maclean's attitude, and now when Cousin Emmie mentioned her name I was struck anew by her unerring gift for bringing up the unpalatable. "I suppose that Mrs. Maclean will be in a temper too. I've never seen such people for getting into tempers about things that are none of their business. I wouldn't."

"I suppose this is another one in a temper," Twice said, "for here's the Rolls coming," and in a few seconds Sir Ian was on the veranda.

"Good God, you here again, Emmie? Look here, Missis Janet, what's this about this engagement being broken off? Mother's fit to be tied!"

"It's none of her business," said Cousin Emmie.

"It's broken off," I said.

"Why?"

"Because they don't want to get married, I suppose," I said, taking a leaf out of Cousin Emmie's uninformative book, and at once finding it very effective, for Sir Ian dropped his hectoring tone and said: "Miss Dee didn't say why?"

"No," I lied. "After all, as Miss Morrison said, it is none of my business or yours, come to that."

"But what do they mean carryin' on like this?"

"If you can tell me what anybody means by half the things they do I'll be very grateful," I told him.

He turned to Twice. "She's as bad as Mother. You'd think all this perishin' muddle was *my* fault!"

"It's your fault as much as anybody's," said Cousin Emmie. "I heard you, that time at Christmas, telling that young man that what he wanted was a nice young wife. You and your interfering."

"Look here, Emmie, you've no business sittin' here drinkin' coffee. You'd better be gettin' ready to go on that boat next week and mindin' your own business."

"I am minding my own business. I am not going on that boat."

"Now, look here, Emmie, your passage is booked on — "

"I didn't book it. You did. But I'm not going on it. She popped a biscuit into the bag and rose from her chair, turning to me. "Are you driving round to my cousin's? I'll come round with you."

"Right," Twice said. "I'll get the car."

"My car's outside," snapped Sir Ian. "Take it and send it back," and he turned his back on us in a pointed way while we went down the steps and got into the Rolls.

We sat in silence throughout the few minutes of the journey, for Cousin Emmie seemed to be wrapped in some secret contemplation of her own and I had nothing that I wanted to say. Madame, who was already at her big desk, greeted me with: "Good-morning, Janet" and said "Go away, Emmie!" all in one breath. Cousin Emmie, however, did not go away but sat down in a corner, which made Madame give an exasperated sigh and move her chair so that her back was to her cousin, as if this dismissed her from our presence.

"I am most upset, Janet," she said then, "about the termination of this engagement between little Dee and Roddy Maclean. What happened?"

"They seem to have quarrelled, Madame."

"How is Dee's cold this morning?"

"Much better, thank you."

"Do you suppose that maybe this tiff was because she wasn't feeling well? Mightn't they come together again? It seemed so very suitable."

"It wasn't a bit suitable, Lottie," said Cousin Emmie. "She is a wealthy young woman and that young man hasn't even got a proper job."

"Be quiet, Emmie! What do you feel, Janet?"

"I think it is very unlikely they will come together again, Madame. In a way I am not sorry the engagement is broken. Dee is very young and immature."

"In some ways," said Cousin Emmie.

"Hold your tongue, Emmie! You know nothing about it."

"I know more than you, Lottie."

Madame compressed her lips and drew a long sighing breath through her nostrils.

"Oh, well, there is little point in discussing it further at the moment, Janet. All is fair in love and war, I suppose."

"There's nothing fair in either of them," said Cousin Emmie, and Madame puffed out her chest, got up and went to look down upon this haunting one-woman chorus. "Emmie, there are a number of other rooms in the house."

"Too many. You couldn't keep a house this size in England now and quite right too. Nobody needs a house this size. I don't like big houses."

"Emmie, please to retire to the library."

"No. The coffee will be here soon and I'd just have to come back."

Defeated, Madame plumped herself back into her chair, drew a pile of papers towards her and said: "Janet, let us get on with this list."

Madame and I worked for perhaps half an hour before the coffee was brought in, and in the same moment, Nurse Porter arrived with her weekly report.

"Good-morning, Nurse," said Madame. "Janet, please attend to the coffee for me while Nurse and I do the Clinic Report. Sit here, Nurse. Monday, General Clinic," Madame read from the sheet while I poured coffee. "Yes. Tuesday, Venereal Clinic. Treatments, male thirteen, female nineteen. Dear me. Thursday, yes. Friday, Emergency call three-thirty p.m. What was that, Nurse?"

"A young woman, Madame, threatening miscarriage. Doctor is up there again this morning."

"Oh dear. Poor woman. Who is she?"

"A girl called Freeman who worked in the Estate office, Madame."

"That little girl? I didn't know she was married!"

"The girl is not married, Madame."

"Not married? And *who* is the father of the child?"

At Nurse's words, Madame was immediately enraged and embattled against what she saw as one of the great social evils of the island, the major hindrance to social progress, the problem of the illegitimate child. The Freeman family, being "Paradise people", were what Madame regarded as territory won for social law and order, and that this girl of the family was "in trouble" was the equivalent of the island enemy having, by sneak attack, retaken a part of that territory back into outlawry and disorder.

"I don't know, Madame. They would not tell me, but I understand that the girl's father knows and will see Sir Ian about it himself."

"I see. Very well. I shall mention the matter to Sir Ian," said Madame, making a note. "This is most upsetting. Goodmorning, Nurse."

The nurse went away and Madame sat staring balefully down at the name she had noted.

"If it's that little girl called Lucy that used to bring the letters over from the office," said Cousin Emmie through a mouthful of biscuit, "that's in trouble, Ian doesn't have to go anywhere to find out the man's name."

"Be quiet, Em — " Madame spun round like a fat little humming-top in her swivel chair. "Emmie, *what* did you say?"

"That man's name that got that girl into trouble. I can tell you that."

"You?"

"You won't like it." Cousin Emmie masticated and swallowed the biscuit and took a sip of coffee. "But I can tell you."

"Then *tell* me!" Madame brought her hand down with a slam on the desk top.

"It's that young man Maclean," said Cousin Emmie, taking another bite of biscuit, "the one that this little girl has just broken off her engagement to."

"*Emmie!*"

The voice nearly made me jump out of my skin, but Cousin Emmie went on unmoved with her own train of thought. "I shouldn't be surprised if that's why that little girl broke off the engagement. She should never have got engaged to him in the first place. I wouldn't have got engaged to him."

Madame rose from her desk, stumped across the room and stood menacingly over her cousin, who, quite unperturbed, went on eating biscuit and sipping coffee.

"Emmie, if you knew all this — this rubbish, for I don't believe a word of it — why didn't you mention it before?"

"Why?"

"Why what? What do you mean?"

"Why mention something just for the sake of mentioning it? I didn't know before that you wanted to know about this young man and this girl from the office, Lottie," and she took another bite of biscuit.

"Emmie, stop chewing biscuits and listen to *me*!"

"I am listening, Lottie. And biscuits won't digest if you don't chew them. I have to be careful at my age."

"Emmie, this is scandalous rubbish about this girl and Roddy. What makes you say a thing like that?"

"Lottie, you think that any woman who isn't married is a fool, but I am not such a fool that I don't know about babies. I was a nurse once, after all. I know how babies come to get born, don't I?" She stared up at Madame. "I nearly told those two they must stop misbehaving themselves on your property and disturbing me on my walks. I don't like that sort of thing."

Madame sat staring at Cousin Emmie while she finished her biscuit and drank the last of her coffee. Madame was obviously marshalling all her forces for an attack on her cousin that would throw everything she had said into discredit and she radiated a force that held me rigid in my chair. Not so Cousin Emmie. She put down her cup and rose to her feet.

"Emmie, where are you going?"

"Out," said Cousin Emmie, and went, turning the corner of the doorway to drift away along the veranda like a withered leaf in a light breeze.

"Janet, do you think my cousin is mad?" Madame asked me.

"No, Madame. Dee told me that she had seen Roddy with a coloured girl. I didn't see any point in mentioning it."

"Janet! I do not understand how you can say such a thing so calmly!" I noticed that she was very pale and that her hand shook. "You don't seem to realise what this means. Roderick Maclean is the son of my *manager*!"

"There," I thought, although I did not say it, "you are only partly right. Roderick Maclean is first and foremost Roderick Maclean."

"I realise that, Madame," I said aloud, "but Roddy is a very handsome young man and Lucy Freeman is a very pretty young girl."

Suddenly Sir Ian came striding in, his white brows drawn down over his eyes, the eyes themselves at their fiercest.

"Mother, I'd like a private word with you."

The old lady looked up at him. "Yes, Ian?"

"Well — " He looked at me.

"Is it about Roderick Maclean, Ian? Freeman the Millman has been to see you?"

"Good God, Mother, how did you find out about this?"

"Emmie has just told us."

"Emmie? How did *she* know, dammit?"

"That doesn't matter, Ian." She sighed. "Is it true?"

" 'Fraid so, Mother. There's a bunch o' letters an' everything — young fool!"

The telephone rang and Madame said:

"Please answer the Instrument for me, Janet."

"Nurse Porter here," the voice said. "Mrs. Alexander? Would you tell Madame please that that Freeman girl has lost her baby. Doctor says she will be all right. I am leaving for Running Cut now."

I put down the receiver and conveyed the bald message to Madame and Sir Ian.

"Oh, well," Madame said, "perhaps it is for the best."

"By God, I'll take my ridin' stick to that young bounder!" Sir Ian blazed. "Never liked the fellah! Never could fathom him." He swung round on me. "Twice never liked him either although he never said anything. Poor Missis Marion! Poor Rob!" He strode to the door. "By heaven, when I catch him, I'll have the hide off him! Mother, I'm goin' up to Olympus to see Rob."

"Yes, Ian."

I wanted to get out of the place, away from Madame and the Great House.

"Will you drop me on your way, Sir Ian?" I asked.

"Yes, yes," he said impatiently, but I did not care.

12

"A QUESTION OF KNOWING ENOUGH"

"SIR IAN isn't coming in for a beer?" Twice asked, looking up from his drawing-board as I came up the steps and the car drove away. "What's up?"

"You may well ask. How is Dee?"

"All right. I was up half an hour ago. She is studying wine catalogues, and last night might never have been. Come on, what goes on?"

I told him what had happened at the Great House, and after giving a long low whistle he began to smile and said: "The more I hear of that young devil, the more I like him."

"You react in a peculiar way. I don't say I don't agree with you, but the rest of this place is against us."

"It's a question of knowing enough, as you are so fond of saying. He simply didn't hang together as an engineer, but as the bloke who wrote *But Not For Love* he hangs together more and more."

"Implying that engineers are nice respectable types while writers go whoring about getting girls in the family way? People aren't that easy to sort into groups or that hackneyed as personalities."

"It isn't like that exactly," Twice said. "It was more that he was all out of kilter as an engineer."

"In other words, you had a *feeling* that he wasn't really an engineer?"

Twice grinned at me with his teeth clenched. "All right. You win. But you never suspected him of being S. T. Bennett?"

"Never. Thinking back, he was at the greatest pains to lead me away from any idea like that."

"I wonder why?" Twice said. "I've always understood, though, that people who write, artists and so on, think along different lines from the rest of us. There is no guessing at his motives."

"Tangerines," I said, following, like Cousin Emmie, a train of thought of my own.

"Huh?"

Looking at Twice's puzzled face, I realised that I had spoken the word aloud. "When I was a child at Reachfar," I explained, "old Aunt Betsy used to have a box of tangerines sent to me from London every Christmas. They were the only oranges I ever saw in those days. It was a flat wooden box and held about twenty, and Tom and George used to open it very carefully and ceremonially, levering the lid up with the screw-driver. Inside, there were napkins of soft white paper, printed with gold curlycues, and when I lifted the four points of the napkins, there were the tangerines, every one wrapped in thick silver foil with just its dark orange top showing. Sometimes a thick, oval-shaped, dark green leaf had got into the box."

"Go on," Twice said.

"That box was the essence of mystery — beautiful exotic mystery. It had the look, the smell, the colour, the whole atmosphere of another world, a world a million times removed from the human one that I lived in. It made no difference when I was told that peasants beside the Mediterranean Sea grew tangerines for sale as we grew potatoes at Reachfar. At that time tangerines remained for me a manifestation of a more mysterious, more wonderful world." I hesitated, feeling suddenly shy. "I feel a bit like that about people who write. It's not the romantic Byronic image I have of them or anything about Bohemians being sexually loose in slovenly rooms on the Rive Gauche. It is that those people live in their minds in a world exotically different from the world my mind knows, like the tangerines when I was a child. I shall be a little scared of Roddy when I see him again. Shall you ?"

"Not scared exactly but sort of awkward. It's queer, the Macleans producing a son who writes."

"Old Mr. Carter wrote and so did Sir Richard," I said, remembering people from my past, "but with Mr. Carter it was shipping and with Sir Richard it was history and these things are sciences as much as arts. It's the arts that give me the tangerine feeling."

"I think there is a great deal in our being what you might call first-generation-educated," Twice said. "To people like Monica, it is a commonplace to have writers and painters in the family and among their acquaintance. They probably had tangerines every evening with the dessert too, when you think of it. But Rob and Marion are people like us. Their fathers were farmers who left school at fourteen. I wonder how they feel about their writer son?"

"I don't think they know."

"That's another thing. Why this secrecy?"

I rose, looked out through the mosquito mesh and spoke with my back to him. "In a way, I can understand Roddy's secrecy although I can't explain it. It is something to do with being disapproved of — like my grandmother saying that tangerines were all very well but that potatoes were a better staple crop. Maybe Roddy feels that his first-generation-educated parents feel that engineers are a better staple crop than writers. . . . There's the Rolls coming down from Olympus!"

Twice joined me at the mesh screen and we watched the big car come out of the trees of the Olympus drive, streak along between the fields of cane, pass the gates to the Great House and leave the Estate by the south approach.

"The Bay, horse-whips and all," Twice said.

"How I hate this place and these people this morning!" I said. "And how I loathe all their bloody certainty that they are so right! I'd rather have old Cousin Emmie than any of them."

"Here is a change indeed!" Twice jeered.

"Well, at least she sees straight. . . . What about lunch?"

"As soon as you like. I have to go down to the Bay office this afternoon. Want to come?"

"No. I'd better stay with Dee."

"That reminds me. She asked me to ask Isobel Denholm to come up this evening. Do you mind?"

"Not me. If they are going to join forces, if that is what you call it, the sooner they do it the better. I'd like to have the house to ourselves. I tell you what — ask Isobel to come up for the weekend. They are moving up to Mount Melody on Monday, anyway, and she will keep Dee out of my hair, maybe. But tell her not to come before six in the evening. I'd like to have the afternoon in peace. And then, Twice, let's swear a solemn swear to have no more house guests."

"There's not much point. We're bound to get involved with the first stray dog or cat we see."

After lunch we both went upstairs to see Dee, who seemed to be very happy and looking forward to Isobel's visit, but I noticed that there was about her an air of imminent departure, despite the fact that she was in bed, immobile and still sniffly with her cold. Parting sometimes does not wait for the moment when the good-byes are said, and this was one of those times.

It was my habit in the afternoons, between lunch and tea when the day was at its hottest, to lie on my bed with a book, but today, after Twice had gone, I decided to stay downstairs to be on hand should there be any enquirers after Dee, and I settled myself on a sofa in the drawing-room that stood at right angles to the french window, and opened *But Not For Love*, which I was starting to re-read in the light of my new knowledge. The hot afternoon died down to the customary silence. Dram and Charlie had moved from the hibiscus clump, which gave no shade from the overhead summer sun at this time of the day, on to the veranda and lay spread side by side on the tiled floor; Caleb had set his garden hose in the notch of a forked stick so that the trickle of water ran down the slope by the roots of a hedge; Cookie, Clorinda and Minna rattled the last saucepan and slammed the last cupboard door before all four servants vanished to the dim cool quiet of their quarters for the afternoon. There was no sound from the factory on this non-working, out-of-Crop afternoon; no voices echoed from the canefields, and even the insects were silenced in the heat of the sun. I was reading, with admiration, an evocative description of Glasgow in cold November fog when I became aware that the light in the room had become even more shaded, and, looking over the top of the book, I saw at eye-level where I lay a pair of legs in khaki-drill trousers that ended in feet that wore dirty white tennis shoes. Sitting up and looking up in one movement, I found Roddy Maclean in the frame of the french window.

"Why, hello," I said.

"Quietly does it," he said, coming into the room and sitting in a chair on the other side of the window from my sofa. "You see before you a fugitive on the run."

Out of the shaded dimness, his teeth flashed a smile, his eyes gleamed under the ruffled shock of black hair, and his brown skin shone with sweat above the soiled white shirt that stuck to his chest. In that moment the thought came to me that I could well understand Lucy Freeman and that I would never understand Dee Andrews. This was a bold reckless young man, a creature with only the barest veneer of so-called civilisation, maybe, but vitality, courage and gaiety sparkled all about him, seeming to light with a bright glow the dim corner where he sat, seeming to make the humid inert air vibrate with energy.

"So well you might be on the run!" I said, but I could not help smiling at him. "What are you doing here?" My attempt at severity was not a success. "How did you *get* here, anyway?"

"Got a lift on a truck and then walked in through the cane. I didn't want to risk coming in by car."

"Why come here at all? Especially here?"

"This is the last place they'll look for

me," he told me with an impudent grin. "Where's Dee?"

"Upstairs. It's all right," I reassured him. "She is in bed with a cold."

"Good."

"What have you come for?"

"To meet the kid — Sandy. He hasn't been here?"

"No."

"He is bringing me a suit-case from the house."

"What made you choose to meet him here?"

He reached a long arm across to my sofa and picked up *But Not For Love*. "This. I suppose you know it's mine?"

"Yes. Dee told me last night."

He looked down at the book. "I came because of this and because you gave me the keenest pleasure I have ever known when I saw you reading it on the ship and you said it was good. You said it was good in the right way and for the right reasons — I mean *my* way and *my* reasons. That made me think you wouldn't sell me down the river today."

"I won't sell you down the river, Roddy. What are your plans?"

"There's a lumber boat sailing for the Gulf tonight — I've shipped on her as a hand. I've sailed that way before. It's cheap and I like it."

"You are making for the States?"

"Yes."

"Your passport?"

"It's in order, visa and all. It's among the stuff the kid is bringing."

"Money, Roddy? Dollars?"

"I'm all right. That first slim volume" — he nodded with a smile at the book — "has hit the best-selling lists in the States as well as England."

He looked so gaily on top of his world that I felt I must bring its reality and general intractability to his notice. "I suppose I ought to raise a general alarm about your being here."

"All you have to do is to call your yard boy," he said, laughing, and I suddenly began to wonder why someone as bold and reckless as he was should be running away like this.

"How did you know that today was the day to clear out?" I asked.

"The kid phoned me at the office that Sir Ian was at the house talking about me and Lucy Freeman and horse whips, so I told him to meet me here with the locked suit-case from under my bed."

"Roddy," I said, holding the book between my hands, "with this book to your credit, why don't you stand your ground and face things out? You are not the first man to get a girl into trouble, as it is called, and you won't be the last and — "

"Just to clear the ground," he interrupted me, "I am not responsible for Lucy's trouble. That is the result of an encounter she had with a seaman in Victoria Court. Paradise office doesn't know that Lucy spends most of her nights in Victoria Court."

"But you *could* have been responsible?"

He grinned at me. "As my Glasgow landlady says: If you go among the crows you must be ready to be shot at. Yes, the infant could have been mine, I suppose."

"Anyway, she has had a miscarriage."

"I knew she was doing her best about that."

"Roddy, why are you running away like this?" I asked point-blank, for I felt that he was trying to lead me away from this question and I was very much more wary of Roddy now than I had been formerly.

"Because I am a coward," he said.

"Look here," I said angrily, "the least you can do is to be honest with me!"

His face changed, became naked and vulnerable as if he had allowed a protective mask to drop from it. "It is true," he said. "I am a coward — not a coward-and-a-bounder-by-Gad-God-dammit . . ." he parodied the voice of Sir Ian, " — perhaps — but I am cowardly about a scene with my father. I don't want it to happen. If my father and Sir Ian came at me in a horse-whipping frame of mind, somebody might get hurt. I am younger and more agile than they are. And that would be a pity." As he spoke, his jaw tightened, cording the muscles in his neck, and I knew that Roddy, with his temper out of control, would be a formidable adversary. "It's better to get out and let everybody cool down," he ended.

"But this?" I held up the book. "If you tell them about this?"

"The damage would be done before I could get round to it." Another change came over him. He seemed to withdraw into himself, even to lose physical colour, as if his vivid eyes and brilliant hair were merging away into the dim shadow where he sat. "I have been trying to tell my people about that book ever since I came home in December. I've never got round to it. I've missed my chance now." He stared straight at me, frowning, as if he were trying to come to a decision. "Have you a cigarette to spare?" he said then. I gave him a cigarette, and, as he struck the match, he seemed to make up his mind. "All this is difficult to explain, Missis Janet. You see, when I wanted to read English at the university, I was asked at home if I wanted to be a bloody school-master. I didn't. I wanted to be a bloody poet, but I had enough sense not to say that. I went to university and read English at the parental expense for five years. I reckoned if they had the money for me to do what *they* wanted, which was engineering, the same money would do for what *I* wanted. The chances are that I shall have to go on living with me for a long time, and, with all due respect to Twice, I find engineers pretty boring."

He gave me his impudent grin again and I felt that, very subtly, he was beginning

391

to lead me away from the main issue once more, and it irritated me that this six feet of vibrant blood, bone and muscle should be as elusive as a brown trout in a Scottish stream. I am not quick of wit, but I think I have a certain tenacity.

"I still think," I said in the voice that Twice calls "hammering" and in which I could myself hear the beat of persistence, "that if you told your people about this book — "

He expelled a long sigh, as if giving up. "In the light of all that has happened," he said, "you probably think I have got cheek for anything. I haven't. Not about my writing." He pulled his shoulders forward, tucked his elbows close to his sides and he made me think of myself scribbling at the writing-table, when Twice came in unexpectedly and I hid the papers under the blotter, screening them, protecting them while, physically, I seemed to feel myself shrivel and grow smaller as I shrank towards the core of myself. "My writing makes a coward out of me, a real coward," Roddy went on, talking more to himself now than to me. "It is the fear that they will laugh or the look of non-comprehension on their faces or with that" — he pointed to the book I held — "the fear of how they will try to value it, ask how much money I got for it, and when I am going to get on and write another one. I — I get *craven* at the thought of talking to them about it, of seeing them pick it over as if it were doubtful fish lying on a slab!" His voice shook as he spoke the last words, but with a physical jerk he broke away from the thoughts he had spoken aloud and said: "God, I wish that kid would come!"

"When does your boat sail?"

"Six."

"There's time yet."

I passed my cigarettes to him, noticed that his hand trembled as he took one, and now I felt a little ashamed that I had forced him into this exposure of himself, and I also felt embarrassed, as we tend to feel when someone steps outside the mental image we have held of him. It was easier for me to sit opposite and talk to the devil-may-care Roddy I had always known and to wait until I was alone before trying to encompass this new image that had emerged.

"What in the world made you propose to Dee Andrews?" I asked him after a short silence.

"I didn't."

"Didn't?"

"No. It was her idea. She suggested it and I was brought up to be a little gentleman after all, but please believe me when I say that it was a marriage that I never intended to take place."

His strong white teeth showed in a mischievous grin, and the Roddy of the *Pandora* was before me again, but after a second he became grave. "That poor brat is in hell's own muddle, Missis Janet. I've meant to tell you this before, but it's a bit difficult and I hadn't the guts, but I'll tell you now. If you throw me out, it doesn't matter. I'm on my way, anyhow." He grinned again, became grave again. "That girl is a-sexual, Missis Janet — maybe a Lesbian like that Denholm beanpole down at the Peak — but a-sexual, anyway."

"I know," I said, hoping to astonish him and succeeding.

"You know?"

My satisfaction was only momentary.

394

"Yes, now. But I didn't know until Cousin Emmie drew a diagram for me last night," I confessed. "I think she drew a diagram for Dee too — a diagram of Dee for Dee."

"That was what was needed, but I hadn't the guts to do it," Roddy said.

"Anyway, Dee is now going in with Isobel Denholm on the Mount Melody project."

"Dear heaven! What goings-on here in Paradise!" said Roddy and began to laugh uproariously.

"Hush! She is upstairs, remember!"

"Think of that old Cousin Emmie — " Roddy began.

"Yes, just think of her. It was she who blew the gaff about you and the Freeman girl, by the way."

"Damn it, I might have known it! One couldn't have a tumble anywhere without her happening along. She makes me think of the chorus in a Greek play."

I laughed, thinking that this was as apt a description of Cousin Emmie as I had yet heard. At that moment I saw from the window a suit-case being pushed on to the garden wall from the cane-piece beyond.

"There's Sandy!" I said, and Roddy sprang up. "Wait here. I'll go."

I could see only Sandy's red head on the other side of the wall and the head of Samson, his pony, as he asked: "Is Number Three here, Missis Janet?"

"Yes."

"Will you give him this case? And tell him good luck. I gotta go back — Mother's only at the Great House."

"All right, Sandy."

There was a rustle among the sugar-cane, Sandy and the pony became invisible, the afternoon sun blazed down and, feeling that I was caught up in some absurd melodrama, I lugged the heavy suit-case across the lawn and into the house.

"I feel a perfect fool," I told Roddy.

"As long as that's all, it's all right," he said, kneeling down by the case, taking some keys from his pocket and checking what it contained.

"And now what?" I asked as he relocked the case and stood up. "How do you propose to get from here to the Bay carrying that?" I pointed to the case and glanced at my watch. "It's twenty-past four."

"I'll manage all right."

"Take these," I said and gave him a packet of cigarettes and a box of matches. I held out my hand. "Good luck!"

"Thanks." He shook my hand and jerked his head at the book that lay on the sofa. "I'll send you a copy of the next one for free." I picked up the book and held it between my hands again. "Shall I tell Paradise you wrote this one?"

"Tell them if you like. What's one more sin among so many?"

Suit-case in hand, he stepped out of the french window. In the sunlight, he turned to smile at me, the bold, reckless smile that comes only to those who have the world before them and no old debts to the past and no old doubts from the past trailing behind them.

"My cousin is out looking for you," said a voice at the door at the other end of the room and I swung quickly round from the sunlit figure in the garden to the brown shade of Cousin Emmie, the parasol in one hand, the canvas bag in the other, so that the book slipped from my hands and fell at my feet. "There will be trouble — " she began but broke off, sat down and disposed bag and parasol about her chair.

When I looked back to the window there was nobody there. The lawn was empty, but the heat of the day was over and the insects were waking to their clicking, chirruping, rustling life. I picked up the book, walked down the room and laid the volume aside.

"My cousin is still in a temper," Cousin Emmie said, "so I thought I would have tea with you."

"Of course, Miss Morrison. I'll just call Clorinda." When I came back into the room, I said: "Let's go out to the front veranda. It will be cooler there now."

As we settled in wicker chairs at the end of the veranda, there was a movement behind me and, looking round and through the mosquito mesh, I saw Dee's Daimler slip past, rolling of its own momentum down the slope of the drive. When it reached the gate, the engine purred into life and Roddy's brown arm waved from the window as the car turned the corner and sped away.

"Oh, heavens!" I said. "Look at that!"

"He'll leave it in some safe place,"

Cousin Emmie said, quite unmoved, re-disposing her bag in a more convenient spot. "He has a respect for cars — that seems to be about the only thing he has inherited from that engineering father of his. In any case, I always said it was a mistake that little girl bringing that car out here with her. You never know what might happen."

"No. You don't, do you?" I said.

"Where is he going?"

"The States, I think."

"Just the place for him. A fine big place for a young man like him. But I wouldn't go to the States."

"No?"

"No, I am too old. I'll go back to England."

"Oh? I thought you didn't want to sail next week."

"I'm not going to sail. They play Scrabble on boats. I don't like playing Scrabble. I am going to fly. It's all over in about twenty-four hours."

I have a long, hard Highland memory and I remembered now how she had croaked about the danger of flying when Twice went off round the islands. "I

399

thought you didn't trust aeroplanes?" I said spitefully.

"Neither I do, but I'd rather travel in an aeroplane than on that boat with that man Cranston."

"And will you go back to live in London when you land?" I asked, pouring tea.

"If I land," said Cousin Emmie, looking facts in the face. "Yes. I'll go back to our flat."

"With Miss Murgatroyd?"

"No. Miss Murgatroyd is dead. She died last October," said Cousin Emmie, taking the cup of tea from my arrested hand and helping herself to a sandwich. "That's why I came out here on that boat. It is difficult to find yourself alone after fifty years."

"Very difficult — it must be," I said gently. "But wouldn't it be better to move to another flat, perhaps? Won't it feel very lonely?"

"No. Not the way things are. I am going to marry Miss Murgatroyd's brother. He asked me to marry him just after Fanny died. I came out here to think things over."

She took another sandwich and began,

thoughtfully, to eat it. I did not interrupt her cogitations.

"It's an odd thing," she said after a moment, "but I don't really know why I am going to marry Martin. When you get to our age there's no sex, just people. It's Martin that wants us to be married. He is in holy orders, you see. Of course, he is retired now. We will be company for one another and he plays a splendid game of chess and bridge and it is a sensible arrangement for two elderly people like us, but, you know, I don't believe I would bother to get married to him if it wouldn't annoy my cousin so much."

"Madame Dulac?" I breathed.

"Yes. She has always looked down on me for not getting married."

She chewed thoughtfully at her sandwich for a further moment. "I just wish I were sure that she isn't forcing me into something I may regret. I have never liked Lottie."

"I am quite sure," I said with conviction, "that what Madame may or may not think has not had the slightest effect on your decision, Miss Morrison."

"You never know," she said distrustfully. "People do things for all sorts of reasons. Look at that little girl upstairs getting engaged just to please you and Lottie and people. Look at you helping that young man to get away from Ian today just because you like books and so does he." I was silent in the face of this acuteness of hers. "You were always talking to him about books on that ship. Of course, you like young people too and you like good-looking people — all that would have something to do with it." She lapsed into silence, and after a moment I dared to revert to the subject I found most fascinating: "Have you told Madame that you intend to marry Mr. Murgatroyd?"

"Yes," said Cousin Emmie, and for the first time since I had met her it seemed to me that her face and voice were animated by some emotion, if, that is, malicious glee can be called an emotion. "That is why she is in such a temper. The way she was about that typist girl carrying on with that young man Maclean is nothing to it."

"Let me give you some more tea, Miss Morrison," I said with a rare and genuine pleasure in speaking these words to her.

She and I were still sitting on the

veranda, comfortable if rather silent companions, when Twice came home about six o'clock, but almost before he could greet us Clorinda appeared and said: "Please, sah, Charlie cryin' an' Dram gettin' in a state."

"Oh? Where are they?"

"Out de back, sah. Charlie up in de laundry roof an' cryin' an' Caleb think him stuck up dere, sah."

"All right. I'll come and see, Clorinda."

"Excuse me a moment, Miss Morrison," I said and followed Twice to the back garden.

In St. Jago, daylight and dark are as sudden as all else, and the bright afternoon had turned into the five-minute twilight as we rounded the corner of the laundry building where Dram was looking anxiously up at the roof and whining. In the gable, there was a small square hole between roof and ceiling and Twice climbed the garden ladder up the gable, looked inside the hole and then put his hand in. Then he quickly jerked it out, shaking it, and cursed: "You bloody brute!" He then peered in through the hole again and slowly descended to the ground.

"What happened?" I asked. "Has he a mongoose up there?"

"No he hasn't," Twice said. "*She* is very busy having kittens."

"I always said — "

At the voice that croaked from the twilight behind me, I turned round. There she was, a greyish-brown shade, the parasol in one hand, the canvas bag in the other.

"I always said Charlie was a silly unnatural name for that cat," said my friend Cousin Emmie.

THE END

FICTION TITLES IN THE ULVERSCROFT LARGE PRINT SERIES

The Green Years	*A. J. Cronin*
Flowers on the Grass	*Monica Dickens*
Mariana	*Monica Dickens*
Magnificent Obsession	*Lloyd C. Douglas*
My Friend My Father	*Jane Duncan*
The Bird in the Chimney	*Dorothy Eden*
Hornblower in the West Indies	
	C. S. Forester
The Ship	*C. S. Forester*
Flying Colours	*C. S. Forester*
The Gun	*C. S. Forester*
Blood Sport	*Dick Francis*
For Kicks	*Dick Francis*
Rat Race	*Dick Francis*
Bonecrack	*Dick Francis*
Flowers for Mrs. Harris and	
Mrs. Harris goes to New York	
	Paul Gallico
Love, Let Me Not Hunger	*Paul Gallico*
Edge of Glass	*Catherine Gaskin*
The Swan River Story	*Phyllis Hastings*
Sandals for My Feet	*Phyllis Hastings*
The Stars are My Children	
	Phyllis Hastings
Beauvallet	*Georgette Heyer*
The Convenient Marriage	*Georgette Heyer*
Faro's Daughter	*Georgette Heyer*
Charity Girl	*Georgette Heyer*

Devil's Cub	*Georgette Heyer*
The Corinthian	*Georgette Heyer*
The Toll-Gate	*Georgette Heyer*
Black Sheep	*Georgette Heyer*
The Talisman Ring	*Georgette Heyer*
Bride of Pendorric	*Victoria Holt*
Mistress of Mellyn	*Victoria Holt*
Menfreya	*Victoria Holt*
Kirkland Revels	*Victoria Holt*
The Shivering Sands	*Victoria Holt*
The Legend of the Seventh Virgin	
	Victoria Holt
The Shadow of the Lynx	*Victoria Holt*
Wreckers Must Breathe	*Hammond Innes*
The Strange Land	*Hammond Innes*
Maddon's Rock	*Hammond Innes*
The White South	*Hammond Innes*
Atlantic Fury	*Hammond Innes*
The Land God Gave to Cain	
	Hammond Innes
Levkas Man	*Hammond Innes*
The Strode Venturer	*Hammond Innes*
The Wreck of the Mary Deare	
	Hammond Innes
The Lonely Skier	*Hammond Innes*
Blue Ice	*Hammond Innes*
Golden Soak	*Hammond Innes*
The River of Diamonds	*Geoffrey Jenkins*

We hope this Large Print edition gives you the pleasure and enjoyment we ourselves experienced in its publication.

There are now 1,000 titles available in this ULVERSCROFT Large Print Series. Ask to see a Selection at your nearest library.

The Publisher will be delighted to send you, free of charge, upon request a complete and up-to-date list of all titles available.

Ulverscroft Large Print Books Ltd.
The Green, Bradgate Road
Anstey, Leicester
England